The King's Scapegoat

by

Hamilton Drummond

Double9 BOOKS

The King's Scapegoat

by Hamilton Drummond

ISBN: 978-93-62765-05-5

Published by

DOUBLE 9 BOOKS

2/13-B, Ansari Road
Daryaganj, New Delhi – 110002
info@double9books.com
www.double9books.com
Tel. 011-40042856

ABOUT THE AUTHOR

Hamilton Drummond, a master of intrigue and historical fiction, presents "The King's Scapegoat," a riveting tale that unfolds against the backdrop of political turmoil and royal conspiracy. With meticulous attention to detail and a flair for storytelling, Drummond captures the essence of the era, immersing readers in a world of treachery, betrayal, and redemption. Set in a time of shifting alliances and power struggles, this masterpiece delves into the complexities of royal politics and the sacrifices made in the pursuit of power. Through vivid characters and intricate plot twists, Drummond weaves a gripping narrative that keeps readers on the edge of their seats until the very last page. "The King's Scapegoat" stands as a testament to Drummond's literary prowess, offering readers a captivating blend of history, suspense, and drama. With its rich historical detail and compelling storytelling, this book is sure to leave a lasting impression on all who dare to embark on its journey.

CONTENTS

CHAPTER I
MY CLAIM TO BE HEARD FOR TRUTH'S SAKE

Of the many ways, worthy or vile, honourable or ignoble, whereby men, as my excellent friend the Prince de Talmont has shown in his history, may rise to court favour, few, I think, are more curious than that by which fate led me. Led me? The word is too soft, too gracious, too solicitous: fate kicked me, rather; for it was a vicious cuff of misfortune's contempt which made me a King's envoy; and a gentle stroke of the mercy of God which flung me back again to the humble obscurity of a simple gentleman.

But not without reward. And it is of that misfortune, that mercy, and that reward this story treats. God be thanked! the last was greater than the first, for love is a salve that heals all wounds the world over.

If the embassage committed to me by his late majesty finds no place in the admirable memoirs of the Prince de Talmont, better known it may be, as Monsieur Philip de Commines, Lord of Argenton, it is because at my earnest solicitation he expunged the narrative from his records. These, in his earnest desire for accuracy, he had submitted to me for revision. But, deeply conscious of my own unskilfulness in such matters, I humbly pointed out, first, that the story did not redound to the credit or honour of the late King, his master. Second, that the disclosure could not possibly gratify the son who so worthily fills his august father's throne; and, third, that Monsieur de Commines, having already known the cold shadows of banishment from regal favour, there was a danger—but doubtless the third reason moved him not at all. Historians must be superior to considerations of private advantage.

But if these three reasons were insufficient to warrant the fearless historian to consent to such a suppression, I had yet more to urge. The inclusion of the details served no worthy purpose. No political result followed my mission, which was abortive for reasons I hope to make clear. France and Navarre were neither of them a penny the better or the worse for it. Why, then, stir up old ashes? Many a conflagration has sprung from a fool's raking over of half dead embers, which, left to themselves, would have cooled to safety. Stories that are to no man's credit are best let sleep.

That brings me to the final reason that I urged. Perhaps it was the most instant of them all, and the one on which I laid the most stress, since a thorn in our own finger-tip troubles us more than a sword's thrust in our neighbour's ribs: it would give my enemies grounds for speaking ill of me. Little or great, we all have gnats to bite us, and evil tongues are so many that if they burnt like fire the poor would have charcoal for nothing the winter through.

"There goes the man who stooped to such and such an infamy," they would say, wilfully ignoring—but that is the story.

Why, then, do I give that to the world which I have successfully influenced Monsieur de Commines to suppress? Just because of these same evil tongues. Let no man dream that any act of his ever dies: good or bad, it is co-existent with his life, if not with the sun itself. What I had hoped was buried in the dust of the past, ghouls, infamous devourers of men's reputations, have disinterred, and for the sake of those who are to come after me the whole truth must be told. My children's love and reverence are more to me than all I possess, whether in Flanders or Navarre. Partly I tell the tale myself, and partly it is told by another outside of myself, but whether it be Gaspard de Helville in person or that other who speaks, this I solemnly assert, both are alike true.

CHAPTER II
THE BRUISINGS OF A FRIEND

It has been said that the first third of a man's life is the sowing, the second the growing, and the last the mowing, but with seedtime this story has nothing to do. The first more than twenty years of life may be brushed aside. It is enough that in them I lost first, my father; then, fifteen years later, my mother; and for three years had been my own master; if a man could call himself his own who was the slave and worship of his mother's nurse and his father's squire. The story then begins on a late spring day in 1483.

It was curious, though at the time the coincidence passed unnoticed, but so sure as I pressed Roland hard, rasping the poor willing brute's ribs cruelly with both spurs, just so surely did Martin meet with a trifling accident that delayed him. Once, as we galloped down from La Crêle to the river, he broke a stirrup leather. Once, too, he dropped his ash stick and had to go back for it; and once, as we rode round the pinewood at Berseghem, Ninus picked up a stone. At least, Martin said he did, and in face of his anxious concern as he bent over the upturned hoof how could I be angry? Ninus was his faithful servant even as Martin was mine, and that a horse should pick up a stone is no one's blame. The most I could do was to hasten him as urgently as my diffidence dared.

"Even as it is we may be too late," I added.

From the hoof in his palm he looked sourly up.

"That is the girl's fault. What business has a Hellewyl of Solignac philandering after a cow-herd's daughter? Which of you two had the redder face I don't know, hers from honest sun and weather, yours from you know what best yourself. Come now, is it an honest thing to play at courting under the trees with such a girl? What's more, she despised you for it. I saw that in her face when I said 'Solignac's a-fire' 'A-fire!' she cried; 'who fired it?' and her black eyes grew hard as she looked at you. 'Jan Meert,' I told her, and what was her answer? 'God be good to us! but that's great news.' Yes, it's her fault. All you own in the world flaring to ashes, and you philandering miles away." Then, letting Ninus slip his foot down, which he did with no sign of tenderness, Martin said a strange thing. "God bless her for it. We can ride on now, Monsieur Gaspard," and he gathered his reins into his left hand.

Until he had mounted I made no reply. Training had made me a patient man, and Martin, my one follower, was my best friend. I knew his dour, loyal nature too well to be angry at his frankness. For fifty years—that is all his life—he had served Solignac, and I, half his age, was to him no more than a child to be humoured when I could not safely be driven. Besides, if ever men had need for haste, we had, and I was not such a fool as to please my temper at the cost of a solid advantage. That he hated the girl Brigitta I had long known, but that, again, was loyalty to the house that fed him. Martin was still too much of the peasant not to despise his own class.

But once he was in the saddle I went back on my question, in different or more direct words, perhaps, but the sense was the same.

"Are we too late? Jan Meert works quickly, and these mishaps of yours have cost us half an hour."

"Jan Meert works quickly," he echoed; then, though he never looked at me, but straight before him, his face wrinkled, and he broke into a relishing chuckle for which his words gave no warrant till he added, "He'll have gone by this time, curse him, for a thieving Hollander, and these mishaps of mine, as you call them, have saved more than they cost."

Then I understood. He had been playing some of his old campaigner's tricks upon me, and I, like the innocent he knew me for, had never found him out. Thank God! it has always been my way to believe men honest until they show themselves rogues. That was not the King's way; yet of this I am sure, in my humble life I won to myself more love than he did, and more faithful service. Even now love and service were at the root of Martin's trickery, and knowing it was so, I did not turn and strike him. For that control, and remembering what happened so shortly after at Poictiers, I gratefully give God thanks.

"You make a coward of me," was all my reproach.

But when I pressed Roland to a gallop, he leaned forward and caught my rein.

"No, Monsieur Gaspard, no, no," he said, almost crying; "what sense is there in that? Better a burnt Solignac than a dead Hellewyl."

"We may save it. Leave go my rein, Martin, or—or—I'll draw my dagger on you."

"Not you—or I'll risk it, though a man's life is worth more any day than a dry roof. Hear reason. Save Solignac? Save it from Jan Meert and his twenty devils? We two? Curse away if it pleases you, the leather's round my wrist and I won't leave go. Listen now," he went on coaxingly, "what good can you do? What's Solignac but a shell and you the kernel? Why fling away the kernel after the shell? And how could we two face Jan Meert and his twenty brutes, sons of the devil every one of them? Are we to splash water from the Heyst with our palms, or carry it in our bonnets, to drown that roaring furnace? Listen now, listen; this was the way of it. Up he rode at a soft trot, in no haste at all, so safe and sure was he, and when I saw him coming I slammed-to the bolt of the great door, ran out old Babette to the woods behind, she in one hand and Ninus, here, in the other, tied up Ninus out of sight, hid Babette in the oak copse behind the trout pool—not that the wizened old fool had anything to fear but—well—she was part of Solignac, and if once she let loose her tongue upon Jan Meert as she does upon me, he might—Be quiet now, Monsieur Gaspard, don't I tell you she's safe enough? Then I stole back, I, Martin the liar and the maker of cowards—like makes like, Monsieur Gaspard, and a coward makes cowards—I stole back. Hard words are a fine wage to give a man who risks his life—one amongst twenty, and such a twenty as follow Jan Meert! They had the door down of course—all right, Monsieur Gaspard, if it hurts you I'll say no more. D'you think each ripped panel and split jamb wasn't as bad to me as a cracked rib, a cowardly maker of cowards and liar though I am? It was then—for I love the house that bore me as well as you can, but I had sense enough to see that if broken ribs followed stove panels, there was an end to something better than Solignac; there was an end to Hellewyl, there was an end to love, an end to hate, an end to the throttling of Jan Meert. What? Are these not something to live for? Something better than two fools dead before a burnt door? There's your rein loose, Monsieur Gaspard, for it's a loose rein we must have, you and I; a loose rein to ride away from Solignac till we are strong enough to ride back again, and when that day comes we'll shake a looser rein yet, see if we don't. When the time is ripe may God have mercy on Jan Meert's soul. Honestly, now, and man to man—though I am only a servant who would die to pleasure you, only dirt under your feet when it pleases your feet to trample on me, that and no better. I humbly ask your pardon for daring to so much as touch your bridle, Monsieur Gaspard, but I love you as a son, and when all's said it's natural I should have more sense than half my age. As man to man, now, am I liar and cur and all the rest of it? And did I not serve Solignac as well as if I had been kissing and—and—clucking a beggar girl under the beech-trees, a round-faced, bold-eyed herdsman's wench who—be angry if you will, be angry if you will, but the truth's the truth—a wench who might well cook my dinner but never share eating it, and yet I am no Hellewyl of Solignac!"

That he was talking as much against time as to ease his mind I knew, but there was so much sense in what he said that when he dropped my rein and sat back in the saddle I did not ride on. Of all the many leeches who sucked our Flanders' blood, none was bolder, greedier, more ruthless and more reckless than Jan Meert. Even into our remote life, stories drifted at which men cursed, but cursed softly, lest Jan Meert should catch and resent the echo; stories that for shame's sake we dared not tell our women, so wanton were they in cruelty, so brutal in destructiveness, and with such a wading in wickedness for very love of the thing.

A Christian country? A fraction of the Empire? Bah! The Emperor was busy elsewhere, and there was neither law nor justice in the land, nothing but the naked arm of the strong. Those who had the conscience and the power to rob robbed, none making them afraid for this world or the next; in the war of factions the great were striving to grow yet greater, or, if might be, were hard put to it to hold their own, and had no leisure to hold Jan Meert and his like in check. He burned, he plundered, he ravaged, but always with circumspection, preying on the weaker, and who was I that I might hope to outface him even in defence of the house of my fathers?

But, if to Jan Meert I was but a pigeon for a hawk's harrying, to Martin I was Hellewyl of Solignac, and his last words called for a rebuke.

"You presume. Keep your scurrilous tongue quiet, or if you must talk, show all respect when you speak of the lady who——"

"Lady! Has it come to that? Lady! God save us all! Slattern, black-eyed 'Gitta' a Lady? She'll never be that in God's world, it's not in her. Listen again, Monsieur Gaspard. A while back you stared—I saw you—when I thanked God for the woman. And I still thank Him, she kept you out of Solignac when you were best away. I suppose it was to that end the Lord made her—to save a Hellewyl of Solignac, and so even she has her uses. But now I say thank God for something worse than a——a——but we'll let that pass; why fret a green wound! You won't understand me now, still less will you understand me an hour hence, but the day'll come when you will know why I say God be thanked for Jan Meert, God be thanked for a burnt Solignac. From my heart I pray the scoundrel may have done his work well."

There was a solemnity about his earnestness that gave his words weight, mad though they were, and, waiting his explanation, I made no answer. It came promptly.

"See now, here were you day by day sinking lower in the scale, day by day growing liker to the peasant that is so little better than a brute. I should know what he is for I was of the breed till your father, and yet more your mother, drew me from the mud to what I am. Don't think I boast, for I don't. Bad's my best, but it's chalk or charcoal compared with a woman fly-trap! Well then; your land was gone—not your doing, but bread of a father's baking is of ten sour in the children's mouth. For three generations Hellewyls of Solignac have played the fool, always riding the wrong wave till bit by bit they were dashed to pieces. One followed Austria, and France getting the upper hand wrenched a lordship from him as the price of pardon. The next followed France, and Burgundy seized and held what France let go as a makeweight in the next treaty. The last followed Burgundy, and Austria said 'oh ho! Solignac was a fief of mine in the good old days,' and Burgundy in part bought peace with Solignac as a counter in the deal. Now what is left? Ten acres of bad grass, a belt of woods, and a forlorn house; a house fit for a Seigneurie and dripping dank with wet and mould for lack of service, and the last Hellewyl of Solignac philandering after a goatherd's daughter—pray God she's his daughter, her mother had just such another coarse, pretty face of her own—philandering, I say, after a goatherd's daughter by way of mending his fortunes. But Jan Meert has changed all that. Brigitta can sell her red cheeks, her plump white flesh and big black eyes to better advantage elsewhere, and so I say may God show mercy to Jan Meert the day I show him none."

"I don't understand."

"Not understand? And yet it is all so simple. D'you really think that your Brigitta of the bold face would bury herself in a burned house with singed owls and scorched rats for company, all for the sake of a man with a ragged coat? And where are you to live Monsieur Gaspard? With the pigs in the swineherd's mud hut? You! Hellewyl of Solignac! No, no; don't you see that whether you like it or not you're flung out into the world? Or is it by mouldering in the burnt shell of Solignac that you would seek strength to yourself to take Jan Meert by the throat? Shame, Monsieur Gaspard, shame! Five and twenty, sound in limb and head—yes, and in heart too, in spite of the swineherd in petticoats; you, God's own image of a man, and yet content to live like a snipe, sucking mud from a bog!"

"Why did you wait till to-day to throw my *laisser-aller* in my teeth? and why to-day of all unfortunate days? Is that like a friend?"

"Because," and Martin's withered face softened, "I suppose I loved Solignac as well as you did. I was born there as you were, and we poor devils of servants have hearts to suffer and souls to be saved as well as our masters. To-day, too, you say you would put Brigitta the swineherd into my lady's place! With great respect, Monsieur Gaspard, till to-day I had not thought you such a fool; but God be thanked for Jan Meert, and be merciful to him." Then, as if by an afterthought, he added, "God be merciful to me, too, and give me five minutes of Jan Meert's throat though I die for it. Ah! look, Monsieur Gaspard; what did I tell you?"

Above the trees that lay between us and Solignac a pall of smoke hovered, its edges feathered by the wind.

CHAPTER III
FIRE AND SACK

My first dismayed instinct was to pull Roland back upon his haunches, my second to urge him through the wood by the shortest path he could find. But Martin called me back.

"Not that way, Monsieur Gaspard. Never look rogues in the face if you can see their backs, and perhaps old Babette has news."

Caution was wisest, and I followed him upstream. Five minutes' delay could matter little to Solignac, and Babette's curiosity might be trusted to have kept her informed of Jan Meert's doings. But we drew the copse blank, though we hunted through it, crying her name cautiously, there was no answer. To me silence was assurance. Jan Meert and his fellow-rogues had left the chateau, having done their worst, and the way was clear. No doubt we would find her waiting helplessly before the ruin wrought by the Hollander, for she, too, loved Solignac. The wonder was we had not already heard her outcry.

"Come," said I, driving Roland through the bushes.

"Better leave the horses behind," advised Martin.

But I would not.

"No," I answered curtly. "If Jan Meert is yonder we shall need their legs; if not, why leave them?"

The time, be it remembered, was the verge of summer, almost summer itself, with the foliage full and green, so it was not until the trees thinned that I got my first sight of Solignac, a grey bulk of weather-beaten stone between the columns of the oaks and pines. But it was only when we had fairly cleared the wood that it dawned upon me what and how much I owed the Hollander.

Through Martin's message, delivered at a time when no man likes to be interrupted—for I talked with Brigitta in the shade, Roland's bridle hooked over my arm—there had been a covert satisfaction that blunted its edge. My recollection of what passed there differed from Martin's.

"Come, Monsieur Gaspard," said he, his sour look turned not on me, but on the girl, "Solignac's a-fire, and there's a man's work to do."

"Solignac a-fire?" Not only I, but Brigitta echoed the words. As she said them she laid her hands on my shoulders with a little high-pitched laugh that set my heart beating even more than did the touch. The peasant girl could feel as keenly as any fine lady, though of fine ladies I knew nothing. My own thought was that Martin coined some clumsy excuse to draw me home, anywhere away from Brigitta, whom he hated malignantly, as only a narrow peasant can hate. So I added, joining in the laugh, "Let who lit the fire put it out, and go thou and help him."

"That's not Jan Meert's way," answered Martin, his voice rougher than I had heard it since I had grown a man. "Come Monsieur Gaspard, come for God's sake. You can find a face of brass any hour, but there's only one Solignac."

"Is it serious?"

"Is Jan Meert serious? Is the devil serious? Solignac is hell, I tell you, hell to-day, and Jan Meert its devil."

Even then, being, thank God, a man of no imagination, I did not understand, and though we rode fast enough—too fast to please Martin—it was the gallop that warmed my blood and not rage against Jan Meert. Understand! How could I understand? How could any man understand who has not seen the like? But now, as we broke the last cover, I cried I do not know what curse, and spurred Roland forward at a pace that cared never a jot whether or no the devil Jan Meert had quitted that smoking hell of his own making. What three hundred grim adventurous years had failed to do three hours had done, and the house of my fathers was a hollow wreck. The walls still stood sheer, even Jan Meert's malignancy had not strength to thrust stone from stone, but the hewn mullions that divided the Norman windows were cracked with fire, and from every blackened casement smoke blew out in little vicious puffs as the great heat within poured up and out where once the roof had been. There was neither flash nor glow of flame, no cataract of fire, no roar of life swelling in destruction, nothing but the sullen, steady flooding upwards of the reek. Solignac was already dead, stripped and stretched on its funeral pyre, and the smoke of its ashes cried to God for vengeance.

Martin, riding at my elbow, was speechless, but I could hear him whimpering and whinging under his breath, as if a rough finger on a new wound fretted him. To me, almost a peasant, as he had said, the sight was a new one; but Martin had been my father's squire in wars south, east, and west, and had seen both sack and siege. Then it was a matter of course that the pride of ten generations should dissolve in one hour's smoke and men and women go homeless, a thing to be borne philosophically being the loss of others; but this was Solignac, this was the birth-house of us both, and the cradle of his master's race, and though he spoke no words, I knew well that every choked fret in the throat was a curse that language could not match for expression or better for force.

Round the north-west of the smoking house we dashed, our horses' mouths frothing even in that short furlong; round to the grey façade where stood the great door flush with the huge stone pillars from which it hung.

"Babette!" I called out as we pulled up, "Babette! Babette! Where are you, Babette?"

"Jan Meert!" cried Martin. "Lord God! Give me Jan Meert! What matters Babette? There are a thousand Babettes, a thousand, but only one Solignac, and—heavens of grace! See there!"

I saw, but because I saw, I answered nothing. Babette? At the sight of Jan Meert's work I had forgotten Babette even while her name was on my lips. I would not give a fig for the patriotism of the man who does not hold his father's house dearer even than his country. In it every stick and stone is sacred, hallowed not alone by many a tradition, but by a thousand personal memories. Since the Lord God had taken my mother to Himself Solignac had been the one dearest thing in life, and behind the door that hung fretting on wrenched hinges Solignac lay in profanation, its great square hall a heaped mass of reeking filth. Not much was visible, but through the reeling uprights there showed a suggestion of charred beams, rent furnishings, and half-burnt tapestry strewn and scattered through with rubble from the upper walls; no! not much, but enough! How ruthless would be the destruction, how irreparable the ruin, when a casual clouded glance through sluggish smoke could tell so vile a tale!

Dismounting, we knotted our reins together and turned the horses loose. Blown as they were, they might be trusted not to stray, nor, so soundless was Solignac, its silence broken only by the crackle of fire or the rasp of wood on wood as the wreckage settled down, was there need to provide a way of escape. Jan Meert was no longer to be feared. He had done his worst, and moved on to other mischief.

At the threshold we paused, striving to measure that worst and failing miserably. It was like death, and who, in the first numbness of his sorrow, can weigh death in a balance to appraise the loss, or reckon up the sum of its significance? The method of devastation we could understand, but not the measure of its effects, and the thoroughness, the grim malignancy of the method appalled me.

It was Martin who first made the process clear. As I have said, he had seen war, and much of what was hidden from my ignorance was plain to his experience.

"See, Monsieur Gaspard," said he, as we stood beneath the lintel, and the sullen heat, acrid with the smell of smouldering wood, puffed and eddied into our faces. He was frankly weeping now, but, as I believe, unconsciously, his tears half grief, half rage at his helplessness. "See with what a system and to what an end these devils went to work. Not to burn Solignac, but to gut it beyond use was their object. Good and well if it burned, but to destroy was the chief thought. What have you done to Jan Meert that he should do this thing to Solignac? If there was a debt it's paid and the reckoning is due on our side now. They must have fired the house at a score of places; a score? two, three score, but not to burn. Look how it is always the same; the ends of the beams have gone, and then, pouf! down came the floor, down came the middle walls, down came the roof, beam upon beam, rafter on rafter, tearing the plaster and the copings with them till the very weight of all choked the fire to a smoulder and a smoke. But what mattered that! There is nothing left of Solignac but sheer walls, with here and there a splintered spear of wood thrust out for the bats to swing from, and that's what they worked for."

"In three hours?" said I helplessly; "three hours or four; how could that be?"

"What Jan Meert does not know at such work no man knows. A smear of fiery stuff here, a smear there, a touch under this beam, a touch under that; the furnishings piled to the middle of the floor for weight, the wood dry with the the dryness of three hundred years—but what does it matter how he did it; there it is."

Yes, there it was, and neither guesswork nor cry of the heart could make the disaster less complete, or lighten the weight of the blow. Three hundred years of tradition, three hundred years of life and death, man's honour and woman's pureness, mother's love and child's reverence, all ended, as it were, in a breath, ended by a brutal rogue's undeserved, unnatural, and unprofitable violence. Such an end to such a place was as horrible as a wolf's rending out the life of an innocent babe.

The heat was less than would have been supposed from such a pyramid of smoking stuff, and, Martin leading by a foot or two, we crossed the threshold. God! What a sight it was! Solignac was no mean house, and there upon the flags lay not alone the roof, but the ruin of two floors heaped in a pile whose ragged crests almost overtopped the jutting points of the nearer joists. Beams, rafters, marble panelling, roof tiles, rubble, rough-hewn masonry that had not seen the light for ten generations, all flung together in an inextricable confusion that beggars words. But whenever I hear it said that the glory of this world perisheth, and my mind gropes for a picture of the last and awful day of the Lord when the elements shall melt in fervent heat, back there comes a vision of that sheer and naked shaft crammed high with formless ruin, its blackened walls hung here or there with tattered curtain-ends, the shredded gauds and remnants of our pride, and over all a heavy pall of smoke whose acrid vapours stank smarting in the nostrils. Over all? No, not quite. At times the drifted reek eddied aside, and through the rift God's clear blue shone down.

Martin had entered a foot or two in advance, and that position he still held, one arm thrust out and behind in the unconscious attitude of protection. Suddenly I felt his hand shake with a jump, and his fingers, still unconsciously, closed on my breast, pressing me back.

"We have seen enough, Monsieur Gaspard," said he, looking vaguely round, "this thing hurts; why—why—stay any longer?"

Why indeed, seeing that I was beginning to understand, and every sharp rasp of the disordered timbers as they settled down was the galling of a wound, every smouldering glow of the grudging fire an eye of derision? Only because his very touch was a warning, and that day was Gaspard Hellewyl's second day of birth.

CHAPTER IV
BABETTE

To every man they come, sooner or later, these second days of birth in which at last he knows himself to be truly alive and with a purpose in the world. In some the ushering into a life of the knowledge of good and evil comes by way of a woman's kiss, in others the pangs are as keen as those that forerun the first gasped filling of the babe's lungs; but whether by way of sweetness or by way of pain, by the glory of love or by the enfibering dignity of grief, by gain or by loss it comes to all. Nor is it a slow process. In an hour that which was not is, and so, being at last a man, the touch of Martin's hand, the trembling of its grip where no grip should have been, was a sinister alert to watchfulness, and I would not go back.

Putting his arm aside I drew level with him, and through the general chaos searched out a something to justify his presumption, a something that overshadowed with its terror the common exalted level of disaster. But I missed it; search as I might, I missed it, not knowing what to look for, and turned at last to Martin, who stood watching me. There was a new look on his face that puzzled me, so softened was it. What could there be left in Solignac that made for gentleness?

"Well?"

"It was a good end, Monsieur Gaspard, the finest end in the world; I could ask no better myself."

Out of the blackening ruins of my home a puff of foul vapour blew smarting into my face.

"A good end? That! Are you mad?"

"Hers," he answered, "Babette's; she died for Solignac."

"Babette? Dead? Where—?"

I broke off, following the direction of his eyes, but without comprehension. I had forgotten Babette, and remembered her now with a rush of shame. From a triangular patch of gloom where a transverse fallen beam, propped against the wall, buttressed up a mass of wreckage, a sleeve of homespun woollen stuff was thrust. Motes of wood ash and dust of rubble were strewn so thickly over it that I had passed it by as only another wisp of Solignac's torn hangings. Even now it was not until Martin shook these off and Babette's dead hand hung limply down that I understood.

"Poor Babette!" I whispered, "Poor faithful Babette!"

I spoke to myself rather than to Martin, and yet he heard me above the crackle of the pyre settling inch by inch.

"Why would she not be faithful?" he said as roughly as if he grudged her the remorse of my regret; "you make too much of it, Monsieur Gaspard. This is but a little thing to have done, and for what else was she born? We must lift her out somehow; though, but for one thing, I would say leave her where she is."

"Leave her here? Leave Babette in this hell of a place?"

"Where better, with Solignac for a tomb, and the dust of the house she loved to cover her? But we must have her out."

Going down on his knees, he crawled across her into the hollow where the body lay, while I stooped by her, her hand fast in mine as if she were alive and I comforting her. From within came the sound of ripped cloth, and Martin returned, coughing and choking with the dusty smoke.

"A joist pinned her," he explained. "Stand aside now, Monsieur Gaspard, and I'll carry her out."

God be thanked for fresh air! The three greatest blessings in the world are fresh air, pure water, and a clean life. Not even the ruin behind us nor the dead at my feet could make stale the sweetness of the breath that filled my lungs. A dozen steps from the door, Martin had laid her on the grass, and for a moment we stood one on either side of her, motionless. Then Martin went down on one knee and deliberately began fumbling at the loose ends of the bow that knotted-in the kirtle at the throat. Everywhere in the dress there were marks of Solignac's disaster, powdered ash, jagged dents with frayed edges, blotches of charcoal, smouldered holes even, but the stern hard face with the set teeth and wide-open angry eyes was unbruised. It was only when he had the two upper couple of tags unfastened that I guessed at his purpose and it revolted me.

"Leave her alone!" I cried, leaning across her to push him back. "What does it matter how she died?"

"It matters much," he answered. "D'you think it was for pure love and pity that I grovelled in the heat yonder? Wait and see."

To his unaccustomed fingers—Martin knew as little of women or women's gear as I did, and that was nothing—the knots were hard to unravel; but at length he had enough undone to satisfy him, and he looked up.

"That," and he laid his hand upon a brown stain that stretched above the ribs to the left, "is why I do it. You must see all Jan Meert's work, Monsieur Gaspard, or how can you hope to pay all?" Loosening the kirtle slightly, but no more than showed the withered muscles and cordy sinews of the neck, he pushed his hand slowly, reverently beneath it. "Aye! I thought so!" and again he looked up at me, sucking in his breath with a gasp as we all do when we are hurt. "Not even her grey head could save her. See here, Monsieur Gaspard!"

Drawing the edge of the stuff aside an inch or two he showed what I have seen many times since, but never before, the smooth straight lips of a sword wound. In the dry heat the skin had shrunk aside, and the red flesh looked broadly out of the cut.

"Murdered! Babette murdered?"

"Jan Meert's way," answered Martin, and drew back the kirtle. "It was like this," he went on slowly. His hand still rested on the brown stain, and his face, like my own, was bent over that of the dead woman between us. "Even in the copse she heard the noise of the devil's work going on, and it drew her home, for love of Solignac it drew her home. She came back, that was her duty, being alone." He stopped, and his hand slipped up to the face. He had never loved Babette; chiefly, I think, because of her love for me: but now, with a strange tenderness he smoothed the wrinkles of her withered face, and I knew it was his repentant amends for many a hard word and harder thought. She had loved Solignac, she had died for love of Solignac, and if there had been strife between them it was forgiven for the sake of that love and death. "I could not," he went on, half to himself and half, it seemed, in humble, apologetic explanation to her. "I was not alone, and so I could not come back. Monsieur Gaspard came first. Thou understandest, dost thou not, thou quiet one, that Monsieur Gaspard is always first? She came back," he resumed, looking again up at me and speaking briskly, "came back raging! My faith! don't I know the mood well! She found Jan Meert and his crew busy and she let loose her tongue. Solignac has failed in wit now and then, but it never bred cowards even in its women. Rats fight when cornered, and Babette was no rat. She fought with what weapon she had, and it cannot hurt her now to say she was bitter-tongued beyond all reason. Another man would have let her rail, but not Jan Meert. That was never Jan Meert's way; he answered her back, and there's his answer!"

"It was a foolish thing, that coming back," said I, my brain in such a whirl from the conflict within; rage, grief, resentment, hate, warring to so confused a tumult that I hardly knew what I said.

"Is love foolish? Is duty foolish?"

"What could one, and that one a woman, what could she do?" I answered sourly. It was not that I did not love old Babette, it was not that I did not mourn for her, but realization was as yet far from me.

Martin made no reply, but the reproach in his eyes smote me. Down I went on my knees, my palms on either side the withered face.

"Old friend, old friend, how can I pay thee? How? How?"

"Look in her face for the answer and then look here," he said harshly, "Pay Jan Meert. Love takes no payment for love. Pay Jan Meert."

From the hard passionless face of the dead I looked up to the hard passionate face of the living, and laid my hand on the wound Jan Meert had made.

"By God! I will!"

As if there was no more to be said Martin rose briskly to his feet. Babette had done Hellewyl of Solignac a last service and one, in his opinion, worth dying for.

"That settles it, and hey! for Ghent," he cried gaily, as if there were no such thing as ruin or sack or death in the world, and stooping, lifted her once more in his arms.

It was an ugly gruesome sight, and it made me shudder, that leathern, wrinkled, smiling face of his looking satisfaction at me over that frowning mask of death, blind-eyed, and still staring defiance. But Martin was as unconscious of indecorum as he was of offence. Nor was there even cause for mourning. Why should there be? The woman having done her duty, had fallen on sleep, and there was no more to be said.

Still briskly he retraced his steps the way we three had come, but it was only as he paused before the forced door that I divined his purpose.

"Not there!" I cried; "for God's sake not there, Martin; the thought is horrible."

But he only stumbled on up the step. Martin was losing his youth, and the burden in his arms weighed heavier than he would own.

"There's neither pick nor spade; would you leave her to the wolves? Horrible!" and again he paused, panting; "never a Hellewyl of them all,

Seigneurs though they were, had so fine a burial. Look at the smoke, Monsieur Gaspard, and listen to the wind in the tree-tops."

The pall had lifted, and a steady flow of grey vapour flecked with sparks was already streaming east towards Courtray. With such a wind abroad the charred ends still smouldering in the heart of the pyre would yet set flying such a flag as would tell Jan Meert, even were he ten leagues away, that his work was well done. Martin was right. Better that than the wolves. The God who is Himself a consuming fire might be trusted to see to His own, and that which the cold earth gives up, flame will surely not hold back.

With all reverence we cleared a space as near the heart of Solignac as the heat and smoke and danger would permit. There we laid her, piling in—still with all reverence—the torn silks and tapestries that were the brightness of our house, the shattered spoils of raids by more than one generation of Hellewyls, intermixed with rafters and rough timber; beauty, glory, strength, all that was left of Solignac to round off the red grave of almost its last servant.

There we left her, and as we ended, there came the sudden roaring as of a furnace springing into furious heat from a dozen centres. Flame, fanned to sudden birth, spurted, strengthened, leaped from splintered joist to shattered armoire, caught beams and flooring, sucked strength from their three hundred years of dryness, licked up in an instant the gaudy fripperies that hung like rent flags amidst the wreck, soared up, soared outwards, and streamed in smoke-tipped spirals flapping down the wind. Truly Martin was right; never had a Hellewyl of Solignac so grand a funeral as we gave to old Babette.

"It's hey for Ghent!" said Martin again, as we stood on the grass watching the sparks fly, but with hearts less heavy than might have been supposed. The very greatness of a catastrophe can be its own alleviation. The spirit of a man rises within him to watch the crisis and face it down. "Hey for Ghent! or maybe, Cologne? And the sooner we are on the road the better. Which shall it be, Monsieur Gaspard, burgher or Emperor?"

"Neither," I answered; "the King and Paris."

"Paris?" and he looked his incredulity. It was a new thing for Monsieur Gaspard to have a will of his own. "Why to Paris?"

"How can we two face Jan Meert and his twenty brutes?" I quoted. "We need backing, and we'll get it from Louis of France."

"From that old fox? From Louis the treaty-breaker? A cunning, coldhearted, cruel—for the Lord's sake, Monsieur Gaspard, let us keep out of his claws. When did Louis of France ever back anything but Louis?"

"Never, and that is why he'll back us. Listen, and see if I am as much a fool as you think. The Dauphin marries our Margaret of Flanders. The Dauphin's father, that cunning old fox, will desire excuses to meddle in the affairs of Flanders; we give him one, and to gain his own end, he helps us to gain ours."

"What right has he to meddle with Flanders?"

"The right of every just man to put down lawlessness, the right of The Most Christian King to right the wrong, the right of Louis of France to please himself—when he is strong enough! and the right of the third is greater than the other two."

"But he shuts himself up like a rat in a hole; no man goes near him."

"Monsieur de Commines is the King's good friend, Monsieur de Commines was my father's good friend, and is my cousin thrice removed. Monsieur de Commines will open the rat hole and let me in. The one thing that troubles me is how we are to reach Paris, scarecrows as we are and penniless."

"Scarecrows," answered Martin, looking ruefully at the stains and tatters that either from fire, smoke, or the ragged edges of splintered timber so disguised us that whether we were clad in silk or stuff, browns or crimsons, no man could have told. That morning, even though the tryst was only with a peasant girl, I had put on my finest splendour, and now it was a thing of derision; "scarecrows, but not quite penniless; wait for me, Monsieur Gaspard."

Chuckling, he half ran, half shuffled off into the wood in the opposite direction to that in which he had hidden Babette, and in five minutes was back, breathless, but his face still puckered with satisfaction.

"What came from Hellewyl goes back to Hellewyl, and where better could it go?" said he, holding out his hands. They were open, hollowed to a bowl, and in the hollow lay a little heap of coins to which patches of moist earth still clung. They were mostly silver, crowns and three-crown pieces, with here and there the red glint of a ducat. For thirty years Martin had served Solignac, heart, head and hand, and now, as the shadows of age darkened round him, the gains of his service failed to cover his two palms.

The thought of how we had taken so much and given so little smote me, and the tears that filled my eyes were in part shame.

"What are these, old friend?" and I put my hands behind my back.

"Bread and meat for the road to Paris."

"A Hellewyl of Solignac travels at his own charges."

"'Tis the right of the King—" he began.

"But I am no King," I cut in, "nothing but a homeless, ruined man."

"My King," he answered. "Take them, Monsieur Gaspard; would you shame an old friend? Your pardon, but the word is your own. Take them, of what use are they to me? If I had died last night, they'd have lain in the earth till some lout ploughed them up a hundred years hence."

But we compromised. They were my debt, but he should keep them, paying our way as we rode to Paris as friend and friend.

Thus it was that I turned my back for the first time on Solignac, travelling at the charges of my own servant and with no more gear in the world than the ragged, smoke-stained suit upon my back. Brigitta? To be frank, I had forgotten Brigitta, and Martin was too cunning a diplomatist to remind me of her.

CHAPTER V
PARIS IN "EIGHTY-THREE"

Of all the virtues that adorn mankind, none is so common as the virtue of necessity—or so little sought after. By reason of that virtue, and because a slender purse is a great persuader to modesty, we kept by the villages, avoiding Bethune, Arras, Montdidier and their like, though omitting the last of these, at least, was little mortification of the flesh, for the town had never fully recovered from its harrying in '75 when the King took it from the Burgundians.

For the most part, these villages were mere warty outcroppings of filth upon the face of a fair country, some not even with a wine shop so poor were they. But if we lay hardly, ate coarsely, and at times carried out in the morning more than we had brought in at night, we paid little; so that our bloodletting was where we could most spare it. Boorish roughness we met in plenty, but no discourtesy. The poor folk were more accustomed to being robbed than paid, and where the company was more villainous than common we slipped our bed across the door, and so rested in peace.

"Wait till we reach Paris," was Martin's nightly cry, as we stayed our hunger on sour bread and sourer wine. "Five nights more—four nights—three nights—and the Star of Dauphiny pays for all. Such an inn, Monsieur Gaspard! My late master, your father, gave it all his custom. It was neither too grand nor too common, too dear nor too cheap. My Lord Duke found amusement to tickle his greatness, and a poor gentleman could be at his ease and no questions asked. May the devil choke these scoundrels, but I think they've drawn the wine from the vinegar butt by mistake."

It was late in the afternoon when we entered Paris by the St. Denis gate, and made our way to the Rue du Temple, off which, the first turn to the right as one faces the river, and immediately fronting the huge crenellated outer wall of the Temple precinct, opened the street in which was situated Martin's famous inn. Of its gay surroundings, its cheery brightness, its constant bubble of laughter, he had spoken so often and so joyously that the sordid frowsiness of the Rue Neuve Saint Martin, a crooked, ghastly byeway of blistered walls, was a dismal surprise. So narrow was it, so filthy, so full of evil smells, that any question as to the reception of such a pair of out-at-elbows as ourselves vanished. The inn that could thrive upon such squalor could not afford to be nice as to its guests.

In my ignorance of life the natural deduction from that premise never struck me; that the guests would be such as could not afford to be nice as to their inn. But as we wound into an ever-increasing gloom, an ever-growing sinister suggestiveness, a doubt arose that Martin's whole story was a legend of his imagination.

"Are you sure," I began, waving a hand before my face in the vain hope of drawing a sweeter breath, "sure that my father—?"

"I give you my word," he protested. "The Sieur Hellewyl, Monsieur de Commines, Monsieur de Vesc—" the name attracted him, for he was Dauphiny born—"Monsieur—Monsieur—oh! a score of them. But Paris has changed since then, or I have."

"Monsieur de Commines?" I repeated, "are you really sure?"

"Certainly; Monsieur de Commines, did I not say so before? He was little more than a boy at the time, but a bold one. I say, friend," he shouted, stooping to peer into the black vacancy of an open door out of which there came a burr of voices. It was significant that in the Rue Neuve Saint Martin there were no windows on the ground floor. "Whereabouts is the Star of Dauphiny?"

Un the instant the rumble of talk ceased, but it was not until Martin had repeated his question that a man came to the door, a whitefaced, underfed fellow, whose sinewy arms were naked to the shoulders. Without replying he leaned against the door, half within the house and half without, eyeing us and our horses critically.

"Does your master lodge there to-night?" he asked at last, lounging forward to the middle of the street that he might examine us the better.

Before Martin could answer, saying, perhaps more than was wise, I cut in with a curt, "Yes." But his curiosity was still unsatisfied.

"And are there many more of you?"

"My friend, we asked a question."

"And I another."

"You are impertinent."

"And you a dolt! What hedgerow bred you? Don't you see the place might not have room for you all? Are there more of you?"

"No."

"Then your master has the fewer clods. How far have you ridden to-day?"

"Come, come," I said impatiently, "that, at least, has nothing to do with how many beds there are at an inn. Where is the Star of Dauphiny?"

"There's no such place," he answered coolly.

"No such place?"

"No. Ah ha! Now you're civil, my stout clod-thumper. No such place. Fifteen years ago it became the Star of Provence, and since then it has been the host of heaven, but with none of the angels. Now, with the Dauphin's marriage to his three years' baby of a wife, it is the turn of the Flemings, and you'll find the Star of Flanders on the right hand round the second curve of the street."

"Then good day to you, and a civiller tongue in your head," cried Martin, spurring Ninus forward to drive over the fellow.

But he was too quick, and hopped for his doorway, dealing the poor innocent brute a cruel blow on the muzzle as he passed.

"Good day, clod," he answered. "Chut! You cannot even plough straight. You'll need more wit to your skull than that in Paris."

"I owe you one for that," cried Martin, as Ninus plunged, squealing.

"Owe away! To owe and never pay is Paris fashion," he replied laughing, and barred the door behind him, shutting himself into darkness.

To have hammered against that stout barrier, belted with iron as broad as our palms, would have skinned our knuckles for nothing, so we rode on, Martin swearing as he had not sworn since he cursed Jan Meert. Nor did a sight of the Star of Flanders, though it was the end of the first stage of our journey, bring sweetness to his temper, nor, indeed, to mine either. Instead of the cheeriness, the gaiety, the flash and sparkle of court life, there was a dingy arch in the flat of a dingy wall and six or eight dusty, small paned windows, so veiled by heavy gratings as to suggest groans of the prison-house rather than bubbling laughter. But it was too late to seek other quarters, so we rode on into the courtyard.

Supper? Certainly. Beds? A bed, one, perhaps; were we princes of the blood in disguise that we wanted beds apiece? Supper and a bed, yes, but pay before you stir the horses in the morning; that's the rule of the house. The insolence was galling, but poverty must pocket affronts, nor, let there be ever so many, is the pouch so filled that there is no room for another. We might have blustered, but to trim ragged clothes with airs and graces as if they were so much gold lace is to crown misfortune with folly, so we bore the scorn of the groundling in silence.

One effect it had, it put an end to Martin's insistence on obsequious service; that rags should serve rags could only make rags ridiculous. But even our humility refused to sup in the common room. There any prowler of the gutters who had five sous in his pocket could drink, game, and swear as it pleased him, which for the first two was as deep as these same five sous, and for the last at his foul throat's loudest.

At first the host would have hectored us. But judiciously used, a little money can make a great noise in the world, and Martin rattled his coins.

"Who pays chooses," said he, withdrawing his head from the room. "Lay for us elsewhere, landlord. When we wish to sup with mongrels in a dog-kennel we'll tell thee."

With a grunt the fellow turned back across the open court, round which the inn was built, and led us to a decent, quiet, long-shaped room that bounded the further side. It was dingy, narrow, and low-ceiled, but empty. Two tables, end to end with a break between, and benches at either side, filled its centre.

"Lay here," said Martin pointing to the upper end of that nearest the door.

But I demurred. "No; on the second table and at the further end. It is more private."

"But, Monsieur Gaspard, to be near the door—"

"Is to be near draughts. We have no one to fear in Paris."

"In a city where they strike dumb beasts there are always rogues."

"But not to be feared."

"Feared? No, but to be guarded against."

"Even so, the further from the door, the less the surprise. And what, in all the world, have we to guard? Lay there, landlord."

Midway through our meal of one dish came the first incursion on our solitude. Two men, one slouched and cloaked like a brigand, entered, and at sight of us, would have withdrawn again. But the landlord intervened.

"In ten minutes they are done, Monsieur," said he, a new servility struggling with his old surliness. "We have no other room except sleeping rooms."

"Which would not do. Bring wine and take away that candle," he went on, seating himself at the further end of the room in such a position that he faced the door. His companion, obedient to a gesture, also seated himself, but with a yard or two of space between. "Give it to these—ah—gentlemen yonder; they are almost in darkness."

"They've light enough to see to their mouths," he answered insolently, "and so I'll leave it."

"And I too much to see your face in," was the pat and no less insolent reply, "therefore you'll take it away."

It was the right method to deal with the fellow, for he at once bowed with a cringe.

"I'll fetch the wine, Monsieur; good, I suppose?"

"If you've got it!" and he went, taking the candle with him.

At the arbitrary limitation put upon us, Martin would have flared out had I not restrained him, and though he laughed at the stranger's bitter retort over the disputed light, he whispered, "It is not the landlord's face he loves the darkness for, but his own; see how he hides it."

"Let him," I answered; "a thing may be honest enough, and yet better hidden; look at our rags."

"For them we have to thank Jan Meert."

"And he God Almighty for his face."

Though both were plainly dressed, I could soon tell they were not on a par. Only one spoke, and when the wine came, though he poured some into his glass, he drank none, but pushed the bottle impatiently on to his neighbour as if deeper things to think of gave him a contempt for such toys. As to the man nearest us, he took both the wine and the touch of arrogance as a matter of course, and swallowed each with a relish as men do both gifts and slights of the great.

Thus we sat till the ten minutes were up and we had finished our meal but not our wine. Then, as the host came bustling up to rout us out I bade Martin softly leave him to me.

"Now that you've eaten," said he, "perhaps the other room will be nice enough for your lordships' nobility."

"This is nice enough for want of better," I answered; "but it is dull; bring us the dice."

"Dice elsewhere; this room is bespoke."

"Aye, by us."

"But these gentlemen—"

"Came last."

The man in the cloak settled the dispute.

"Let them stay," he cried out. "Messieurs, an end of the room for you, and an end for us. Will that content you?"

"If the other room were not a doghole— —" I began.

But he interrupted me with an outbreak of the same supercilious arrogance, saying curtly:

"Have I not said it was settled? If I am content, surely you may be," and fell again silent.

"What did I say?" whispered Martin, rubbing his hands that he had at last found confirmation for his tales, "a duke or a simple gentleman, the Sieur Hellewyl, Monsieur de Commines, Monsieur de Vesc; eh, Monsieur Gaspard?"

It was while we were still playing at playing with the dice that the second interruption came. With much politeness but yet more curiosity three further guests were ushered in, and again two of them were hooded like conspirators, but this time with a difference—they were women. Their age or figures no man could guess, so hidden were they, but one was tall, and bore herself with a carriage that suggested lissom activity. The third of their party was as frankly revealed as they were frankly disguised; a sinewy broad-shouldered man, with Soldier written largely on him from head to heel in characters that spoke louder than the weapons at hip and thigh.

The three stood in silence together until—some trivial order having been given and obeyed—the door shut out the landlord's inquisition. Then, as if by common consent, the smaller woman with their guard—for in that capacity he attended them there could be no doubt—moved round the head of the table to where was an open fireplace set in a deep alcove midway down the wall opposite the door. The humbler of the two first comers joined them there, but stood apart, leaving his leader and the taller of the women in comparative isolation at the further end of the room.

At her entrance he had risen, bowing with the careless courtesy of a stranger and receiving in return as negligent an acknowledgment; but though my curiosity had been stirred like that of the landlord, it was her first word that fairly aroused it.

"Narbonne," said he.

"Argenton," was the answer.

CHAPTER VI
THE MUSE IN DRAGGLED SKIRTS

Argenton! That was strange, so strange that I started on my stool at the end of the table, and half rose. Of course they were passwords, but why Argenton? Argenton was the lordship of Monsieur de Commines, to whom I looked for protection; why Argenton?

Bowing again, but with a warmer courtesy, he motioned her to take his place at the inner side of the table while he, drawing the end of stool a foot or two back towards the corner, sat, half-concealed by her shrouded bulk.

"Mademoiselle will excuse me uncovering?" he said, touching his slouched hat, "and will also remember we are not alone."

Turning, she glanced down at us as we sat in the light of our one guttering candle. It was my first glimpse of her face, but so deep was her hood I saw no more than an oval of pallor in the darkness of its cavity.

"I think," said she contemptuously, with a glance at the scattered group in the alcove, "we could soon be alone if Monseigneur thought it desirable."

Of the hint and the contempt I alike took no notice, of the latter because of the former; the threat that underlay it fixed me to my seat. To have moved then, was to move upon compulsion. But as we continued our play with the dice as if the words had never been said, her companion interposed hastily.

"No, no. I confess I thought of that before you came. But brawling would serve neither you nor me, no, nor those who—who—trust us."

"That there is trust between us, Monseigneur, I am glad to know," she answered, "for as yet, I have not seen much of it—on one side."

So far they had spoken with no pretence at concealment, their object, I surmised, being to disabuse us of all suspicion of deep matters. But now their voices fell to a murmur, over which the click of the dice on the wood of the table sounded to my tense nerves like a clash of swords. Let it be remembered that I was but a country lad. All this was new to me, and the pricking threat of danger, the secrecy, the very air of Paris itself, fired my blood.

And so the minutes passed; the girl—I was sure she was a girl, so sweet was her voice, so gentle, and with a stirring music in it that was strange to me in women's voices. Since then I have heard a like music throbbing from a bird's song in the pure blue of a summer's noon, and been thrilled by it as I was then; yes, I was sure it was a girl.

The girl it was who spoke most, spoke with a varying mood that charmed and angered me; even when mechanically flinging the dice I feigned not to see the eagerness, the insistence, the passion, the pleading whose murmured words fell like tears. What right had that stolid clod—clod was what Paris had called us in her streets, and the name stuck—what right had he to be so coldly unmoved, so silent, that he only answered her by a word or a gesture of denial? But she would take no denial, and with the brave spirit of a good woman returned to her pleading, pushing the petition home urgently, even strengthening her arguments by two outstretched arms, and a hand upon his shoulder. How did I know all that? Ah! every clod on which the sun strikes has a soul within it, and so I knew.

Yet what did he answer?

"All must be as the King wills," said he, his words roughening with distinctness as if he were not altogether sorry to be overheard. "All as the King wills, remember that, Mademoiselle. He is the potter, I the clay; he is everything, I nothing—nothing."

"Nothing!" she echoed, her voice rising level with his own, "why! all France knows that you are the King in everything but name. What you say to-day, Louis says to-morrow; why deny it? Let us come to the bare truth. We desire peace, desire it with all our heart, and you say you will do nothing. Is that to be your answer, Monseigneur?"

"Not that I will do nothing, but that I am nothing. If all France thinks it knows better, then all France is a fool. I sleep in his chamber, I tend him, I wait upon him, I valet him—I think no shame of that; he is the greatest King and wisest man in Christendom—I do these things, but—I am nothing. Or," he went on, after a pause, "if I am something—anything, it is because I am careful to be nothing. By a breath he undoes me, and I would not have it different. France grows great by the greatness of its Kings, and if France falls, it will be because the King has let the shadow of the people fall upon the throne."

"Then—is it ruin?" I do not think she meant the words to be heard, but she was shaken out of herself, and spoke louder than she knew. "Must a great house fail that greatness may grow yet a little greater? And so little greater, so very little! Much to us, Monseigneur, ah! you can never guess how much, but so little to France. Is that your answer, ruin, ruin, ruin?"

A silence fell, and I will not deny that though I still fingered the dice my breath was held to catch the reply. It came slowly, gravely, spoken as a man speaks who knows his own weight, and the weight his words cannot help but carry.

"I, too, desire peace, but all is as the King wills."

Whether she would have urged him afresh I do not know, but opportunity was wanting. All through supper, and afterward, sounds of carousals had come across the courtyard from the common room, hoarse bursts of song, hoarser laughter, roared out oaths, and the occasional scuffle of feet stamping on the sanded floor. Then came a time of quiet, and had I but known my Paris better I would have guessed that then was the time of danger. While Paris is noisy, Paris, by a paradox, is safe and tranquil; when Paris thinks, and speaks under its breath, then Paris is dangerous.

But of the many wild beasts that couch in France, Paris was the one of which I knew the least, and when I thought the night drew to peace, Paris was already on the spring. A door opened more quietly than a door is commonly opened with a half-drunk reveller's hand upon the latch; from the courtyard a voice or two spoke out, spoke shortly and without clamour. Then, unheralded by warning, came the third interruption of the night. Both wings of the door were flung open, and in the space a figure showed itself, which, apart from its sudden appearance, must still have drawn our eyes.

It was a man so beragged, and so variously bepatched as to be ridiculous, were it not that aged poverty is always pathetic. Every stuff of the looms had gone to his clothing, every shade of the dyer, faded and weatherstained, peeped and twinkled in the mendings of his tatters. But the eye soon shifted from these frank advertisements of starved penury, and wandering to his face, stayed there, fixed by a fascination that defies analysis. Let a soul but look out of window, and whether it be naked Priapus plastered to the crown with filth, or Saint Francis of the birds—are there not many gods in the Olympus of the mind?—they who see it must needs look back, and never heed what are the drapings of flesh through which it peers.

From under a dirty linen cap, from which, in a derision of gaiety, drooped a draggled red feather, three or four grey locks strayed across a noble forehead till they met and thickened a line of delicate brows. The nose was thin, hooked, and cruel, pinched in at the nostrils to a fixed sneer; the cheeks lean and smooth, but covered with a network of fine wrinkles branching from below the eyes. Over a loose, full-lipped mouth, red, sensuous, and smiling, fell an almost white moustache, caught up into an audacious curve at the ends; the chin was bearded by a straggle of thin silver hair drawn to a point.

But, more than all the rest, the eyes marked him for a man of brains, so full were they, so lustrous, and yet so piercing; age might whiten him, shrivel him; an evil life, hard lived, might shake his nerve, but the eyes and the brain and the soul of the man bated no jot of their strength. Behind him—strangely like, and yet strangely unakin—tiptoeing or stooping low to see the better, was such a gathering of rabble as a casting of nets will draw from the denser, fouler slums of any great city.

Laying a long-fingered, delicate, much-soiled hand upon his breast, he bowed satirically.

"Mesdames and Messieurs, and you, the disguised princes of the blood in the dark yonder, you sweepings of the hedgerows who cannot eat in the presence of men more like Almighty God in intelligence than yourselves, you are welcome every one of you. We looked for tribute from two of earth's scum," he went on, posing himself negligently, one foot advanced, a fist doubled on a hip, the fingers of the other playing with his straggled beard point, "and lo! there are seven great and small; therefore, as seven is to two, and the product to the emptiness of our pockets, so is our welcome."

By this time all, whether within the room, or without, were on their feet, but the seven of which he spoke so gibingly were still in three groups. But he who called himself Narbonne was naturally the spokesman of us all and he it was who answered.

"Take your jest elsewhere, and your filthy crew with it," he said coldly. "Piff! your very smell is an offence."

But the other never stirred, nor did the smile leave his face; only his eyes narrowed, and his full mouth grew hard, the lips tightening till the stumps showed in the gums.

"'Tis the oil of the student," he answered suavely; "the literary flavour as we in Paris know it, or maybe, your nostrils are unaccustomed to the sweet-smelling flowers of Parnassus? To some poor souls the perfume of poesy is as strange as the odour of sanctity. They have my pity!"

"Again, I tell you, take your jest elsewhere."

"Jest! My friend, you cannot have lived in courts. Now, I know court life as I know my barren pouch. Jest? Does our brother Louis jest when he knocks at the door of high and low and says, Pay me my taxes? His is a door of wood, mine that yet harder, more tightly fitting door, the human heart! You do not understand? Listen then! Francis the First, King of Divine Song, Prince of all Poets, Elder Brother to the Nine Muses and Father of the Lord knows what, levies tribute, and by God! Messieurs and Mesdames, he'll see it paid! These," and he pointed, thumb across shoulder, to the tattered slum bullies, thieves, cut-throats, and night-walkers, who had pushed him forward almost to the edge of the table, "these are our honourable tax-collectors, lambs almost as gentle as our brother Louis' own. Do you pay, Messieurs, or must the law take its course?"

From his place in the alcove, he who had been the women's attendant stepped forward.

"Let me deal with the rabble, Monseigneur."

"Silence, sir, know your place—and mine," he added significantly. Then, turning to the fellow across the table he went on sternly, "and you, leave the King's name out of your mummery, or your fool's wit may not save your neck."

"I have looked through a halter ere now, and come away neither sadder nor wiser than you see me. God forbid I should ever be one or other. I have even given my Testament to the world, a thing few men do and live. Alas! How the world changes. But that is past and the bird sings no longer.

Ou sont les gratieux gallards
Que je suy voye au temps jadis,
Si bien chantans, si bien parlans,
Si plaisans en faicts et en dicts?

Hung, I sadly fear, hung, every mother's son of them! But the bird still sits upon the bough, and if in age it sings less, still needs must that it fills its craw, so, come, sir, pay up! Like my brother Louis, I try smooth means first, but, also like my brother Louis, I do not stop there; and, again like my brother Louis, when I squeeze I squeeze hard.

Necessité fait gars mesprendre,
Et faim saillir le loup des boys,

"François, the one and only King of Song, has spoken!"

"François? What? Art thou that François Villon?"

The fellow laughed as he bowed with a flourish.

"Monsieur has said it!"

"François Villon? And not hanged yet?"

Again he laughed, but this time without merriment; the gibe and the contempt were alike bitter.

"Again Monsieur has said it! Twice, no, when I come to think of it, thrice Montfauçon has sighed for me, and yet I live. By my faith! I begin to think I shall die in my bed if I do not first starve in the streets!"

"François Villon——"

"I have said it, I have said it; King François Villon, François the first, François the last, François Villon, the lover of all the Muses and every pretty woman in the world! And now that you know me, Monsieur, your purse, that François Villon the man and his tax collectors may drink and bless you. What? You will not? Ah, be persuaded, be gently persuaded, what is a purse or two, a handful of beggarly coins, compared with—Mademoiselle is with you, is she not? Then God forbid that I should finish the comparison. As a poet I hate ugly realities, as a man I love pretty women, and François Villon the man—Alas! we all have our passions, our frailties, you understand; eh? Look at us, we can be rough at times, just as our brother Louis can, and not having seen Mademoiselle's face I do not know if it is worth our while to quarrel. One peep, Mademoiselle, one little glimpse for the poet; the man, whose delights are not altogether pleasures of the mind, can come later if it is worth his while; one look, just one," and leaning across the narrow table he stretched out a long arm as if to twitch her hood aside.

"*Mon Dieu*! Monseigneur," she cried, not shrinking back, but holding herself erect just out of reach of the foul and twitching fingertips. "Is there no one to kill this infamous wretch?"

In a flash her neighbour's sword was out, and with its point at Villon's throat he cried;

"Another inch, and she shall see it done!"

To do him justice, Villon never flinched, but stood there silent, rigid as a statue, his loose lips parted in an evil smile, his eyes searching the shaded faces of the two fronting him. But if he held his peace, those about him did not. Look on us! he had said, and said wisely. It was a frank warning, a cynical invitation to repulsion and disgust. From noisome cellars and crazy garrets, down rotting stairways, by crooked sunless lanes, from thieves' dens and nameless stews of vice where neither law, honour, or sweetness of life ever went, they had come, these garbage rats of the sewers of Paris, of which he said, Look on us! And the brand of their lives was red on them, as if stamped by the hangman's iron. Weasel face, rat face, wolf face; look on us! human brutes every one. And like brutes they bore themselves, growling, snarling, spitting; their teeth bared to bite.

Little by little they had pressed in after Villon, little by little they had spread themselves through the room, but mostly at the upper end, guessing that the sweetest pickings lay there, and in a herd, as if they drew a natural brute courage from the feel and jostle of numbers. Never for an instant were they still, but shifted restlessly like wolves in a cage; never for an instant were they silent, and when the chief brute of them all, he of the God-given brain, laid upon the altar of service to the devil, said, Look on us! a guttural chorus rose that gave point and barb to the menace. They knew the power of evil and gloried in it. Arms were shaken in the air, arms in sleeves, arms in tatters, arms bare, women's arms, men's arms, and in every fist was a weapon, a knife, a cleaver, a bludgeon, anything that could maim or bruise, even cobble stones torn from the streets were flourished above shock heads, the slime of the kennel still wet upon them.

With the blade at Villon's throat the chorus swelled to a roar, and I was passing up behind Martin's back, my own sword half drawn, when he stopped me.

"No, no, Monsieur Gaspard," he whispered, clinging to my sleeve as he had clung to Roland's bridle the day Solignac was burned. "Let them settle it among themselves; our way is by the window opposite. What have we to do with other men's brawls. Once in the courtyard and——" He stopped short and swung round on his heel. "*Dame*! there is the fellow who struck Ninus across the muzzle! With you, Monseigneur, with you! A Hellewyl! a Hellewyl! Only for heaven's sake, let the women stand back." And before I could follow his change of mood he had flung our candle into a corner and was leaning across the table side by side with him I have called Monsieur Narbonne. "We pay no debts in Paris, do we not?" he cried, jerking a knee on to the table with his left hand while he lunged with the right, "My faith! but we do, we of Flanders!" and his blade went home.

It was first blood for us. From behind Villon was drawn back out of reach of the point at his throat, over went the table between us—Martin saving himself by a backward leap—and what happened thereafter I cannot tell. Twice I was hurt; once by a stone on the shoulder, and once by a stab instinctively parried in the dark by my left arm. But the putting out of the light saved us. Through the windows a straggle of moonbeams fell on the yelling, rascally mob, but left us in gloom. If they were outlines we were shadows, so like the fuller darkness as to be hardly visible, and the shadows had the advantage. Of two things the room seemed full; noise, the din of cursing voices, shuffling feet, groans, obscenities, and a faint play of light like the flight of dull fireflies as the moon caught the twisting flats of steel.

Then the end came, but from without, not from within; a knocking at the inn door that grew louder and louder, and as it grew the babel within sobered. The kennel crew knew its meaning better than we. By ones and twos, and then in a swarm, the mob fled. François the First and Last, King of Song, and High Priest of all the rest of his blatancy, heard Montfauçon call for the fourth time, and had no heart to dance upon nothing to the music of that sinister voice.

CHAPTER VII
THE SHREWDEST BRAIN IN FRANCE

By the provost's lantern we were able to count losses. Martin had a cut upon the forehead which, dribbling down by the corner of his mouth, gave him a pitiful appearance, but meant little. The thickness of his skull, he said, saved him. Monsieur Narbonne's companion had his own wounds to lament, and Mademoiselle's guard was cursing softly in a language I did not understand over a palm slashed in warding off a two-edged dagger. If it was French he spoke, it was no French that I had ever heard. Monseigneur was unhurt, and my own bruises were no worse than three or four days would see cured.

Beyond the table the damage was not much greater. Of the three on the floor, and the two afterwards found in the court, only he who had received Martin's first thrust had forestalled the hangman. For the rest, *Toute beste garde sa pel,* had been Villon's motto, and his fellow rabble had echoed it.

At first it seemed as if we would join the other four upon the gallows, and so settle our quarrel with equal honours. But drawing the provost aside, Monseigneur showed him some token which turned the midnight of his face to a smiling noon, and if we had but expressed the wish, he would have dangled his four prisoners from the newly-painted sign there and then. "In any case it is but three days' delay," said he cheerfully, "and if the first loiters but a little, all five can travel home together."

Next he was anxious to see Monseigneur safe to his lodgings, but was met by a firm refusal.

"I know my Paris. In the open street so large a party is safe. These," and he paused, looking doubtfully at us, nor, in the faint yellow light of the smoky lantern was our appearance prepossessing, "these—um—gentlemen had better join my friends."

"So, so!" And in his zeal that the extreme justice of the law might not be cheated three days later, even by such pitiful wretches as we, the provost caught Martin by the arm. "Monseigneur does not know these—um—gentlemen?"

Before either Monseigneur or I could answer, Martin cut in, the ominous grip of the sleeve quickening his tongue, and the seeming trivial interference bore its fruit later on.

"We are Gaspard Hellewyl of Solignac in Flanders, and his servant," said he, shaking off the persuasive hand.

The thiefcatcher promptly replaced it.

"That is for Monseigneur to say, not you—Do you know these men, my lord?"

The answer and the action that foreran it startled me. Taking the lantern from the provost's hand, Monseigneur, still keeping himself completely in shadow, threw the light brightly on to Martin's face.

"Yes," he said slowly, "I know Hellewyl of Solignac in Flanders, but—" he stopped.

"I am—" began Martin, only to be checked by a wave of Monseigneur's unoccupied hand.

"That will keep," he said curtly. "For the present it is enough that I know and vouch for Hellewyl of Solignac. You have horses? Get them, then; I give you ten minutes. Mademoiselle," and he turned to the hooded woman who, with her companion, had remained in the shelter of the alcove throughout the *melée*. How she had borne herself I could only guess, for her face was still hidden, but she had neither uttered cry nor hampered us in any way, "this is a lesson, a book without words, and a child may read the pictures. I desire peace, and war is forced upon me."

What she answered I do not know. He had such a curt, masterful way with him that when he said, I give you ten minutes, self-interest advised, Take eight or less. There was not even time to ask ourselves, Who is this that knows Hellewyl of Solignac here in Paris? That it was Monsieur de Commines himself we never guessed. I, for I had never met him, nor had Martin seen him for nineteen years, while he was still a lad in the service of Charles the Bold, and then not often.

Nor was it so strange that we should meet as we did. Martin had only told the truth when he said the Star of Dauphiny had been a rendezvous in the old days, and now, when Monsieur de Commines had need of a trysting place where all might go without remark, the memory of his youthful experience had come back to him. Of the changes for the worse twenty years had in the inn worked he knew as little as Martin.

It was a procession of two and two, headed by Monseigneur's companion, that presently turned westward down the Rue Neuve Saint

Martin. Mademoiselle's guard and woman attendant went next, then Monsieur de Commines and Mademoiselle, Martin and I bringing up the rear, the only mounted members of the party. We men had our swords drawn, and all kept the middle of the streets. These were mostly dark and empty, ill-lit by a cloudy half-moon. When a band of night-prowlers met us, our numbers were passport enough, and they slunk away into the gloom of a side lane. If up these we heard the noise of a scuffle, a cry, a clash, a blasphemy, even an appeal for help, we marched on as if we had not heard; murder and theft were the common events of the night, and the weak must pay the penalty of their weakness. With women to guard we did not divide our party, and to have penetrated into the unlit ways was to court destruction. In the midst of most open spaces bonfires blazed, round which the watch gathered, and across certain streets chains were drawn to break the rush of the mob in times of disaffection.

During their long tramp, those immediately in front of us spoke little. To avoid the offal flung on the streets and the holes half filled with slime strained all their attention in the dim light. But as we paused where the Rue des Poulies joins the Rue Saint Honoré, I heard Monsieur de Commines say:

"Is it wise, so near the Louvre?"

"The nearer the church, the further from grace, Monseigneur," she answered bitterly, "and I suppose I may adapt the saying to The nearer the foe, the farther from danger. Besides, who knows we are in Paris?"

"Few things pass in Paris that my master does not know; he has eyes at the end of the earth," was the reply as we turned down to the left.

But only a little way. Opposite a darkened house, a few steps down the Rue des Poulies, we again halted, and as Monseigneur bent over Mademoiselle's hand in farewell, she held him fast.

"Is it ruin, truly ruin?" she said, the tears trembling in her voice. "Oh, Monseigneur, Monseigneur, can you not give us some hope? So much to us, so little to France; give us some hope to live upon, Monseigneur, for the love of God!"

Monsieur de Commines made no attempt to withdraw his hand, nor, in his place, would I. But his voice had a cheery ring through its gravity as he answered—

"Take comfort, Mademoiselle, take comfort. Though all must be as the King wills, two things fight for you; I desire peace, and time is on your side."

"Ah!" she replied, still bitterly, "that is cold comfort, cold as—as—the love of Louis." Then her voice sharpened as if she had caught a meaning in his tone which the bare words failed to suggest; or it may be a pressure of the hand had passed in the darkness; had I been in his place, I think it would, "unless, indeed, Monseigneur, you have some plan in your head, you, who are so shrewd, so far of sight, the cleverest, clearest brain in France, ah, then—then there would be hope."

This time he dropped her hand as if its touch scorched him.

"A plan? Who am I to have plans, Mademoiselle? No, no, not a plan, hardly that, hardly that. Farewell, Mademoiselle, farewell, Madame; my last word is this, forget Paris and the Star of Flanders. Come, gentlemen, our way lies forward," and he walked briskly on towards the river just showing its silver between the darkness of the walls on either hand, leaving us to follow.

But a few steps further on, the door having closed behind the women, he turned and called sharply,

"Monsieur Hellewyl, here, if you please. No, no," he went on, as I drew up to his side, "not you, but that weasel-faced fellow who calls himself Gaspard Hellewyl of Solignac in Flanders. It is he I want."

"But I am Gaspard Hellewyl of Solignac."

"Thou? Then how came he to call himself Hellewyl?"

"That was your misapprehension, Monseigneur. He is my—what shall I say?" and I laughed a little bitterly, a little forlornly, "my squire, my servant, my retinue, the last friend left to the last Hellewyl unless Monsieur de Commines can help me. You cut him short in his explanation."

"A misapprehension?" he repeated. "My word for it, young gentleman, but you rubbed shoulders with the gibbet for that misapprehension. If I had not been a trifle in your debt I would have left you to the provost's mercies for what I took to be an impudent lie. I knew Hellewyl of Solignac of old, but you, who are you?"

"Gaspard Hellewyl, son to Philip Hellewyl who was in Paris nineteen years ago, and died in 'sixty five.'"

"Turn your face to the light. In these unsettled times we must run no risks. Yes, the age fits, and you have a look of Philip. I took you for a pair of night-hawks, and that such sorry clothing bestrode such well-bred beasts strengthened the thought." Long before this we had walked slowly onward, still in the direction of the river, I by his side, with Roland's bridle in one hand. "But the story of the incongruity can wait," he went on; "Monsieur de Commines? What claim have you on him?"

"He was my father's friend——"

"Nineteen years ago!" he interrupted cynically. "In an age of short memories have you no claim more modern?"

"He is a far-off cousin."

"A relationship Monsieur de Commines has apparently never remembered or recognised; anything more plausible than a German cousinship?"

I shook my head.

"Yes," and he laid a hand on my shoulder, pressing it warmly, "I know better. You have five claims, one dead, and four with three days' life in them. I am Philip de Commines."

"Monsieur de Commines? The Prince de Talmont?"

"The same, and in all sincerity let me add, at your service. But we can talk of that later. Do you know your whereabouts? No, how could you! This is the Louvre, and our lodging for to-night."

Monsieur de Commines! The Louvre! I could only stare. As we talked we had walked on, to the right by the Rue du Petit Bourbon, to the left down the Rue d'Hosterische, bordered on the one side by a wide fosse beyond which rose a palace of disenchantment. The Louvre! When one spoke of the Louvre I had imagined I know not what, but a vague glory fired the fancy. The Louvre! These frowning walls of dirty grey were a prison house, these little pierced windows the shot-holes of a threatened fortress, that rounded donjon in the centre the King's clenched fist menacing Paris, those pointed towers at the corners—But Monseigneur cut the catalogue short; we were already at the moat.

Late though it was, the drawbridge was lowered, a guard of three standing at the hither end. To these Monsieur de Commines gave the password, and we crossed to a small postern that pierced the walls to the right of the sunk gateway. Through this he led us.

"You will come with me, Monsieur Hellewyl. Morlaix will see after—is it Martin you call him? Only, remember this, all three. You heard my farewell to Mademoiselle? Take it to yourselves, and forget the Star of Flanders. To-night I have been on the King's business, and Louis has but one cure for loose tongues. I ask no promises, your risk is my best assurance."

Some men would have said "your honour," but not Monsieur de Commines; he had lived long at courts and preferred to rest his claim on the surest foundation.

It was not until my wounds were dressed, and garments of I know not whose ownership provided in place of my mired rags, that Monsieur de

Commines—we being in the privacy of his own suite of rooms—asked for my story. Nor did he interrupt me in its telling, but sat like a statue, his face turned up to the painted ceiling. The failure of our fortunes, the burning of Solignac, the murder of old Babette, moved him no more than if a stranger had bidden him good day. But as I ended he lowered his eyes, looking at me keenly but not unkindly.

"And why do you come to Paris?"

My answer was as curt as the question.

"To move Monsieur de Commines to move the King to give me justice on Jan Meert."

"I might as well hope to move the Louvre to carry you to Plessis les Tours—unless the King willed to be moved. And on Jan Meert!" a little grim smile dashed with a tolerant contempt, broke over his lips; "a Hollander, eh?"

"You know him, Monseigneur, you know him!" I cried impetuously, moved less by the words than by the look on his face, "Oh, then, it will be easy."

"I know many things," he answered, the smile deepening. "I know this, my friend; you are very innocent. Did it never strike you that the King of France has many agents—no, agents is too strong a word, it implies a kind of intimacy, a private confidence,—call them tools?"

"Agents? Tools? Monseigneur, Monseigneur, what commerce can a King of France have with a Jan Meert?"

"Commerce? Pish! this time it is you who use too strong a word. Monsieur Hellewyl, do you know how kingdoms are built? how varied, how complex, yes, and at times how opposite, the elements of construction? Loyalty at home, treason abroad, a bribe to avarice, a threat to cowardice, flattery to pride, men's blood, tears of women, babes made fatherless, the wisdom of a Louis, the rashness of a Charles, the I would but I dare not of a Maximilian, the brutishness of a Jan Meert."

"The Most Christian King and Jan Meert! Oh! Monseigneur, the conjunction is impossible, the thought is too contemptible."

Commines' face darkened as he leaned towards me, his arms resting on his knees.

"Learn to guard your tongue, Monsieur, when you speak of the greatest monarch now upon earth. How can you, a green and weedy sapling out of a Flanders hedge, judge the oak of the forest? Is a gardener unclean because he raises a flower of nobility and strength from the outscourings of a stable?"

But the wound to my hopes galled me, and I was obstinate.

"I do not see the King's gain in such an honourable partnership."

"I will tell you. But first, why should the King do justice for you on Jan Meert?"

"It might give him a hold on Flanders."

"You must have a great mind, friend Gaspard, for you and the King thought alike, only he before the event, and you after. Anarchy in Flanders creates a need for the strong hand of a better government, and so—Jan Meert!"

"Then Monseigneur," said I helplessly, "my quest is ended before it is well begun."

But Monsieur de Commines shook his head. The sudden sternness that had flashed into his voice had passed away, and he was once more the friend and patron.

"You go too fast. Never try to take all your ditches at one stride. Some tools are only used once and then flung aside, others of their kind being never far to seek. There are many Jan Meerts in the world. As I said before I say again, All is as the King wills. What is your plan? Except Monsieur de Beaujeu, the officers of state, and myself, the King sees no gentlemen. That is his humour. Are you very proud, Monsieur Hellewyl?"

"Not too proud to serve—"

"The King?"

"Myself, Monseigneur," I retorted, for I had caught his meaning. He laughed and nodded.

"Good, I see you have learned your lesson. There are times when a man must stoop that he may rise. That will suit the King's humour. I will be frank with you. He spends his time raising men up and casting them down again, that France may understand her master's life is still strong in him. He loves new faces, but soon tires or grows doubtful. There lies your opportunity. To have a gentleman of ten generations serve him as a servant will please him. Before he tires, or grows doubtful of your fidelity, your chance may come."

"To move him to justice?"

"No, no; I said you were very innocent. To earn your wages: Jan Meert's life in your hand, a new Solignac on the ashes of the old, your lost lands restored."

"Large wages, Monseigneur," said I, drawing in a breath, and catching something of the spirit of hope throbbing high in his words, "almost too large to dream of receiving, except in a dream."

"Pish! Now you are modest! When the King gives, he gives royally, only, remember this, large wages mean great service. If the pay is to be earned, the task will match the pay. Are you afraid?"

"God helping me, Monseigneur, no!"

"Just so," answered he, drily, "God helping you. It is a help most men need who wade in King's waters," and sat looking at me in deep thought.

CHAPTER VIII
THE DOORS OF THE LOUVRE ONLY OPEN INWARDS

I have always been uncertain whether or not the task, as he phrased it, which ultimately became mine, was already taking form in Monsieur de Commines' mind. His attitude of incisive contemplation gave colour to the supposition. But, on the other hand, it was never quite clear with whom the idea truly originated: not, I am convinced with Monseigneur in its final shape. When questioned, Monsieur de Commines always took shelter behind his favourite formula, All was as the King willed. In a sense, that, no doubt, was the case, especially in my last instructions, but from much that happened when my stewardship was accounted for I have always believed that Monseigneur admitted a liability to his conscience. If that were so, then, let me say, he discharged that liability to its last shadow of a claim, discharged it generously, fully, without reserve, and at a time when he had much need to give his whole thought to his own danger.

But, interesting as a man's affairs are to himself—and there is nothing he loves better to talk about than What I have done, What I am doing, and What I shall do to-morrow—there was a curtness in his last words that warned me off to other subjects.

"Shall we see Mademoiselle again?"

"Mademoiselle?" Into Monsieur de Commines eyes there crept a look a uncomprehending but tolerant amusement. "Alas! I have reached the age when Mademoiselles cease to interest. But with youth it is different, and youth, as usual, is always right. If she has a fortune she may put a roof on Solignac sooner than the King will, and at a less risk. I have known many a broken house patched-up by a woman's hand, slender and white though it is. Has she a fortune, my friend, and—who is Mademoiselle?"

"Oh! Monseigneur, I have been indiscreet."

"Young and yet indiscreet, oh! no, no! Besides, indiscretion is the venial offence of lovers. If it were not so long since I had kissed a maid I would almost say it is their privilege. But you see, I am ten years married, and have forgotten. If Mademoiselle is satisfied, why should I complain? Indeed, I would almost doubt that a man were a true lover, and had veins aglow with the dear fires of Venus, if he were not discreetly indiscreet at times. It has the sanction of great antiquity, for it dates from the garden of Eden. Adam, I am sure, was indiscreet—he spoke to the lady without an introduction. Or perhaps the Devil acted as Master of Ceremonies? What do you think? That also would be a precedent, and one followed many a million time since then. The Lord God threw Adam into a sleep, and the Devil waked him, eh? To this day, sleep is the greatest gift of God,—blessed be sleep!—and waking, at times, is the very devil; have you not found it so yourself?"

"Oh Monseigneur," I cried again, deeply hurt by his jeering banter with its pretended misapprehension. "I repeat, I have been indiscreet. I am in the wrong."

"And being there, Monsieur Hellewyl, you are where no gentleman should ever put himself."

I shrugged my shoulders. For a man who knew the world so well Monsieur de Commines was going the wrong way about gaining his end.

"To put myself right, then, I had best answer my own question; I shall see Mademoiselle—to-morrow."

He only bowed, waited a second or two, then, saying carelessly that the hour was late, called a lackey to show me my quarters for the night, and we parted with constraint. Yes, Monsieur de Commines' lesson had gone too far. I do not say it was not deserved, but youth loves to think itself above laughter, and few things bite deeper through its sensitive skin than does a barbed jest. That I was not only a fool, but an ungrateful fool, I am now the first to admit. But a wound to self-esteem has this quality, it blinds as well as galls and I could see no farther than my temper.

As I leaned out of the narrow window that overlooked the river, my indignation was too hot to be cooled by the night air, my irritation too raw to be soothed by the beauty or strangeness of the scene. And yet, to a man fresh from the outskirts of a Flanders wood, how much there was of beauty and strangeness.

Underneath me, beyond the fosse, lay the garden, bordered on either side by the thin stream of the water that fed the moat; beyond that swept the river, broad and full and a-swirl with strength. Here it gloomed to blackness, there it flashed bright and smooth as steel where the moon caught the soundless slope of the currents as they met below Ile Notre Dame. To the left the Tour de Nesle rose on the further bank, black and sinister with its tradition of murder, the water lapping almost to its buttresses. Still farther to the left was the huge bulk of the Chateau Galliard; farther yet, and Notre Dame melted into the vapours of the night, lost against the background of the Ile des Vaches and Ile de Javiaux. Out of the vapours rose spires, towers, and sloping roofs innumerable, shining with dew or edged to a white effulgence as the full lustre of the moon glorified them.

But if the river slept, writhing and turning in its sleep as though ill dreams of drowned men plagued its rest, Paris was awake. But Paris never sleeps. It is a body possessed of many souls, many spirits—devils, some would say—and when slumber nurses one to quiet another rouses to carry on the fevered actions of its life. It is a forest of many beasts; those of the day couch to their rest at sunset, and in the same hour the prowlers of the night creep from their lairs, foul beasts of prey that love the darkness and thrive on deeds from which men hide their faces. The *pad, pad, pad,* of their stealthy feet may be heard in the byeways, the growling of their hunger, the crash of their spring. To and fro they wander, never satisfied, and seek their dens before the coming of dawn when the creatures of innocent labour awake to the burden of a new day. No! Paris never sleeps!

The wakefulness was least to the east side where, beyond the Rue d'Hosterische, the Hotel de Bourbon sulked silent in its great square courtyard. There men both waked and slept, but waked watchful and on guard lest the prowling beast, desperate from famine, should spring at higher game than common. From the south, over the river, came a murmur as of bees, a murmur that hoarsened with the livelier play of the wind, as when one taps the hive, or fell away to a thin drone with the dying of the breeze. Westward, life was sharper, more individual, and with swift surprises, of which one came as I watched; the loud patter of running feet in the Rue Froid Mantel just beyond the fosse, a woman's scream, the roaring out of a rough oath, and dwindling sobs cut through and over-borne by a far-off drunken roysterer's mirthless song.

But the obscure tragedy never moved me; a midge in a man's own eye is more hurt to him than a live coal in his neighbour's. Morning might have brought counsel, but that another small fret flecked the raw of my irritation, and kept the sore open—my borrowed finery had disappeared, and in its place lay the sorry garb, yet sorrier through travel, in which I had quitted Solignac. Clearly that was Monsieur de Commines' cynic response to my challenge of the night before, and was in itself a challenge.

Seek Mademoiselle, will you! he said in his heart, grimly jesting, then seek her beggar-fashion, and if your tongue asks no hire for your sword's service your rags will hint an importunity. In the glimmering light of the Star of Flanders she may have taken you for a gentleman; go, if you will go, in the broad light of day, and let these rags speak for you!

But if he thought shame would turn me from my purpose, court life must, for once, have blunted his perception. I hold that a sweet kernel has no need to think shame of a rough shell, and from a quality in her voice, an impulse in her act, I guessed that Mademoiselle was not one to judge a man wholly by the outside. A true and noble womanliness had at all times rung through her pleading, and if that were not enough there was this, she had flung no scorn even on such a feeder on garbage as this François Villon, until the man's foul mind hinted a license. Then, indeed, her soul flashed out. "Will no man rid us of this wretch!" It was the foul mind she scorned, and not the poverty peeping through his tatters. No! Monsieur de Commines' jest, so far from turning me from my purpose, confirmed me in it; I would have been ashamed to feel shamed that I dared not seek her face even in rags.

It was at the gate by which we had entered on the previous night I first learned that to lodge in a royal palace had its obligations as well as its honours, and that Monsieur de Commines had other arrows in this quiver besides that levelled at my self-conceit. One of the three or four on guard stopped me when I would have passed out.

"Your permit, Monsieur, if you please," said he, civilly enough.

"Permit? I have none," I answered. "I am lodging with Monsieur de Commines."

"Ah, I remember now. Monsieur has that droll of a Martin to follow him, and came in with Monsieur le Prince last night? As a form, Monsieur, I will send for my officer; will Monsieur wait?"

What could Monsieur do but wait, fretting and fuming, for twenty minutes. Then a smooth-faced boy came, smiling, cordial, and full of words. Had Monsieur Hellewyl rested well? Were his lodgings to his mind? Was it his first visit to Paris? Had he seen—Pish! it was Monsieur Hellewyl this, Monsieur Hellewyl that, and I answering yes or no, like a country blockhead with a vocabulary of one syllable. But when at last I got my plea in he shrugged his shoulders with a grimace.

"Would you have Tristan hang me? How can I give passes from the Louvre? Let us go to the lieutenant."

So from the east gate we went to the south, and as we crossed the angle of the court, the sun being above the walls, I felt like a half-plucked daw beside a parrot, so gaily plumed was he in silks and laces such as women love, and not a thread out of place. He said nothing, but the corner of his eye burned holes in my rags, and for the twitch of his mouth I could have shaken the life half out of him with exultant satisfaction.

The lieutenant of the southern gate was Monsieur de Commines' companion of the night before, limping slightly from a wound in the thigh, and again my greeting was most cordial. There is no introduction like a common danger. But the whole Louvre seemed in league to make me welcome, nor could even my impatience resent such friendliness to one who was a stranger. My wound and his had to be enquired for, and for the first time I learned that we had received them in a scuffle in the streets. Such brawls, it seemed, were of nightly occurrence, and I had to listen to a long complaint of how badly Paris was governed.

Then came the whole catechism over again; Had I slept? Was I rested? Did my wound still burn? Had that fire-eating weasel of mine been well cared for? And so on for a score of questions, all so kindly, so genial, so courteous, that I would have been a Flemish clod indeed to have cut them short.

But at last he asked:

"Now, what can I do for you?"

"Give me leave to pass the gates."

"What! You want fresh adventures?" he answered gaily, "then we must go to the captain."

He, it seemed, was on guard at the west gate, and there the comedy played itself for another half-hour. If his cordiality was colder, it was because age, in grizzling his beard, had chilled his exuberance, but it seemed none the less sincere. I must breakfast with him. What? I had breakfasted? Then I must try the King's wine, and for ten minutes we talked vintages, the thing, next to women and their own doings, on which men love best to gossip. Then, at last, came the belated request.

"So, so, Monsieur Hellewyl? But for that we we must go to the Governor."

"*Dame,*" said I pettishly. "It seems as hard for a man to get out of the Louvre as for most to get in."

"You are wrong," he answered, looking me straight in the eyes; "a simple word does it, Monsieur; one word, a simple promise."

It was then, so drily significant was the tone, that I began to understand the dance I was being led. Monsieur de Commines had no intention that I should leave the Louvre. No doubt the Governor would have to appeal to the Chancellor, the Chancellor to the King, and the King was at Plessis les Tours. Or it might be they would refer the momentous question to Monseigneur himself! Was he not the King's Commissioner? To play the comedy further would be to play the fool.

"A single word?" said I and pausing turned back, "I think I have it, Monsieur! It is Commines, is it not?"

Promptly he also turned.

"You have a shrewd wit when you choose to use it," he answered, laying his hand on my shoulder. "Take an old soldier's advice and follow where it leads you."

That meant, Make your peace with Monseigneur; a thing not hard to do, for he met me as if I had just risen from my bed instead of having spent the better part of two good hours trying to out-manoeuvre him.

"You are come in good time, for we dine early," he cried, holding out both hands; "sit down, now, and let us make haste, for we leave Paris at noon:" nor through the meal, or at any time, did he hint displeasure. Only, when the servant, who at the close brought us water to wash our fingers, had left the room, he said suddenly:

"Do you know why I did it? For this reason, to teach you that a man who is on the King's service has neither love nor hate, pride nor pique, no, nor even eyes or ears except for that service. It is a teaching you may have to follow before long."

Now it was my turn to hold out my hands, but with a different impulse.

"Forgive me, Monseigneur— —"

"I forgave you even while I taught you," he answered, not letting me finish. "What? Am I so old that I cannot remember I was once young? And now I shall answer you the question you asked me last night; will you see Mademoiselle again? I think so—if the King wills."

CHAPTER IX
HOW I MET MADEMOISELLE THE SECOND TIME

Though Monsieur de Commines travelled, as he said, on the King's service—a service which, I have since concluded, had it been known, might have cost him his head—he travelled without ostentation. And yet our train of twelve mounted guards, six led packhorses and as many body servants was a royal progress compared with our entrance to Paris.

We crossed the river by the ferry that plied from the Louvre gardens, landing near the end of the Rue de Seine, a hundred paces below the Tour de Nesle. Thence we followed the same street till we reached the Rue du Bussy, where we turned to the right, keeping straight on till we reached the pillory which stands, as a terror to evil-doers, at the junction of the Rue du Four and the Rue des Boucheries. There, in the triangular open space used as an occasional market, we were joined by Monsieur de Rochfort, the Chancellor, and Monsieur de Commines, who, so far, had ridden by my side pointing out this or that of interest as we passed, drew apart.

"It is for your sake," said he, with a kindly nod. "The Chancellor and I are both too near the King to wish well to the other's friends."

Once or twice thereafter through the day he reined back alongside Roland, just as he did with each of the three or four gentlemen in his train. But, unless we were out of earshot of the Chancellor's friends, there was an indifferent coldness in his manner which, more than any words could have done, warned me how warily men must walk whose paths lie near a throne. So plain was this coldness to himself that he half-excused it.

"There are three parties at court," said he waving his hand aside as if indicating some point in the landscape. "I call them the party of the present, of the early future, and for all time; or, to put it more clearly, of the King, of the Dauphin, and of France. I am of the last, and so most truly for the King, though all do not see as I do. When the King is well, Monsieur de Rochfort is of the first; when the King is sick, he is of the second; and never, to my thinking, of the third. Now, such a man rarely,—oh ho! here comes one of his friends slipping back to catch what I am saying. Good-morning, Monsieur de Bueil, there is an urgent matter on which I wish to consult you, but without advertisement. Do you think the Chancellor would consider it wise— —" and lowering his voice he drew aside, plunging into I know not what story, having in a single sentence flattered not only the Chancellor's wisdom and influence at court, but also Monsieur de Bueil's intimacy with his master.

That night we lay at Anneau where, because of the inn's cramped space, I slept on hay, and was glad of its softness for my wound still stung me. Next night our quarters were at Vendôme, and so Tours was reached before dinner on the third day. There Martin and I dropped off; Plessis, which lay a mile or so to the south-west, was not for us as yet.

"Put up at the Cross of Saint Martin," was Monsieur de Commines' last advice. "It is not the best inn in the city, but the other is in the Rue des Trois Pucelles, and so too near Confrère Tristan's for comfort, unless you have a strong stomach," a hint which, in my innocence, I failed to understand. "Give me a week," he added at parting, "but remember, I promise nothing except that I am at all times the friend of your father's son," and so rode on.

Later I was grateful for his choice of our lodgings. As we gaped about the streets, Martin a discreet half-pace behind me, but talking across my shoulder without a break, touched me.

"Monsieur Tristan's," he said, nodding at the other side. "That a man should make a gallows of the house where he eats and sleeps, and, it maybe, loves his wife and children."

"A gallows? where?"

"For God's sake walk on, Monsieur Gaspard, and don't stare. These nails, and that fag end of a cut rope blowing in the wind make my flesh creep."

That is always the way! The kennel is swimming in mud and a pretty woman crosses the road with her skirts a-tilt; or an unhappy gallant in silks is chasing his bonnet through the self-same mud, and you are bidden to look and not stare! Not stare? That's not in nature; the very warning is a challenge. Of course I stood and stared, though at first there was little to look at, a house, like a hundred others in Tours with a dozen of the kind in the same street. Then, as I looked again, there came a sense of the sinister. It was as when a face, which at the first glance seems one of a score, shows something of a peculiar and personal devil, and with it a fascination that fastens the attention, as all things evil or ugly fasten it.

It was a tall narrow house of four storeys, tapering as if by steps and stairs to a point at the ridge. The wall of the floor on the street level was pierced by two unequal windows, heavily barred. The larger was to the left, and in its position it balanced the stout door raised two steps above the pavement. Above these were three windows, the largest again to the left, and all with similar significant heavy defences; whoso lived there was careful of his safety. The two upper storeys were in the contraction of the roof. Each had but one outlook, and in the case of the lower it was again to the left, leaving a wide expanse of blank wall, and when I understood the tale it told, my gorge rose. Here was the sinister threat, the foul vice writ on an honest seeming; François Villon in stone and mortar stared across the road.

The whole wide expanse, and it was a very wide one, for the windows were small, was studded over by stout nails driven between the joints of the masonry. From these fluttered rope-ends, some short, some long, some weather-frayed to rags, others—horrible to think of—newly cut, and there men and women had choked to death while the King's Provost Marshal ate, drank, or took his pleasure within to the music of the dying wretches clattering their boot heels against the wall!

Shuddering and half-sick with disgust I swallowed down my loathing as best I could. And yet it was nothing more than the sordid commentary to the comedy of the Louvre and a plain warning. Everywhere I turned the law of the King's will was a handwriting on the wall, inexorable, inevitable, callous.

Perhaps because of this newly reawakened sense of the dangers that lay behind the walls of Plessis, or perhaps—and I trust it was so—because to the heart of every man who thinks at all there comes the desire to give God thanks for mercies undeserved and unlooked for, and to seek His strength and guidance in the uncertainties of life, I shook off Martin about vespers, and made my way alone to the great church of Saint Gatien. Behind the grated screens of its dim aisles there rarely fails a priest to ease a burdened spirit of that which grows too heavy to be borne.

But before a man can thus cleanse his soul it is fitting he should pray, and so I knelt, but not before the great altar. No! its hard brilliance and gorgeous extravagance of this world's passing splendours repelled me. What had a poor crushed soul in common with such proud display? The God who loved these flaring lights, silver lamps that swung by silver chains, gilt candlesticks of many branches all ablaze, who took complacent pleasure in such ostentation of gold vessels, broidered draperies, fretted carvings, gems that flashed and gems that glowed, how could He stoop to a worm of the earth? True, the pure, pale Face of the suffering Christ looked out from it all, but looked out as if to ask, What have I, the Man of Sorrows acquainted with grief, Who had not where to lay His head, what have I to do with all this arrogance of flaunted wealth? Either I am the Son of God in My heaven of heavens, and what to Me are your tinsel glories! or I am the Son of Man working out salvation in anguish and alone, sweating, as it were, great drops of blood, no man ministering to Me, and what have I to do with all this splendour! The God of the high altar is either the God of the very great or the very poor; of the man who says in his pride, I, too, am a god, a god to myself, a god upon earth for the people's worship, and so we are a-kin, thou and I! Or else it is for those ignorants who find the incense of heaven in the smell of the unsnuffed guttering candles; for myself, I could not pray there. I found instead a small remote chapel, where a single rushlight trembled before a darkened shrine, faint and small like a soul facing the unknowable; shrinking, and yet persistent because of the Love unseen that watched and waited, yearning to be gracious. Nor was I alone. A woman knelt upon the altar step, her head bowed forward till it rested on the wooden rail.

Seeing her rapt worship I kept back, and in the quiet of the little sanctuary lost myself. The world, with its drone of life, its careless callous tread, was behind my back, and I forgot everything but that Solignac was in ashes, Babette murdered, and that God had prospered me on my way to retribution. What He begins He finishes, and not a thousand Jan Meerts, no, nor Louis of France, could turn back the hand of His justice.

But how diverse are His attributes, how infinite, how inscrutable, is the greatness of His powers. As I, through His justice cried for vengeance, another kneeling at the same footstool sought peace through mercy.

"Not the King's will, but Thine, O Lord!"

It was the voice of Mademoiselle, and as I heard it, my heart leaped! Our paths had come together through no seeking of mine, and there was now no question of disloyalty to Monsieur de Commines. Nor, I remembered with satisfaction, being a frail man, was I any longer in rags.

It may be asked, What was Mademoiselle to me, who had never so much as seen her face clearly, never spoken three words to her, never touched her hand? I answer, Nothing! And yet my heart leaped; perhaps because Monsieur de Commines' interference piqued me, perhaps—but at twenty-five one does not stop to analyse a perhaps that makes the heart leap! It is still the age of impulse and half-blind instinct, and these ask no questions. Rising, I slipped out into the growing dusk and waited without a thought as to whether or no there was a priest behind his grille ready to give comfort to the sinner.

Presently she came.

"Mademoiselle!" and I bared my head.

With a little twitch of her skirts she stood aside, straightening herself.

"What?" she said. "Even on the very church step? Oh, for shame, Monsieur, for shame!"

"No, no," I protested, "you mistake."

"Prove it, Monsieur," she retorted; "prove it by going your way while I go mine."

But as she had moved so had I, and the waning light fell sufficiently strongly on the gay greens and yellows of my bruised forehead for her to see them.

"Ah!" she cried, drawing in her breath, "you come from—from—Monseigneur? You were with us in the Paris inn and are the servant of that Monsieur Hellewyl he said he knew? What is your message? Has he seen the King?"

"I have no message, Mademoiselle, and it is I who am Gaspard Hellewyl."

"You? But it was the other——"

"That was a mistake and——"

"No message? Then whoever you may be, Monsieur, what have I to do with you, or you with me?"

"Nothing, Mademoiselle, except——" and I stopped, not knowing how to answer her.

The pain of her disappointment was written on her face, and I, in my blundering want of thought, had brought it there. The optimism of her youth had jumped to the comfort of the hope that Monsieur de Commines had already good news for her, and that I had brought it. Now the reaction galled her like a blow; I could have cursed myself for my tactless want of foresight. But her gentle womanhoods found an excuse even for that stupidity.

"Except—?" and her face softened.

Have I described her face? I think not, no, I cannot have since till then I had not seen it, and God forbid that I should describe it now. No two faces are alike in the world, and that in almost every one some other finds a sweetness others fail to see is the recurrent miracle of life. I could tell you much of the face that looked up to mine in the twilight, but I could never tell its sweetness, and failing that, the rest is little better than dead flesh. What do so many inches matter except in a man who may have to use their strength? It is not the inches a wise man loves, nor yet the eyes or lips or cheeks, but the Spirit that uses all these, and more than these, as God uses the cold dead things of stone and wood, the perishing things of the world, to point a promise of eternal life. And yet, understand me; I did not, at that time, love Mademoiselle, nor had I totally forgotten Brigitta, as will be seen. But I had begun to compare the two, and when a man begins comparing a new interest with an old love a change is not far off.

"Except," she said, her face softening, and, I think, a little moisture shining in her eyes, "except that we owe you a life—perhaps even more than a life."

"No, no," and I drew back, wounded that she should think I traded on her gratitude, and yet with the wound salved by her wakened warmth of kindliness; "it was not that, it was that in Tours—in a strange city—at this hour—Mademoiselle might have trouble——"

"And that Monsieur might have the pleasure of killing some one else? Bah?" and she searched me gravely with her eyes a second or two. "I can guard myself. What does Tours care for a serving maid! Had it been my mistress, there might have been a need for your gallantry."

"Oh! Mademoiselle, but Monseigneur said——"

"Nothing to you, of that I am sure; and besides Monseigneur knows there are more cloaks in the world than go on the shoulders."

A serving maid? Her mistress? Of course it should have been an evident folly; but remember I was no more than a Flemish clod. I suppose it was that same cloddishness in me, for even while I staggered at what she said I kept my hat in my hand.

"But," I persisted, "Tours is still Tours, and you are still you. With your leave, I will see you safe home."

Turning, she looked over her shoulder with the first glimpse of coquetry I had seen. We had, of course, quitted the Place Saint Gatien, I following her a foot or two behind, as Martin earlier in the day had followed me. But now she slackened her pace, and without increasing mine I drew along side.

"Madame will laugh when I tell her how Monsieur Hellewyl—you said you were Monsieur Hellewyl, did you not, and not that other? I think I prefer the exchange, but it is hard to be sure on so short an acquaintance—how Monsieur Hellewyl, Monseigneur's friend, squired a serving maid through the streets of Tours!"

"Let her laugh!" answered I bravely, "better she should laugh than that a woman left alone in Tours should have bitter cause to weep."

"One woman!" she cried with a sudden pained sharpness, "oh! what does one woman matter? If your King has his way it will not be one woman who will weep but thousands; yes, thousands, thousands."

"Not my King," I answered, and again I will say, answered bravely. More bravely than I knew. To say such words on the streets of Tours risked more than the being laughed at for a woman's sake; Tristan's House of the Great Nails was grim warrant for the danger. "Not my King, I am of Flanders, and so—not my King."

"The better fortune yours!" she answered curtly. "I would rather trust the grossest bully in Tours than Louis of France."

"Then," said I, giving tongue to the thought that had troubled me these ten minutes, "why come to Tours at all, with Louis only a mile away?"

"Because it was safest so. Do you think he would look for me under the shadow of Tristan's gallows? And because, too, I am a woman, Monsieur Hellewyl, and hoped—hoped I might bring back a message of peace to my—my—mistress."

With the words in her mouth, words caught by a half-breath of tears, she turned into a little covered archway opening off the street, and dropped a curtsey.

"I lodge here, Monsieur, and my mistress and I both thank you for your care—though this time there was no man to kill!"

"To-morrow——" I began.

"To-morrow?" echoed she, looking back at me with her foot on the doorstep, "I hope there is no To-morrow for me in Tours, for if there is, it will be passed dangling from one of Tristan's flesh hooks!" and with a little gesture of farewell, she was gone.

Nor had Tours a To-morrow for me either; by midday I was behind the triple walls of Plessis.

CHAPTER X
PLESSIS-LES-TOURS

That, of course, was Monsieur de Commines' doing. He had said, Give me seven days; but he took no more than one, and added to the favour of haste the grace of coming himself to tell me of his success.

I had just returned from a fruitless enquiry at Mademoiselle's lodgings when the landlord met me at the door. To see his change of countenance was a vision of the contemptible in human nature.

"Monsieur is a friend of Monseigneur the Prince de Talmont and I did not know it!" he said plaintively, his hands lightly crossed upon the servile hinge below his chest. "His Excellency is within asking for your Lordship. Ah! Monsieur, had I but known! What a supper I could have served, what a room I could have prepared——"

"And what a bill would have followed! Be easy, a man can only sleep on one bed at a time. Where is Monsieur de Commines?"

"Monsieur le Prince does me the honour to wait in the garden. He has already given orders——"

But Martin, who had heard my voice, pushed him aside.

"Monsieur Gaspard," he cried ruefully, "tell him you cannot have it so. He says the permit is for you only and that I must bide here. I told him, No! Where you went, I went. But he laughed at me, and said every babe must leave its nurse and walk alone some day, and that your time had come."

As he talked we had walked on into the garden that lay to the side and back of the inn, a pleasant place of prune trees well set with young fruit; pinks and roses grew underneath the boughs, and after rain the air was heavy with the sweets of lavender. To these thyme and early gillyflowers added their scent, making the morning air a king's luxury with perfume. Here Monsieur de Commines was waiting for me, a great bunch of newly-gathered flowers in his hands.

Catching Martin's last words he looked up.

"Fie!" said he frowning, though a twinkle in his eyes belied the gravity of the rebuke; "a soldier and preaching cowardice?"

"No coward for myself, Monseigneur, and I'll prove it to you," answered Martin sturdily. "If that fox in Plessis must gnaw his bone, then let him gnaw me, not Monsieur Gaspard."

The spasm of fear that swept across Monsieur de Commines' face startled me, so sudden was it, so abject, so unlike the man who had within four days faced a howling mob unflinchingly, with no more than a table's breadth between. His cheeks had gone white even in the sunlight, and the flowers fell from his hands as if the fingers had no longer strength to hold them.

"Christ's life! man! hold your fool's tongue!" he screamed in a harsh high-pitched voice more like a shrewish woman's than a man's; "who are you to take the King's majesty into your mouth and mangle it? Would you ruin your master? Would you ruin me? Would you hang yourself and that gaping idiot behind you there on Tristan's gallows? By the splendour of God! but I've a mind to swing the two of you! You that dared speak, and him that he dared listen and not cry out upon you! Eh, master host, eh?"

"But Monseigneur," cried the poor shaking wretch, "I heard nothing, I—I—I swear I heard nothing."

"Nothing at all? You are sure, eh? You are sure?"

"Sure, Monseigneur," he repeated in an agony; "do you think I would hear our gracious King miscalled a—a—sneaking beast, and not resent it? But how could I hear when there was nothing said?"

"Then go bid them saddle the horses; but remember this, if I hear you repeat what that fool never said, then——"

"Never, Monseigneur, never; have no fear."

"Fear? I? Use civiller language, rascal; what have I to do with fear? Do as thou'rt bid, and thou of the loose tongue, finish thy master's packing, and make haste."

Too cowed to do more than look piteously at me, Martin turned away to obey, and as the pair went about their business, Monsieur de Commines drew the deep breath of a man who for one terrible minute has hung by a single handsgrip above a gulf of death.

"I think I played my part," said he, forcing a smile. "Martin has learned his lesson, and the other—yes, for his own sake the other will be silent. But one thing is sure, even had the permit been for two, only one would have used it."

Played a part! My heart was still beating double tides from the sick fear I had seen in his face, and he called it playing a part! No warning, whether of direct words or tongueless flesh hooks with fragments of freshly-used dangling rope could urge discretion in the affairs of His Most Christian Majesty with half the emphasis of that agony of terror. If the King's friend, who tended him by day, and slept at his feet by night, had such cause for circumspection, how warily must he walk who came to urge the King to fling aside a soiled tool still keen for the royal service?

Naturally I accepted Monsieur de Commines' half apologetic explanation without comment, but when I would have asked about the progress of my own affairs he motioned me to silence.

"When we are on our road," he said curtly. But when Martin brought out Ninus saddled, as well as Roland and the pack-horse, his angry mood again burst constraint. "What fresh foolery is this? Did I not tell you the permit was for one only?"

"Yes, Monseigneur," answered Martin humbly, "but with your leave it is my duty to see Monsieur Gaspard as far as—as—as maybe."

De Commines' face cleared.

"Right, my friend! Love and duty are the pillars of the world; happy is the man who holds by them. Thou shalt see thy Master Gaspard as far as—as maybe. Ride thou behind with Benoit and my fellows and tell them to keep their distance; they know what that means. We will travel at a foot's pace," he added to me; "for there is much to be said, and the way is short."

"The first thing," he went on, as, side by side, we wound our way through the narrow streets, "is that you must change your name. Hellewyl smacks of Flanders, and the King hates—Good-day, my lord; we are all jealous of you at court. This marriage of the Dauphin will put you gentlemen of Flanders in such high favour that we poor ancient servants of the King will be forgotten in the cold—God grant he thinks so! As I was saying, we must drop the Hellewyl and henceforth be Monsieur Gaspard de Helville. In the King's present health and peevish mood—Yes, Monsieur le Conseiller, I rejoice to say His Majesty is in excellent health and spirits, excellent, excellent, but I do not think he receives to-day—with the King in his present mood it would be unwise to cross his prejudice. After all, a name is but a little thing, and the permit is for Monsieur de Helville. Next grasp this; the King is never ailing, except under the breath, you understand? To you I will tell the truth. When he sleeps we do not know that he will wake again, and when he wakes we do not know but that his next sleep will be eternal. He eats—as I have just said to Monsieur Chasse, excellent! You should have seen him break his fast this morning! I am a fair trencherman, but His Majesty surpasses me in that as in all things—eats nothing, only sucks the juice of an orange or two, so that we can almost see his bones sharpen daily. No man dares cross him—ah, my lord! you ride our way? To Plessis no doubt? Then a friendly word in your ear; the King was asking for you this morning, and you know his impatience is not always—H'm! I thought that would put spurs to his horse and so rid us of his company. It is true, too, that His Majesty did ask for 'that fool, de Baux,' but it was to forbid him the gate! It was no business of mine to tell him unpalatable news. Through life I have made it my rule to serve not only my friends but my enemies. Courtesy is a seed that bears fruit in all soils, even the roughest and least kindly. But there are so many interruptions I had better wait till we are beyond the walls."

To which I cordially agreed, so bewildering were the diplomatic contradictions which a plain man would have called blunt lies.

So, for the remainder of our ride through the city he bowed, smiled, saluted, talked; and was grave, gay, suave, stern, cordial, cold, as the person and the occasion demanded. There is nothing like being a courtier with a reputation for favour to win a man acquaintances, friends I dare not call them, for one half are ready to turn upon him for envy, and the other half are thinking their hardest how they can climb upon his back to their own advantage.

But once clear of the gate the throng slackened, and he took up his parable as if there had been no break in the thread.

"No! no man dares cross him. That does not mean there is need to cross him, by the Spirit of God! no! The King may be frail in body, but his brain burns as with fire, and when his thought blazes out in offence upon a man it consumes him. I tell you that, Monsieur de Helville, lest it should flash out at you and shrivel you and your petty vengeance out of the world. In your twenty-four hours in Tours rumour must have whispered many things in your ears; whispered, I say, since to speak outright is to court an outside lodgings at the Chateau Tristan, for all these rumours buzz round and round the King. The King is half dead; the King was never more alive; the King is crazed; the King's policy is keener witted than ever; the Dauphin goes in terror of his father; the King goes in terror of the Dauphin; these, and many more, and all of them true by turns, for he is compounded of contradictions. For instance, so coward is he that no man dares say Death! or The Grave! in his presence, and yet, when a few months back Death jogged his elbow and sent him staggering to the Grave's mouth, the King never winced, but thrust out his chin, and stared the Terror in the face, unafraid."

"But, Monseigneur, how can I, a stranger, and no courtier, walk safely through these pitfalls?"

"For seven days you will share my quarters; make the most of your chances. The King will then put you to service, God knows what, for he has strange whims at times, and again I say, make the most of what he offers. Your time in Plessis will be short. It is his wisdom to change his servants often lest they should learn too much and be dangerous. As I have told you, he spends half his days making and breaking men's fortunes; only what the King finally sends you to do, do: or else tear up the permit now and ride back, not to Tours, but to your charnel house of Solignac, lest he reach after you. There stands Plessis!" he added abruptly.

Drawing rein, we sat in silence and as we waited Martin slowly drew up with us. It was our first view of the—what shall I call it? Chateau? Palace? Prison? Fortress? It was all four in one, or something of all four. But perhaps Martin's summing up fitted the case best.

"God have mercy upon us!" he said under his breath; "it's a rat trap!"

"There is no cat in Europe with claws strong enough to scratch it open," answered Monsieur de Commines; this time we were alone, and he had no rebuke for Martin's freedom of speech. "No, nor wolf either! Look at its strength. First there is the iron paling set on the near bank of the fosse; next, the fosse is twenty feet deep and is no mere ditch, but a lake for breadth; then comes the outermost wall, bristling, as you see, with four-pointed hooks that would rip a man's flesh to the bone and hang him up by joints like a sheep in a butcher's shop. These two towers flank the gateway. It faces the river, and can only be approached by that zig-zag path which is set on every side by springes, traps and gins cunningly hidden. May the world to come show mercy to the man they grip, for in this life there is no longer hope for him! Within that outer wall there is a second which dominates the first and is also bounded by a moat; within that again there is a third yet higher and again girded by water. You see them there, terraced, one, two, three; and if the first gate were forced—a thing hard to believe—the second stands not opposite but aside, and the third yet further aside, so that to reach the core, where the King lies, there must be a transverse straggle along the bank under fire both back and front, then the fosse to cross and another gate to force. That grim black shaft rising from the centre is the donjon; strength within strength, defence defending defence, and these four iron-sheeted towers crown and govern all. Monsieur de Helville, your late master, saw war, and you with him, Master Martin, did either of you ever see such a King's house before, or was there ever such seen since the world began?"

"A rat trap," repeated Martin, "and God have mercy on——"

"Monsieur Gaspard!" said Monsieur de Commines, and rode on laughing. But not for long. While we were still more than a bowshot from the outer walls he turned to Martin. "Now, friend, get back to the Cross of

Saint Martin, and wait there in patience. Do not go far from the inn door; your master may need you any hour by day or by night. God knows when! It is all as the King wills, and remember this, curiosity is a fatal vice at Plessis. If you approach too near the Castle those fellows you see on the walls will shoot you like a mad dog first, and enquire why afterwards, and so the saints keep you!"

Dropping the reins on Ninus' neck, Martin jumped to the ground, and went on his knee in the dust.

"The Lord, He knows, Monsieur Gaspard, that the leaving you is none of my doing," he said between the mumbles of his mouth upon my hand. "If I'd ha' thought it would come to this then the Lord again He knows I'd ha' sooner faced Jan Meert and his twenty devils and so never have been here to taste the bitterness. There were but three of us, Monsieur Gaspard; Babette is gone, now you will go, and I only shall be left, a poor, miserable, dried skin of a man that—that—would give his life to go first," and he broke down, weeping.

Laughing, but in no laughing mood, I leaned aside, and tried to pull him to his feet. But he would not move, and when at last I drew my hand away—for Monseigneur was waiting for me—its back was wet with his tears. Nor, so long as we were in sight, did he rise from his knee.

"Ah!" said Monseigneur, as we rode on, "Master Martin has a heart in him for all his years, and is not ashamed to show it. I fear he would never make a courtier, he has not learned to forget love, and be ungrateful."

CHAPTER XI
THE PLOT OF THE FOUR NATIONS

When, out of his experience, the devil formed schools to teach apt humanity, he set them in the extremes of life, the noisome dens of packed cities and the courts of kings. Misery forgets God, that by theft and murder it may live out yet one more unhappy day, and greatness climbs upon its own shame to yet more dishonoured honour.

Never was there such a place as Plessis for intrigue. From Monsieur de Beaujeu, the King's son-in-law, down to the kitchen scullions, there was not a man but mined or countermined to gain some private advantage; nor, in all the palace, was there a finger-nail—mine among the rest—but itched to scratch the King's favour. That much I learned in my seven days of waiting.

Through Monsieur de Commines' influence almost every door was open to me, and by his instructions I used my liberty freely.

"Who knows to what service you may be put," he added; "Plessis is not to be turned inside out in a week, but a week may teach you not to show yourself a fool."

So day by day I went my rounds by the outer, middle and inner walls; the courtyards, the galleries, the anterooms, the sparrows' nests, the towers, the donjon, even to the bear-pit and the sheds where were housed that varied collection of strange beasts His Majesty had gathered from the four corners of the earth to distract his thoughts, and show the world how active was his mind. The quarters of the Scottish archers I avoided as far as possible. Though Monsieur de Commines did not love these interloping Northmen, nor they him, they were civil enough to me for his sake, or, rather, for the sake of his influence. But I could not understand half their guttural jargon.

The King I also avoided, and only saw from a distance until the day he sent for me; once, far off, his scarlet satin cloak and heavy furs showing like a giant poppy with the brown capsule half pushed off; once sunning himself in a narrow court, his elbows on his knees, his chin in his hands, his shoulders hunched to his ears, decrepit, shrunken, every muscle in collapse; and once, not an hour later, on the parapet of the outer wall, bowing a gracious acknowledgment to a group of the good folk of Tours who saluted him from a discreet and safe distance; the half-dead man was then very much alive, and so rumour was justified of her children!

Tied though he was to the King's girdle, it was Monsieur de Commines' custom to steal an hour nightly, and listen to my rehearsal of the day's lessons.

"What strikes me most," said I, as my week drew to an end, "is the confusion of tongues within the walls. There is the liquid music of Provence, the iron rasp of Normandy, the clipped French of Paris, the uncouth burr of Gascony; I even heard a Flanders oath or two to-day."

"Eh?" said Monseigneur, looking up at me; "Flanders? Did you say Flanders?"

"Yes, Jehan Flemalle the bearward. The brute clawed at him as he fed it, and he drew back swearing; I know a Flanders curse when I hear it, and so, I think, should you," I added, laughing.

But, so far from breaking up, the gravity on his face deepened, and for a full minute he sat with pursed mouth and narrowed eyes, staring into vacancy out of window. When I would have spoken he shook his head and snarled an incoherence, warning me into silence with a little impatient twist of his hand. But suddenly his face lit up, and he turned upon me, his eyes shining.

"Jehan Flemalle—Jan Flemael! By the splendour of God, I begin to understand!" then he checked himself, and sat watching me, as he had sat that night in the Louvre, when I knew to my discomfort that the keenest brain in France was reckoning up not my strength, but my weakness. "Do you know," he went on at last, his voice suave and smooth, with all trace of excitement gone from it, "I distrust this Jehan Flemalle. What if he starves the King's beasts to his own profit? He is an Angevin, and—Yes, here is your chance to do the King a service. From time to time these wild creatures have cost immense sums. I hate them myself, but the King loves them, and visits them almost daily. Watch this Jehan Flemalle; watch him when alone with the beasts, note whom he consorts with, and if they meet in secret try and catch them in talk."

"What, Monseigneur? Play spy upon a butcher?"

"Ay! on a butcher," he said harshly; "the word is a good one, and you could not better it in a year. As to playing spy, I'd have you understand, Monsieur, that if I bid you lay your ear to the crack of a maid's door for the King's service, you must do it, or quit Plessis. There are two types of useful men in the world; those who think and are obeyed without question, and those who obey without question, but do not think. For the present, be content to be the second, that one day you may perhaps be the first. What! Monsieur Hellewyl, do you, who as yet are not a little finger in Plessis, presume to call yourself a brain?" Rising he strode to the door, and turning, shook a monitory if not a menacing forefinger at me. "Remember," he went on, "in this thing I am the King and you have your orders. If your dignity is not supple enough to stoop to a little thing, how can it rise to a great? And who are you to dare to question whys and wherefores in the King's business?"

Without waiting for an answer he was gone. And what answer was possible? Ever since Solignac was burned the whole force of my schooling had been, None dare cross the King's will! It was written in the ashes of my father's house, it was taught by the mouth of the King's friend, it met me at the four gates of the Louvre, the dangling-rope-ends on Tristan's house called it aloud, and even at the altar of God Himself, Mademoiselle caught the echo and bowed in an agony of prayer before its force. Or this order of Monsieur de Commines might be a test, a trap of the King's own devising. It was notorious that Louis loved crooked methods. Stoop that you may rise! Monseigneur's words had hinted as much. Perhaps—but excuses are never hard to find, even for a meanness, when that meanness serves a personal gain very near to the heart.

Though I have said little of him, Jan Meert was never long out of my thoughts. Dead Babette called to me across the smoke, and with both blood and fire to avenge my weakness of poverty could afford no luxury of qualms. It must lean where it could, even upon a foul staff. In a word, what Monsieur de Commines bade me do, I did, nor was the execution difficult.

A menagerie was as much part of a royal palace as were the kitchens. Why, I cannot say. Perhaps it tickled a King's pride to know that even the wild beasts were under his heel. That of Plessis at this time lay to the south-east; cages, stalls, dens, pits, as were required. These the King was continually adding to or enlarging, and behind the planks laid for their repair, slanting against the wall, there was perfect concealment.

Was I ashamed of the situation into which Monsieur de Commines had forced me? Frankly yes; but, also frankly, still more ashamed of the risk of being found out.

The stalls and cages were side by side, bordering both walls of an angle facing me not ten paces distant; nowhere in Plessis was there space to spare, and the poor, free-born beasts suffered from the congestion with their betters. In these were the King's true favourites. Monsieur de Commines might sleep at his feet, Monsieur de Beaujeu minister his affairs, the Chancellor, Rochfort, have his ear and his confidence, but their tenure was no stronger than a loose whim. These others held his love and his interest, and to such an extent that, ailing or well, he visited them almost daily; Barbary lions no larger than great cats, elk-deer, reindeer, a strange medley.

But oftenest of all he would stand opposite the cage that prisoned four great wolves from Auvergne. These he would bait till the savage brutes, bigger than month-old calves, flung themselves howling against the bars, raging but helpless, their fangs bared, their chaps dribbling foam and slaver. He had even names for them.

"Burgundy," he would say, pointing from one to the other, "Spain, The Empire, Rome!" Then, tapping his breast, add significantly, "France! Snarl, my friends, froth, howl, eat your hearts out in hate, France is unafraid," and they, as if they understood his jeer, would fling themselves afresh against the side of the cage, tearing and biting the bars to get at him. So, in jest, this cage came to be known as the cage of The Four Nations.

Presently, as I waited behind my pile of timber, Jehan Flemalle came. In Plessis there were no idlers. Even the four hundred archers of the guard had their duties, and discipline was iron. Jehan Flemalle, therefore, came alone and with no loiterers at his heels to watch the feeding of the animals. In either hand was a great basket of kitchen offal, and at the smell of him a howl arose whose echo rumbled in the confined space like a winter's thunder.

From cage to cage he went, dealing out the day's rations, here a half loaf such as few in France set teeth in from January to December, there a bone such as still fewer in France saw even once a month in their pots, and little by little the howls died down to a grumbling purr of brute contentment. If other days were as this, then Monsieur de Commines need be under no doubt; the King's beasts were not starved, let happen what might to the King's subjects. Then a curious thing struck me, spurring my jaded watchfulness; Jehan Flemalle in his feeding had passed by the cage of the Four Nations, leaving Burgundy and the rest to howl their hungry lamentations unheeded. He even goaded them to louder complaint and stronger protest, for, setting down their dinner in full sight, he gibed them as the King had done.

"Howl, Burgundy, snap your jaws, Spain! Tear at the bars, Rome, tear! tear! Perhaps one day the way will open, and then—eh, my sons? then we shall see, shall we not? That is the one thing needed, an open door, and, Christus! but it is creaking on its hinges if the world but knew it!" It was good Flemish, and not the mumbling jumble of a half-baked Angevin clod! "Here's to make it creak louder," he went on. "Here's to help it open with a crash that will shake all France from the Nivernais to the three seas."

From under his leathern jerkin he drew an armourer's file such as is used for cutting rivets, long, flat, and coarse, and through the howls of the frantic brutes came the steady rasp, rasp, rasp, while the sweat grew cold upon me at the cunning devilishness of the villian's purpose.

"Your dinner to-day, Burgundy," said he, plying the tool steadily under cover of the howling din. "Your dinner to-morrow, but the third day you must go a-hunting. One spring and you're through, my children; Rome, Burgundy, and the Empire all on France at a leap, and Spain crawling in behind to claim her share of the spoils. Good!" as one of the famished brutes, crouching, thundered against the bars, "that is the trick to play when a man jeers your empty belly. Spring! and you're through! but not to-day nor to-morrow. When the third day comes, then, God with us! poof! You're through! you're through!" and again the rasp, rasp, rasp arose, harsh and strident, his body swinging in rhythm to the grind of the tool.

CHAPTER XII
MONSEIGNEUR'S COUNTERPLOT

If ever there had been a doubt of the scoundrel's treacherous purpose there was none now and, the beasts being at last fed, and he gone, it was with a humbled heart I slipped from my hiding-place. My God! What a secret to hold! Truly those who net in King's waters sometimes land strange fish. For a moment my purpose staggered. Jan Meert was the King's tool. Let me but hold my peace for two days, and the hand and brain which set that tool working would pass to judgment by as red a road as had dead Babette. I owed the King no loyalty, no gratitude, no love. Love! Who in all France or out of it owed Louis love? Mademoiselle? No, hate rather; for in some way which I did not understand, Louis stood to her for ruin and the wreck of all she held most dear.

Again my purpose staggered. Once already I have said I was not in love with Mademoiselle, but she had stirred my sympathy, and except Martin, and perhaps, no, not perhaps, certainly—Brigitta and the dead Babette, no one had touched me so nearly as that since my mother died.

But that mood passed. I have always believed that the finger of God is closer to the lives of men than some think. You are blind and do not see it, hardened and do not feel it, self-guided and so misunderstand its directings, but whose fault is it that we fail to read the signs, or are unconscious of the pressure of spirit on spirit? By silence I could secure my private vengeance, but at what a cost?

If Louis died, died murdered in such a fashion, war would surely follow. A picture of The Four Nations let loose on France: of Burgundy and Spain, Rome and The Empire, dividing her mangled body, not in type, but in truth, with all the crowded horrors of siege and sack rose before me; cities laid waste, a helpless peasantry ravaged, innocence flung to feed the passions of human wolves; these were mine to permit or prevent; who knew but that God Almighty had brought me to Plessis for this very thing?

"Who are you, to question whys and wherefores in the King's business?" Monsieur de Commines had said, and I had allowed the justice of the demand. Here was the hand of the King of Kings Himself, and who was I to question His whys and wherefores? or to His command. Do this for me! answer, I will not! No! Monsieur de Commines must hear and must act.

He listened without comment, almost without emotion, till I had ended. Then—

"You know our Flanders proverb? Flood, and a high wind, do not go a journey for nothing! No! nor does an Angevin swear Flemish in Plessis at his neck's risk for nothing either!"

"Then I was only a catspaw? When you bade me seek, you knew what I would find?"

"I guessed, but the affair was too small for me to touch. Besides, you have now your claim upon the King, though I think we shall finish the affair ourselves before informing His Majesty. Trifles at all times vex great natures; think how a grit of sand in the eye galls you."

"Trifles? A grit of sand?" I repeated, nettled that he should make so little of my discovery. "Do you call a plot to kill the King a trifle? Do you call The Four Nations trifles? No man who saw these slavering brutes pounding themselves frantic against the half-filed bars could call them trifles!"

"That is just it; you have seen, but I have not, and so, perhaps, I make too little of it. To-morrow Monsieur Jehan feeds them as usual? Good! I shall be there. I think I see my way to do substantial justice, and yet not give Monsieur Jehan the undeserved dignity of a state trial. There again it would be making too much of trifles; or"—he added, shaking a finger in the air—"some one may be behind Monsieur Jehan whom it would not be convenient to unmask."

Though my belief is that next day Jehan Flemalle anticipated his usual time, it seemed to me he lagged in the coming. Even to me, a patient, almost a phlegmatic man, as you must have discovered, the waiting in the half-gloom set my nerves all a-creep. I say half-gloom, because by an alteration in the position of the boards Monsieur de Commines blocked up the space which gave access to our hiding-place.

"It would never do," he whispered, "for Monsieur de Rochfort to catch the Prince de Talmont slinking to cover like a thief behind arras. His laughter would kill as surely as—as—the jaws of The Four Nations."

But even with this safeguard against observation he seemed ill at ease, muttering to himself and shifting restlessly from place to place, so that to us both it was a relief when a louder howl rose from the cage facing us. The wolves scented blood and cried for it.

But their hunger had to wait Jehan Flemalle's pleasure, and as the procedure of the previous day was repeated, here a loaf and there a bone with the cage of The Four Nations passed ostentatiously by, I touched Monseigneur on the shoulder. It was the vindication of the truth of my story, which it seemed to me, he had more than half-doubted. But he shook me off with an inconsiderate petulance.

"*Dame!*" he muttered impatiently, "have I not eyes of my own?"

My faith! but he had, and used them well. With his face pressed against the boards he stared through a crack like a truant child at a peepshow, his teeth clenched and bared, his eyes narrowed, his breath coming in little short gasps. A faint grin was on his face, a spasm of excited emotion rather than of merriment. I have since seen the same look on gamesters' faces when a fortune hung on the fall of the dice and to lose was ruin. But at that time it was new to me, and I stood back a little, watching him curiously.

Here a loaf, there a bone, and back to the cage of The Four Nations came Jehan Flemalle. Nothing remained except the wolves' meat, and straddling his legs a yard or two from the den, he jeered their hunger.

"Hey! Burgundy! Hey! Spain!" he cried, snapping his fat fingers on either side his head while the starving brutes raced howling up and down the cage, pressing their lean flanks against the bars. "Yap and yowl, my sons, yap and yowl! Dine to-day like fed lords, and to-morrow go a-hunting for yourselves, my little ones! An open door, and France in your jaws. France, do you hear?" and he clicked his tongue "France! France! May you find him sweet!"

("*You hear for yourself,*" said I, touching Monseigneur a second time, "*are you satisfied, now?*" "*Peace, fool,*" answered Monseigneur, "*how can I hear if you chatter like a daw?*")

"All France by the throat to tear and nuzzle; God! I would I were a wolf and one of you, if only for an hour! But yapping and yowling are not enough, my children, you must jump for your dinner, jump at the throat of the man who gibes your hunger, and pin him with your fangs. Up he'll come, dragging his lame foot in the dust, dragging it thus, thus, thus, up he'll come, smirking and jeering, ay, jeering, and the Devil waiting for him behind the jowl of The Four Nations. Ah ha! he'll say, fret and fume, curs! You'd tear France, would you? Bah! France is not afraid! and he'll snap his fingers as I do. And you, my sons, what will you do? So! So! that is your answer is it? You'll jump for his throat, will you? Good, Burgundy, Good! down on your belly, boy; flatter, flatter, and get the grip of your claws home for the spring; now, *one, two, three*— —Christus!"

In the half-gloom Monseigneur's hand caught mine, and drew me forward imperiously. Above 7the grumbling mumble of the feeding brutes had risen the howling of the wolves, sinking at last to a sharp, *yap, yap, yap,* broken by a dog-like, complaining whine. Then, as Jehan Flemalle marked time at the last there was an instant's silence, and a rasping crash followed by a deep-chested, hoarse baying like that of hounds on a trail.

"My God!" I cried, "they are loose!"

"I hope so," answered Monseigneur huskily; "they ought to be, for I filed the bars myself last night."

"But there will be murder done?"

"Justice, not murder. Am I a man to do things by halves? Be quiet, and let me look, for this is very curious, much more curious than if Tristan had hanged him. Hanging is common, but I never saw a man die in this way before."

No, nor can many have seen the like, for which God be thanked; it was an awful end. Jan Flemael lay on his back, his limp arms flung out in a cross. Burgundy had rolled aside with the force of the leap, and was picking himself up, cowed by the fall and silent. Behind him Spain had crept, had caught Jan Flemael by the throat, had given one whimpering worrying wrench, had—but that is enough, it was an awful end. Rome and The Empire sniffed and growled uneasily inside the cage, but made no effort to escape.

In three minutes all was over and Monseigneur shook himself with a sigh. His face had gone grey and haggard, and in ten breaths he had aged as many years, so drawn was his mouth, so webbed the corners of his eyes.

"A great sight," he said, shaking himself again, "and one with a moral for more than us in Plessis. Death on the threshold, knocking, knocking, knocking, and a man within call who has no ears to hear."

"With these brutes loose," answered I, as the worrying growl rose afresh, "there will be knocking at many doors, and an answer to be given whether we like or not."

But Monseigneur had already recovered his *sang froid*.

"I say again, am I a fool to do thing by halves? See!" and he pushed aside the boards blocking the entrance.

Little by little a line of men were pushing forward strong nets hung from poles and braced beneath; little by little The Four Nations would be again trapped. Truly, as he said, Monsieur de Commines did nothing by halves.

"My men," he added laconically.

"But this was to be kept from the King's ears, and now—"

"I tell you they are my men," he answered testily, "and what if they do talk? Bars are already prepared to fit the sockets. The old bars will be destroyed, and if men do whisper, Filed! there are so many lies believed in Plessis that a little truth may well be discredited. If necessary we shall say he tampered with the door and a lamentable accident resulted! Faugh! look at the carrion! Jump for your dinners! said he; Saints! how they have jumped, and how they have dined! He told more truth than he knew!'"

Beyond that I never heard that Jehan Flemalle had any epitaph.

CHAPTER XIII
HIS MOST CHRISTIAN MAJESTY

It was Monsieur de Commines himself who came for me as I went my rounds of self-instruction three days after The Four Nations had gone a-hunting.

"The King calls you," he said, out of breath with haste; "I think your chance has come, for he has some scheme in his head."

"The King? What! This instant?" and I looked downward at my dress, plain, clean, and serviceable enough, but hardly fit for a court presentation.

"Bah! Catch fortune as she flies. Besides, silks and satins would not become the man who files a wolf's bars to save the King's life, and then hunts the brutes back to their cage at the risk of his own."

"But, Monseigneur, I did none of these things."

"No, but the King thinks you did, and that is the same thing. I told you the counter-plot was too trivial for me to lend my name to it. It would not hoist a man at the top of the ladder an inch higher; but you, who are at the bottom, it may raise a rung, or even two, if you are politic. Come, the King waits; he has his dogs to play with, but he may tire of them at any moment, and your chance be lost. One last word," he went on, as, hurrying at a trot whose pace was very significant in a man of Monseigneur's age and dignity, we drew near the mouth of the Cour au Soleil, where Louis warmed his cold blood in the sun. "Remember, you climb over my back. It is I who have brought you into Plessis, and there are many who would be glad to see you muddy my shoulders; therefore be watchful. Here in a sentence is the way to win and hold court favour. Catch the King's meaning, and jump with his humour, whatever it may be. Hush! not a word till he speaks, he is often like that."

The court was triangular in shape, and faced south. Across the apex of the angle a couch was drawn, and there, stretched upon its cushions, was Louis. One leg was drawn up under him, the other lay straight out, and where it showed below the edge of his mantle the calf was of a bigness no greater than my wrist. A sleeved cloak or coat of scarlet satin, lined and trimmed with ermine, wrapped him to the knees. A tight-fitting cap of the same colour as the cloak covered not alone the scalp, but coming round the back of the head as far as the nape, caught in his ears, leaving only the face exposed, and, my God! what a face it was! Meagre as a death's head, the smooth-shaven skin a yellow parchment, the nose long and thin as a vulture's beak, the full lips withered and shrivelled to a crumpling of livid skin tightened across broken teeth, the eyes—was he awake or asleep? living or dead? for though these eyes were open they had rolled back in their sockets and showed only a narrow splash of muddy grey shot with blood at the corners. One arm hung over the couch-edge almost to the ground, and the whole attitude was the pitiable collapse of a sick old age and utter weariness.

Three or four dogs stood or sprawled beside him, good courtiers all! for they seemed to know his mood, and lay quiet, waiting for the change. One, a coarse-jowled brindled beast that panted for fatness, cowered on its haunches a foot or two away from the couch-head. No member of the court was present, but knots of the King's archers, half-armoured, but with sword and dagger, and carrying their bows, were on guard at every point that commanded the court.

As minute after minute passed, and the King still lay as one dead, there was ample time for the picture to fix itself in my memory. Then, suddenly, the sightless eyes rolled in their sockets, and he awoke.

"Sire," said Monseigneur, as, hat in hand, I went down on one knee, "here is Monsieur de Helville."

"The compatriot of Monsieur Jehan Flemalle?"

"Your majesty's faithful servant."

"Faithful as England, and for the same cause," answered Louis, beckoning with his fingers to the big-jowled dog crouching near him.

The brute saw and understood, for, though the lips twitched till the fangs showed, it flattened itself on its belly and inched nearer to the thin hand it feared. But though the King called the dog, his eyes never left my face, and as I said of the face a moment back so now I say, My God! what eyes they were! Ice and fire, cold, inscrutable, implacable; dead as grey ash, but with the smouldering heat of the ember not far below the film; remorseless eyes that groped the secrets of a man's thoughts as the delicate fingers of the blind grope a face.

"I call him England, after my dear brother Edward," went on Louis, "because though he shows his teeth and would fly at me if he dared, a sop will always bribe him, and, like the King whose premature decease we all so bitterly lament, he will die at last of over-eating. God and Saint Claude forgive me if I seem to speak evil of the dead! Are you as faithful as this my dog, Monsieur de Helville?"

For a moment I was silent, partly because the shrewd, malevolent, fixed gaze fascinated me as men say a serpent fascinates a bird, partly because he had cleft the truth to the very core. I had told Mademoiselle that I owed the King no loyalty, I had even been in two minds as to letting Jan Flemael's plot run a triumphant course; to gain my own ends, and my own ends alone, had brought me to Plessis. As the King had said, my fidelity was no greater than that of the cowed bull-dog, and thereby came a lesson.

The poor brute had crept reluctantly within reach of the beckoning hand, and the thin fingers that looked so frail, but had so much iron of will in them, had gripped the loose skin of the plethoric neck, twisting it till the dog wheezed in an agony of breathlessness. Let the grip close in another half-inch, and it would choke.

"Faithful as England and for the same reason," said the King, reading the truth. "What is the sop that wins your love, Monsieur de Helville?"

"I desire service, Sire."

He grinned contemptuously, grinned till the thin lips twitched up, showing the teeth as England had shown his.

"Pish, man! Leave useless flattery to your betters! You desire Jan Meert's life. Monsieur d'Argenton has told me. Who knows! perhaps you may have it."

The words stung me, or rather, their contempt. It was as if he gave me the lie, and impelled by the smart, I answered more boldly than I had dreamed I would have dared—

"Why not, Sire? A man's house is his house, and if yours were burned would you not lop the hand——"

He stopped me with a laugh; no thin sarcastic smile at such a childish outburst, but full-throated merriment.

"The torch, you mean, Monsieur Hellewyl, not the hand itself; the hand that held the torch was—elsewhere!"

Groping upward, he patted a little leaden image of the Virgin that hung from a loop in his cap, patted it without reverence but rather as one who would say, God is on my side.

"Mary have mercy upon you if you so much as touch that hand except to kiss it; what it gropes it grasps, and what it grasps it crushes. You mean the torch, eh, Monsieur Hellewyl?"

"The torch, then, Sire," said I, shivering a little, so significant was the threat, and so significant too, when taken in conjunction with that threat, the laugh that foreran it; "would you not set your foot on the torch that burned your father's house? Would you not trample it, quench it— —?"

"I? I am France, while you are— —" He flung aside the half-choked brute with more strength than one would have supposed possible in such a shrunken frame. "Monsieur d'Argenton, take away the dogs, but do not hasten poor England lest he die before his next sop gorges him; and you, Monsieur Hellewyl, wait."

Back he sank upon the cushions, upwards rolled the eyes to sightlessness, and again he lay as one dead, but breathing heavily from the exertion.

Without so much as a grimace of repugnance at his task, Monsieur de Commines caught up a little shaggy Spanish dog, a present from King Ferdinand the Catholic, and nursing it in his arms turned away, whistling softly to the rest. The signal was well known and quickly obeyed, for all at once followed him, England capering clumsily in the joy of dismissal.

I admit my envy went with the wheezing beast. Had I dared, I, too, would have danced lightheartedly out of the sunshine of the King's presence into any shadow in Plessis. But such joyful release was not for me. Wait, said he, and I waited, motionless, still on one knee. Wait for what? To be gripped, so to speak, by the throat, gibed at, and then flung aside like a dog? And yet that was the very fate I craved for Jan Meert, whose only offence was that he had done what he was bid.

How far the King played a part, and how far his weariness was real no man could tell, but it's my belief that through all his lassitude nothing escaped him. No sooner had Monsieur de Commines and the drove of dogs turned the angle of the court than he sat up.

"On your feet, on your feet!" he said sharply, all the weak huskiness gone from his voice. "You asked for service, priests serve with their knees—God be thanked for prayer—but a man with his hands and feet. What service? Jehan Flemalle's place is vacant, will that suit you?" Pausing, he again read my thoughts, read them as a man reads a book, and put them into such blunt words as after his late rebuke I would not have dared to use. "You are a gentleman, and fit for something better than to feed offal to brutes? Perhaps; and then again, perhaps not! What do I know of your fitness? Will you take Jehan Flemalle's place, Monsieur de Helville?"

"If the King bids me," answered I, crestfallen.

"And if the King bids you do him some other service?"

"If my honour, Sire——"

"Honour! God's name sir, I am your honour." The sudden storm that possessed him frightened me, so fierce was it, so malevolent. His dull lacklustre eyes blazed up like powder sparks, and he shook his clenched fist at me as if he desired nothing better than to strike me down. "We have no room for if's in Plessis, no, nor out of it, on the King's service. If?—If?—do you serve me, or do you not?"

"With the blessing of God, yes, Sire," I answered.

"Ah!" and the lean hands went together, the fingers pointing upwards, following the direction of his eyes. "If the blessing of God be not with us we are indeed undone. His mercy forbid we should ever seek aught contrary to His will. But I have often found that what I willed, He was graciously pleased to will also, and this service, Monsieur de Helville, is one peculiarly pleasing to God Almighty. Tell me, why did you file the bars of The Four Nations?"

The question caught me unawares, and for two reasons I had no answer ready; one, that I am unready in a lie and had not filed the bars at all; the other, that my first impulse had been to let Jan Flemael do his own filing, follow what might. Louis was quick to catch my embarrassment, and shrewd to understand it, at least in part.

"So, so!" he said. "You, too, are of Flanders, Monsieur Hellewyl? But let that pass. I judge a man by his acts, and whatever your first thought was in the end you filed the bars. But why? Why? You, too, being of Flanders."

By this time I had my wits at command, and could have lied with a courtier-like straight face, protesting against the imputation, but that I knew he would have scoffed at the pretence. Jump with his mood, said Monsieur de Commines, and as his mood seemed to desire the truth, I told it.

"For the sake of peace, Sire. The wolves would have torn France. Better one man die than——"

"A whole nation perish! My own thought, Monsieur de Helville, of a verity my own thought, as God's my witness." Crossing his breast hastily, he put a hand under him, pushing himself to his feet, and stood facing me, his back arched, his limbs trembling in weakness, but with the virile fire of the eyes unquenched, indomitable in their masterful purpose. "I, too, desire peace, and shall one life stand between to say No! to me? Peace to France, peace—oh yes, yes, yes"—and he laughed a little cackling laugh, nodding his trembling head in time to the merriment—"peace, too, to Navarre; poor distracted Navarre that needs peace even more than does France! It is a Christian act to bring peace, a Christian act. Monsieur de Helville, does the service suit you?"

"A life, you said, Sire: whose life?"

For a moment or two the King stood silent, one lean transparent hand laid across his narrow chest as if for warmth, the other covered his mouth so that the chin rested on the palm while the teeth gnawed at the finger nails.

"There is a child," he began at last, "a miserable, useless, puling child——"

"My God, Sire!" I cried, shaken out of all control, even out of all trepidation, "is it murder?"

Out flew both hands, open, shaking in a passion of menace, and he staggered forward a step as if to claw me in the face, but drew back, panting.

"I cannot! God! I cannot, I cannot!" he muttered, and gulping for breath, stood staring at me with blinking eyes. "Murder? Shame, Monsieur de Helville, shame, shame to think such a thought of a Christian king, such a thought of me—*of me*!" groping upward, he again patted the image on his cap. "See! I swear it, by the Virgin, by the Virgin; God strike me—strike me—eh? You understand? I seek peace, Monsieur, only peace and the good of France, and—yes, yes,—the pleasing of God, that of course, always, the pleasing of God. Again I ask, do you say No! to such a service? Dare any man say No? Dare any—any——"

His voice fell, quavering, his jaw dropped, and a look of abject terror broke across his face. Swaying on his feet he pawed blindly at the air, then collapsed backwards in a heap upon the cushions.

"Coctier! Coctier! Coctier!" he screamed. "For the love of Christ, come to me. Coctier! Coctier! Ah! dear God! not this time, give me a little longer, just a little, little longer!"

Whimpering, he tore at his throat with powerless fingers, and thinking he wanted his cloak loosened at the collar I ran forward to help him. But he dug at me with his nails, spitting like a frightened cat.

"Not you, not you; no man but Coctier. Mon Dieu! will no man send me Coctier!" again his voice rose to a scream. "The King is dying, Coctier, Coctier! dying! dying!"

Turning to seek help, I ran full tilt into the arms of Monsieur de Commines, who, with Maitre Jacques Coctier, the King's physician, was hastening in answer to the cry.

"Monseigneur— —"

"Dolt! You have crossed him and I bid you not. He is never like this except when crossed. If the King dies, by God! you may count Jan Flamael's end a happy one," and striking at me, he ran on.

Down on one knee went Coctier, his fingers busy with the throat of the King's cloak, and as I drew back I heard Louis' voice as if in answer to a question.

"A priest? No, no, not this time, not this time. Priests are for the sick, for the dying—and I must live that there may be peace."

Peace! It was curious how I stumbled on the word. First Mademoiselle, then Monsieur de Commines, and now the King; all desired peace, but it seemed to me that to all peace did not mean the same thing.

CHAPTER XIV
MONSIEUR DE COMMINES EXPLAINS

At what length, and in what terms, Monsieur de Commines berated me I need say little. Those who know his command of vigorous language may judge, but had his tongue been a birch rod, and I a little thievish boy, caught red-handed, I could not have been more sorely lashed. Epithets flew as thick as snow-flakes in winter, but were neither as cold nor as soft. I was a blundering dolt, a thick-headed fool, a self-seeking, ungrateful pick-thank.

But there I stopped him.

"No, Monseigneur, never ungrateful."

"Ungrateful," he persisted. "Here do I bring you to Plessis, vouch for you, sow a thought in the King's mind for you, and when it buds you trample it under foot, never caring that you may trample me down with it. Is that gratitude?"

"A man has his honour, Monseigneur; yes, and something greater than his honour; for when it comes to steeping his soul in a child's blood— —"

"A child's blood? What do you mean, de Helville?"

"What thought you sowed I do not know," I answered bluntly and perhaps without much respect, for at the moment my blood was hot, "but the crop was murder, and I was bid go reap it."

The heavy wrinkles on his forehead, wrinkles in which you might have sunk a bow-string out of sight, deepened yet further, and he stood gnawing his lip in silence.

"Yes, I remember now," he said at last. "There is a child, but his name never passed between us, the King and myself, I mean. Mon Dieu! Monsieur de Helville, you surely cannot think His Majesty meant any harm to the boy?"

"You told me, Monseigneur, that my time to think had not yet come, and so, if it pleases you, I shall think nothing," I answered. "I am a plain man, a stranger to Plessis and new to its admirable court ways. It may be when the King says this is black, he means it is white or red or blue, and that to kill a child is to stuff it with sweetmeats. What passed was this," and I told him everything in as few words as I could.

By the time I had ended, he was reasonable. That is where a man frequently differs from a woman; he can see two sides to a question, she only that which reflects her mood of the moment.

"Thank God he seeks peace," said he when I had finished. "Gaspard, my friend, my tongue was too rough just now, and yet I think you were wrong. You should have played him, and so learned his true mind. What he said was to try you, or, at worst, a jest."

"A grim jest, Monseigneur, so grim that the King nearly died of its failure."

Monsieur de Commines shook an open palm in the air as if to push a thought from him.

"You see how we stand, always on the brink of the grave. Some day, to-morrow, next month, next year, the grave-edge will crumble under our feet and yet we dare not say, Sire! take care! All we can do is to hold him back at all costs and in spite of himself. For when that grave shuts——"

Though my knowledge of Plessis could be measured by days, my ears had been open as well as my eyes, and so the snap of the fingers that rounded off the sentence was more informatory than words. It meant, as far as Monseigneur was concerned, a friend's deep sorrow, a crown minister's despair, a courtier's ruin; bereavement instant and irremediable to heart, brain, and ambition; it meant that the present fortunes and future prospects of the living Commines would certainly be buried with the dead King, and perhaps also the glory and greatness of France. Nor do I think the certainty of the one fretted him as sorely as the perhaps of the others. For eleven years Philip de Commines had been the greatest man in the kingdom, serving Louis, France, and himself, and loving all three. Let the grave close over his master, and at the groan of the sepulchral stone rasping to its socket Love and Service perished. But I think that with him, as with every truly great man, his life's work was dearer than himself, and his heart, as he leaned against the little diamond window panes looking out into the narrow court, was bitter for the loss to France rather than at the crumbling of his own fortunes.

"At any cost," he said, repeating the words over and over, "at any cost, at any—any cost."

"Even of a child's murder?"

"What?" he answered looking back across his shoulder, "are you still harping on that blunder? Oh! you Flemish calves! with but one idea in your head!"

"And is Commines not also in Flanders?"

He laughed, and quitting the window came towards me.

"True, friend Gaspard, and a fair hit; but there are great ideas as well as small ones, and it would be a mercy if you and that Martin of yours could think of more than one thing at a time."

"Martin?" said I, in despair at this fresh blow. "My own folly you have made clear, but what has Martin done?"

Monsieur de Commines shook his head gravely, but it was a relief to see a twinkle of humour shining through the gravity in his eyes.

"Martin has broken that high law of courts which says, Thou shalt run no risks to thyself for the sake of another! Love and faithfulness are dead in Plessis, and who is Martin to dare pretend they are alive? Twice every day he has come out from Tours to glower at the walls that hold his Master Gaspard, and it is not safe for a man to do that for a week at a stretch. Tristan has a keen nose and scented treason, love and faithfulness being perfumes strange to his nostrils, and had I not said No! haling Martin into Plessis almost by the neck, the misguided fool would have tapped his heels against that wall in the Rue Trois Pucelles before this."

"What, Monseigneur! You had this thought for us even when you were scolding me? How can I thank you?"

"Chut, chut," he answered, taking my hand in his, and holding it fast. "You gave the reason yourself a minute back; is not Commines also in Flanders?"

That was Philip de Commines all over. Policy and the mean cunning of court life might crust him round, but underneath were the tender heart, the broad deep mind, the generous sentiment ever ready to break a way to the surface. But when I would have pressed to see Martin at once he refused me.

"Not yet; the King has a claim before even a brother of Flanders, and the King is waiting for you."

"Now?"

"Yes, by this time he should be ready. Rochfort is with him but will be turned out that Monsieur Gaspard de Helville may be received in private audience. How important we are! But for both our sakes do not fall into the same trap a second time. Once was pardonable, but twice savours of suspicion, or what is worse in a man seeking the King's service, a witless foolishness. The one is natural at Plessis, and to be forgiven, but never the other! Take this from me; the man who cannot quickly understand a jest and laugh at it, even when it is against himself, is not fit for nice negotiations."

Leaving Monsieur de Commines' lodgings we turned to the left to the block set apart for the King's use. It lay east and west, with its windows, none of the widest, facing south, for the sun was the only living force on earth that Louis was willing should enter freely. Round the door were archers of the Scottish guard, on every landing of the stone stairway they lounged in threes and fours, and half a company were quartered in the outer room we first entered.

By all three we were challenged in turn, and for every group there was a different password. But even that security could not satisfy the King's jealous suspicion. Beyond the great chamber was an anteroom, where three of the officers of the archers were always in attendance, and well as the Prince de Talmont was known at court the captain of these would have turned him back, had it not been for the famous signet which had already saved our necks in Paris.

But even then the Scot had a scruple of what no doubt he called his conscience.

"It franks you, Monsieur," he said, pushing his scabbard in front of me when, Monsieur de Commines having entered, I would have followed, "but our orders are strict. 'Understand, Lesellè,' His Majesty said to me only to-day, 'you are to admit no one who does not carry the King's token.'"

For a foreigner, he spoke good French, but there was a harsh guttural in the voice that grated in my ears. As to his name, I do not know how it was spelt, but I give it as I caught the pronunciation.

For a moment Monseigneur looked perplexed as he stood with the curtain drawn back and one foot already across the threshold. To argue with the wooden-witted northerner was impossible, and he dared not risk the sound of an altercation at the King's door. Louis might have scented treason and called out to Lesellè to strike, not knowing nor caring who was struck. Nor would Lesellè have been slow to obey. I think I have said there was not much love between Monsieur de Commines and these mercenaries of the guard. But the embarrassment was only for an instant; Monseigneur was not the Prince de Talmont for nothing.

"The King is well served," he said courteously. Slipping the ring from his finger he dropped it into my palm across the outstretched steel and at the same moment withdrew himself into the King's chamber. "Show your token, Monsieur de Helville, and lose no time; already His Majesty has been made to wait."

"The King's signet, Monsieur," said I, catching my cue and shaking the collet within an inch or two of Lesellè's surprised eyes. "Will you withdraw your sword, or must I push it aside?"

It seemed at first as if he would have protested against the trick played upon him; then a saving sense of humour came to his rescue, and with a laugh he lowered his sword. Only, as I let the curtain fall behind me, I heard him say:

"Next time your hand comes so close to my face, Monsieur Whoever-you-are, I hope it will have no King's ring on its finger."

There was no time to reply. Taking me by the arm, Monsieur drew me on, and again I found myself in the King's presence.

CHAPTER XV
A LESSON IN DIPLOMACY

Before ever I had set foot in Plessis I had been warned that Louis was a man of many moods, many contradictions. Some of these sides of character I had already seen, but now a new, and at times a nobler vein, was brought to the surface; I was to see the King who governed. France had had kings who prayed, kings who fought, kings who reigned, but rarely a king who governed.

The apartment at the end of which we stood was long, narrow, and lofty, with windows only to the south. These were wider than the average in Plessis but were so fast barred that the power of the sun was greatly broken even though there were no hangings to shut out the heat. The floor was cumbered by but little furniture. A narrow table stood near the farther end with a few carved chairs surrounding it; a sacred picture or two, with a crucifix between, broke the dull flat of the walls; beyond these there was nothing of ornament. A prosperous merchant in any of the larger cities would be better housed than was Louis of France in his private cabinet.

Beyond the table the eastern end of the room terminated in an apse partly cut off by curtains, a kind of oratory dimly visible by the aid of a single hanging lamp. Facing the table and with his back to the oratory sat the King, a litter of papers spread out before him. He was again dressed in scarlet satin heavily fringed with fur, and there was such a tinge of colour on his hollow cheeks that at first I thought he was in better health than at the time of his seizure. But presently it was clear that this wholesomeness came not from within but from without, and was nothing more than the reflection of his clothing. It was a trivial thing, and yet its very triviality was significant of the King's thoroughness. Louis was as careful of his complexion as any faded coquette, but the deception was one of policy, not vanity. It was not well for France that men should know how ill was the King of France.

At his elbow stood Rochfort the Chancellor, nor, though there was a swift upward glance of the King's eyes, did our entrance turn aside the flow of words.

"I repeat," he was saying, rustling his hand among the papers, "Spain will not trouble us. Her toy, the Kingdom of Naples, fills her mind for the present. What says the Scripture?"—and he crossed himself, bowing with a duck of the head towards the table, and patting at a venture one of the leaden images hung about his person. In his opinion all the saints were on his side, and it did not matter very much which he invoked—"a fool's eyes are on the ends of the earth! Let Spain divide herself in Italy; Rome may be trusted to see she does not grow too strong; there are such things as Estates of the Church! Eh, Rochfort, eh? Well, what next?" again he glanced at us, still standing where we had entered. "England? I think not, I think not. Now that Edward has eaten himself to death—dear Edward—there is no need even to fling a sop to England. Peace in the south, peace in the north, there remains then our beloved—son! Our beloved fool!" he snarled suddenly, both his hands shivering amongst the papers like a wind in dry leaves, while he rocked to and fro on his seat, his head sunk between his shoulders like some painted image of malevolent death. "Oh that such a father should have such a son! Rochfort! It makes me—it makes me—well, well, well, even he has his uses; he reminds me of Flanders. Flanders!" he was gnawing his finger-tips now, his glaring eyes fixed on us, but vacantly, as though he saw us not.

Monsieur de Commines touched my elbow.

"There is a stroke coming, be on your guard," he said, without seeming to speak, "I know the symptoms!"

"Flanders!" went on the curiously roughened shrill voice that vibrated through me like the jarring of a tense chord, "there lies our business to-day. Let Spain grow weak in Italy, let England prey upon herself till only the picked bones are left, the policy of France is to widen her borders near home. Rochfort, we must have Flanders. The Dauphin, our beloved—fool! is contracted to that milk-mouthed Flemish princess of three and a half. That marriage will never come to pass, and we must make good our claim now."

As in the games with these playing-cards which His Majesty had introduced into court use there are certain well-defined rules, so also are there in the greater game of politics. When the King paused, with a challenge in his voice and attitude, Monsieur de Rochfort promptly responded to his lead, asking the question he was meant to ask.

"Flanders? Yes, Sire, but how make good our claim now? Nay, if I might hint a doubt, have we a claim?"

"Yes, yes, yes," answered Louis, his voice rising clear above its common level of sharp huskiness. The Chancellor's astute second question went farther than the King had intended, but not too far, for a smile twitched his lips. "The claim of every just man to right the wrong, to free the oppressed, and bring intolerable disorder to an end. Flanders is in flames and I must quench the fire for my dear son's sake. It has been reported to me— —"

Again his finger-tips were drawn in between the yellow teeth, and again Monseigneur nudged me. "Again I say, be on your guard," he whispered almost soundlessly.

"— —reported on high authority that a certain Jan Meert holds the country in terror, burning, ravaging, murdering, plundering where he pleases, and with none to check him. The peasantry he grinds, the lesser lords he crushes one by one. The subjects of the princess who is to be my beloved son's dear wife go in fear of their lives because of this Jan Meert, and I have a mind to make a sharp end of Jan Meert. Eh, Chancellor?"

"It would be bare justice, Sire," began Rochfort cautiously. This time the lead was not so clear, and Louis did not easily pardon blunders. "Indeed, a righteous act, but—but—"

"We are in Plessis and Flanders is far off? Splendour of God! Rochfort, are my fingers so weak or my arm so short that for the honour of God and the upholding of the law I cannot reach and crush a miserable plundering rogue? By Saint Claude! I'll do it, I'll do it—*if it be worth my while*. Eh, Monsieur le Prince, whom have you there with you? Is it some private business? Perhaps some petition to present? Some news to tell? Chancellor, we will excuse you; de Talmont has something to say, and you know I am always greedy of secrets. Kings govern by hiding their knowledge. *Qui nescit dissimulare nescit regnare*. And your companion? Ah ha! ah ha! it is—Yes, yes, it is Monsieur Hellewyl. Well, Monsieur, do you still desire to serve France?"

As we moved forward, Rochfort retired by a door at the side of the oratory, leaving us alone with the King. But though the question asked was a direct one, I could only answer it by a bow. My mouth had suddenly gone dry, so that I dared not attempt words. But for Monsieur de Commines' hint I might have assumed that our overhearing of the King's reference to Jan Meert was coincidence, but Monseigneur's significance forbade that mistake. Louis was dangling his bribe, but a bribe to what end? It was de Commines who replied for me.

"I can say Yes to that, Sire."

"So, so, but of all men, d'Argenton, you should know we can only employ servants who are faithful."

"I guarantee Monsieur de Helville's fidelity, Sire."

"You guarantee? you! Of what use is that to me? Am I to hang you if this de Helville of yours breaks faith? And yet it is guarantees I want. Have you a father or a mother, Monsieur?"

"Neither, Sire," I replied, wetting my lips, "both are dead."

"That is unfortunate," he said, the sour sardonic smile twitching his mouth afresh, "for I have noticed that a man is sometimes faithful when I can hold and crush his mother, as I hold and crush this," and his fingers shut viciously over a sheet of the paper spread in front of him, rasping it into a crumpled mass, which he flung briskly aside. "But not all men, no! some are superior to such weakness and they mostly rise high—when they are not hung first! Sisters, then? brothers? None? Well, they would not be sufficient, especially if the brother were an elder one. What then? Solignac is burned, there are no lands to forfeit; with you it is all to gain and nought to lose, and yet the fear of loss is a surer guarantee than the hope of gain. Suggest something, d'Argenton."

"There are other women in the world besides mothers, Sire."

Louis nodded and his cold eyes travelled over me thoughtfully. As once before he had searched my thoughts, he was now appraising my person as one would the points of a horse.

"Twenty-five, broad enough, tall enough, comely enough, and not altogether a fool. Who is the woman, Monsieur de Helville?"

Had I been more of a courtier I could have lied, warned by the King's cruel cynicism. But at the sudden question the blood rose to my face, and I stammered:

"There is none, your Majesty, at least there is none worthy——"

"Oh ho! he is modest, this sucking envoy of yours, d'Argenton. Well, all the better. Come, Monsieur, her name and degree? The King speaks."

From mockery he passed into incisive demand, and though what I had already said was true enough in the sense he meant, I was constrained to answer. In five minutes he had dragged from me all there was to know concerning Brigitta and, in his cunning, inferred much more than the truth. With his elbows on the table, and one hand half-covering his mouth, he stared up at me until I ended, the sallow parchment of his face withered into wrinkles.

"A peasant! And he would marry her! What do you say to that, d'Argenton?"

"Only that Monsieur de Helville is a man of contradictory tastes, Sire; but, for my part, I prefer second thoughts."

"Pish! you talk riddles, and I do not like what I do not understand," said Louis. Though he spoke to Commines, his gaze never left my face, and I was conscious that he played with me as a tolerant cat plays with a mouse. "So you would marry her, though she is only a peasant? Some would say, have you no *droits de Seigneur* in your parts! and cry Fie! on you for your honesty. But not I. Her limbs may be as white as any satin lady's, her cheeks as pink, her lips as red to kiss, her breath as sweet, and what more can five and twenty ask! eh?"

He paused, as if for an answer, but I, conscious of Monseigneur's veiled reference to Mademoiselle, and that I was practising at least half a lie, could do no more than stammer an inane something to the effect that he was very good, which was in itself a lie, and at which banality the grin broke out afresh.

"For my part," he went on, "I am well enough pleased. After all, you are a gentleman; the breed will be one degree nearer to the sod and all the better for the mixture. It is from the people that salvation must come to the nation, not from the nobles. Besides she is a hostage, and being a peasant, will be the easier handled. For her sake, be faithful, Monsieur, or by God!" and leaning aside, he shook his finger backwards and forwards at the dim shrine behind him, "by God! I say, those white limbs shall suffer, and those red lips scream, nor will all the love in the world keep a curse of Gaspard de Helville off them. The marriage bed with Solignac as your roof-tree, or the naked rack, Monsieur, and at your own choice."

"I have already promised, Sire— —"

"No, Monsieur, no," he interrupted, "you have promised nothing. D'Argenton has promised for you, which is quite another thing. Promises? Bah! what are promises? I have known even kings break them! Give me an oath." Fumbling at his throat he loosed a collar of reliquaries which hung round his neck and spread it on the table before him with more real reverence than I had ever yet seen him display, even when taking the name of Christ in his mouth. "Now, Monsieur, lay your hand there. No, no, down on your knees, on your knees. What! you kneel to me, and yet dare stand upright in the presence of God Almighty, before Whom you swear? Down on your knees, I say! when you call Christ and His saints to witness. Now, repeat: I Gaspard de Helville, otherwise, Hellewyl, swear by my honour in this life, and by my salvation in that to come, that I shall perform the King's service faithfully to the end, or, failing such performance, will return forthwith to Plessis to confess the failure and its cause, so help me God and His Saints."

Speaking from my knees, and with both hands spread over the little heap of holy things, I repeated the oath clause by clause. As I ended, and while still kneeling, Louis snatched the necklet from under my palms, and touching a spring in one of the reliquaries, pressed the little grey morsel it contained to my lips.

"*Consummatum est!*" he cried triumphantly, "Now indeed we have you, have you body and soul, bound fast for this world and that which is to come. 'Tis the Cross of Saint Lo, Monsieur de Helville, whereon who forswears himself dies within the year and perishes eternally. The guarantees are complete. What a man will not do for a woman's sake he will for his life—if not for his soul. His soul!" he groaned complainingly, the unctuousness slipping out from his voice as suddenly as it had slipped in. "We spend so much time saving our souls that France suffers. Cannot the Saints save us and have done with it! But there's a thought there; d'Argenton, your arm."

Pushing back his chair, the King rose painfully to his feet, a meagre skeleton of a man, bent by more than the weight of years.

"On this occasion when we seek the peace of the world it would be a Christian duty to ask the blessing of Saint Eutropius."

Leaning on Monseigneur, Louis limped towards the oratory, dragging one foot rasping on the floor as he walked.

"It can do no harm," I heard him mutter. "It is always well to keep heaven on our side, eh, d'Argenton?"

"Yes, Sire, but is it wise that the priest should over-hear——?"

"Tut, tut; he never leaves Plessis. Besides, a priest has a neck between his frock and his shaven crown as well as another man."

"But, Sire, his office?"

Louis paused, looking round, so that I saw the profile of his wrinkled forehead and thin nose white against the gloom of the shrine.

"I am faithful to the Church, d'Argenton, no man more so, but, by God! the Church had better be faithful to me, for there's no benefit of clergy to traitors! We desire your prayers, dear father," he went on loudly, "to the end that an enterprise of peace may have the blessing of Saint Eutropius upon it. Only, no Latin, pray in honest French so that I, as well as the good Saint, may understand what you say." Down on his knees he went by the rail, Monseigneur on a faltstool behind him, while I, apparently forgotten, knelt in turn on the bare floor. "To the point, and not too long," said Louis. "Like myself, he is busy in good works, and we must not waste his time."

Out from the deeper shadow at the side of the altar a black-frocked figure stole into view.

"Then you do not desire a special office, Sire?" said a soft voice.

Louis raised his head.

"Anything, man, so that you are quick, and to the point. If I could have spoken for myself, we would have done by this."

There was a brief silence, to allow, no doubt, for a collecting of thoughts. Where a man is accustomed to have prayers put into his mouth it is not always easy to draw them fresh from the heart upon an emergency. But at last the soft voice broke into a murmur.

"Forasmuch, oh holy Saint Eutropius, as it has pleased thee to put into the heart of thy faithful servant purposes of blessed peace, grant, we humbly beseech thee, that the consummation he seeks may richly abound to—to—"

"The greatness of France," interrupted Louis in a loud voice; "make haste to the end."

"The greatness of France," went on the soft voice submissively, "and the furtherance of the Lord's eternal Kingdom. Grant, also, we pray thee, that upon the King, thy servant, may descend with great power refreshment and strength to body and soul——"

"There, there," said Louis, rising heavily to his feet, "cut it short at the body and leave the soul for another time. It is not well to importune the blessed saint by too many requests at once. The body will do for to-day." And once more taking Monseigneur's arm, he shuffled back to his seat.

CHAPTER XVI
A MISSION OF PEACE

"Now that we have the blessing of God we may go on," said Louis, biting his fingernails so closely that the beginnings of what he had next to say were mumbled through a hand upon his mouth. As words they were smooth enough, but when I remembered the King's reply to Monseigneur upon the very altar step the threat behind the flattery could not be ignored. "I am going to trust you, Monsieur de Helville, even as I trust the worthy priest who serves me and the Church at the altar behind us. It is enough for common men that they look no farther than to-morrow or next year, but nations live by generations, and we who think for France must think in tens of years. We have prayed for peace, but through a little seven years' child in Navarre there is a menace." He paused, slipping a level hand up to shroud his eyes, and watched me keenly. But this time Monsieur de Commines' lesson had been better learned and I made no reply. My wisdom was to let the King's meaning unfold itself beyond doubt. Apparently I stood the test to his satisfaction, for he went on, suavely—

"Your outburst of the other day, Monsieur de Helville was very natural, very much to your credit, and though the shame of your most unworthy suspicion nearly cost me my life, you are pardoned. Listen now. Spain is tangled in Italy, and with all her will to trouble France she has not the power; the princes of Italy, Sforza, Visconti, Medici, Este, and a dozen other pigmies, are my friends; James of Scotland and John of Portugal are my close allies; England," and he snapped his fingers contemptuously, "England is a muzzled dog; Austria stands upon its mercenaries, and my pay is better than Maximilian's. Only little Navarre is left, and through my niece, Queen Catherine, half Navarre is already mine. Have you ever had a cinder in your eye, Monsieur de Helville? a speck almost too petty to be seen, and yet it frets, and frets, and frets? That miserable half of little Navarre is the petty speck in the eye of France, and Gaston de Foix, the seven years' son of the Count of Narbonne, is the edge that frets and frets and frets."

Again he paused, and this time I was fool enough to speak.

"I do not understand, Sire, how so young a child——"

"God's name, man, who bid you understand? I said, Listen! And will not the child grow? and is he not in collateral line for the crown? The father is past middle age and spent, but the child will become the man, and through that miserable half of Navarre there will be a way open for Spain to strike France twenty years hence. Who knows what feeble brain may govern France when that day comes? I—I—I can hardly hope—D'Argenton! my cordial; quick—quick—um—um—um—there! that is past."

He sat back in his chair, very white and breathing heavily, while from a wide-mouthed crystal he sucked loudly and with evident satisfaction, long sips of a yellowish fluid.

"Let the rest wait till to-morrow, Sire," said Commines, who bent over him.

But if Louis did not spare his servants neither did he spare himself.

"Will to-morrow be less full than to-day? Besides, I am in a fever until this question of Navarre is settled. We must have the child, Monsieur de Helville."

"How, Sire?"

"Do you hear him, d'Argenton? What kind of a tool is this you have put into my hand, with his hows and whys and buts? How? Do I care how! That is your business. There are a dozen ways, all safe, all sure. Oh, it is the curse of life to have a brain to think and yet be forced to leave the execution to—to—blundering hands. How? Steal him if you like! Next you will ask—you who are so nice and have such charitable thoughts of your King—you will ask, Why? Well, I shall tell you, Monsieur, I shall tell you. Even your scruples will admit the scheme is a worthy one. If France educates the child, France educates him for a friend, France shows him that his interests are French, not Spanish, and so we hold Navarre on both frontiers and may be at peace. The mind of a child of seven is wax, is wax; and to win a child's love is not difficult. This time I ask you, Do you understand?"

"I understand, Sire, that by fair means or—or——"

"Yes, say it, or by foul! How he chokes over it, d'Argenton. Do you truly think him fit for the work?"

"I warrant Monsieur de Helville to be brave, your Majesty, to be prompt, to be devoted, and to be no fool."

"Devoted?" Louis fastened on the word like a starved rat on a bone. "Yes, but to himself or to me? To his own interests or to mine?"

"To you, Sire, to you."

"Ay! he had better. I have his oath, and I'll have the girl; yes, and I would have him too, if he played me false, have him though I bribed every court in Europe to find him."

"Sire, Sire, you mistake your man," cried Monseigneur, his voice full of a generous indignation. "Threats— —"

"But there are promises, too, d'Argenton, promises and rewards. First, let come what may, you shall face Jan Meert; that I set my word to. Were I a man of your inches, Monsieur de Helville, and of that courage for which your patron vouches, I would ask nothing better than that in my own private quarrel. Next, fulfil to the letter the instructions I shall give you and I will not only build you a new Solignac, greater than the first, but for the lands of Hellewyl you shall have double, no matter whether Burgundy, France, or The Empire holds them; to that also I set my word. Talmont, am I a niggard to those who serve me? You know I am not. You came to me with empty hands and now, if every finger were a palm, they would be overflowing. Well, Monsieur, are you satisfied? At one stroke you bring peace to a nation, vengeance to yourself, wealth to your race. Does your oath hold?"

The extraordinary winning powers of the man, the sudden sweetness of tone, the softened kindliness, the generous manner, the vibration of pleading in the voice, swept me from my feet rather than the prodigality of the promises. Nor was it a new thing that a prince should be brought up at a foreign court as a pledge of peace. The novelty was in the method of securing the prince's person, and that, weighed against the advantages, did not trouble me much.

"I'll do it, Sire, I'll do it, though there should be twenty Counts of Narbonne to say No! Nor will there be time lost on the road. Once I have the boy I shall make straight for Plessis— —?

"Tse! Tse!" hissed Louis between his teeth, while he wagged a finger hastily at me. "No, no, you go too fast. Who bade you make straight for Plessis? The hand of France must not appear in this affair at all."

"But, Sire, my credentials?"

"Credentials? What? Parchments with a King's seal and countersign to certify you have the authority of France to go a-thieving? Why not ask for the oriflamme at once! By the splendour of God! d'Argenton, but the fellow thinks himself an ambassador plenipotentiary at the very least! Credentials! Authority under my hand to abduct Gaston de Foix! Do you take me for a fool, Monsieur?"

"Then, Sire," said I bluntly, "if I am caught, I hang."

"Ah!" answered Louis unctuously, and patting a saint's figure haphazard as he spoke, "All is as God wills, and surely it is as honourable to die for peace as to die in war?"

"Then, Sire, having secured the boy?"

"Having, with the blessing of God, secured the boy, Monsieur de Helville, you will then—where is the letter I bade Rochfort seal with your signet, d'Argenton? It should be amongst the papers on the table."

"With my signet?" answered Monseigneur uneasily, "I have no knowledge—the Chancellor did not convey to me—that is, I had not heard——"

"No, no; there was no need you should. Ah! here it is," and Louis, pushing aside some parchments which I do not doubt he had placed where they lay that they might conceal the folded paper he now drew towards him with the tips of his claws, lifted an oblong letter sealed broadly upon the back, and tied with silk, "Rochfort prepared it for me. Write your name across the corner, my friend, if you please. Since Monsieur desires credentials, this will serve him. So! your hand shakes, de Talmont, why is that? Now, Monsieur de Helville, attend; once, by God's grace you have secured the boy, open this and do what it bids you. That is all; d'Argenton, take him away and give him what he will need. Credentials! there are your credentials, money, money, and again money! What man of the world asks for finer credentials? Tell him the route too, as he travels it he will learn now far the arm of France can stretch whether to succour or to strike."

Pushing himself to his feet, stiffly and with evident pain, Louis turned towards the altar behind him and bowed humbly, crossing his breast repeatedly, then faced again towards me.

"The God of peace go with you, Monsieur de Helville, and at all times and in all acts remember Him you serve. Ay, ay," he went on, his voice hardening, "and remember, too, your Brigitta of the white limbs and red mouth, for, by the same God, I'll not forget her or you."

The last I saw of him was a bowed, half-crouched figure, a grey-pale face looking out from between bent shoulders, and a lean hand shaken shrewishly in the air.

I was to remember whom I served! Did he mean God or himself? For all his assumption of servile religiosity, I doubted if Louis set even the seat of the Almighty higher than the throne of France.

CHAPTER XVII
SOUTH FROM PLESSIS

Monseigneur made no comment until we were in the freshness of the open air; then he drew a long breath as if a strain had been relaxed.

"It might have been worse. Come, now, that I may fill your purse; you and Martin must leave Plessis to-night."

"But, Monseigneur," I protested, "this is not at all what I desired."

"What you desired! Who comes to Plessis to do what he desires? And remember this, my friend, there is no turning back from the King's plough. But to tell you the truth, it is not what I desired for you, not exactly what I had in my mind for you, and yet I was a true prophet. All is as the King wills. Keep that truth in your head, walk at all times by its light, and your ten days in the rat-trap will not have been wasted."

I made no reply, and we turned the angle of the royal block in silence. In silence, too, we crossed the court to his lodgings; but with his hand upon the latch, Monsieur de Commines, with a gayer note in his voice, repeated my complaint.

"Not all you desired? Perhaps it is; perhaps it is even more than your imagination groped after. The petulance of ignorant youth starts like a shying horse at the first obstacle, and cries: I do not like the road. It is the method that troubles me, not the end. The end!" and the last of the cloud upon his face dissolved in merriment. "I think I would play the end of the game myself if I were five-and-twenty."

"But to be a thief, an abductor of children——"

"Does that choke you? Then why did you not say No! to the King?"

"There was a glamour about him," I began.

"Did I not tell you he had many moods? He can make any man love him—for the moment—when that is his pleasure or his profit. Besides, you over-state the case; there is only one child, and he a very little one."

"It is theft, all the same."

"Pooh! We are all thieves in court when a theft profits. A reputation, an office, a title, a province, it is all a question of degree. What? If I am His Majesty's ambassador at Cologne or Rome—with credentials, mind you!—is it not that I may steal an advantage? The greater the theft, the greater the honour—if only the theft be successful! There you have the world's diplomacy in a sentence. We lie and thieve abroad for the good of our country. Who are you, friend Gaspard, that you should be more scrupulous than I?"

"But what kind of a household shall I find at—at——?"

"Where you are going? Charming, charming; especially if, as I imagine, it is the frank abandonment of country life without etiquette or punctilio."

His harangue upon the honourable methods of court life was, of course, half jest, but there was also so much of truth in his irony that complacency and self-respect once more lifted their head, swaggering as if there was no such thing as a lie in the world. After all, what was my task but to do in units what for years Monsieur de Commines had schemed to do by thousands, in the transferring of whole principalities from one ruler to another?

As I pushed open the door of Monseigneur's private apartment and stood aside to allow him to precede me, Martin, standing within, caught sight of me. What a cry he gave! "Monsieur Gaspard! Oh, thank God! thank God!" It warmed my heart to hear him. Without ceremony he pushed past Monsieur de Commines and caught me by both hands; nor would Monseigneur listen to my apologies.

"Love is no respecter of persons," said he, clapping him on the shoulder. "I told you Master Martin had a heart in his breast, and so would make a bad courtier. All the same, I wish I had fifty such insolents about me. I would be safer than Louis in Plessis for all its walls and moats. That you will have Martin with you on your journey makes me easier in my mind."

Dropping my hands, Martin bowed humbly, angry with himself that his unceremonious impetuosity had, perhaps, lowered the dignity of his Monsieur Gaspard.

"Your pardon, Monseigneur, and yours, Monsieur Gaspard; I forgot myself. But when one has gone hungry for ten days——"

"That's a fine phrase of yours, my friend; say no more lest you spoil it."

"Then, Monseigneur, if I am permitted? You spoke of a journey—is it soon?"

"To-night."

"But not to Tours, Monseigneur, not to the Street——?"

"The Street of the House of the Great Nails! No, my friend, to the south."

"To the south to-night! God be praised for all His mercies! I'll go for the horses, Monsieur Gaspard."

"Yes," said de Commines, laughing at his haste, but a little bitterly, "go, go, for there is no time to be lost. It's a strange world, de Helville," he went on as the door closed. "Here we have the greatest names in the land, and every ambitious schemer in France intriguing to set foot in Plessis, and this honest heart thanking God unfeignedly that he rides away into the darkness,—he does not even ask where! But now to arrange for your journey. For the King's peace and your own, leave Plessis to-night, late as it is. You will just have time before the gates close, when none can pass. Halt at Ouzay for the night—it is the first of the King's posts, and put up at the sign of the Laughing Man. Say to the host as you enter, 'Is the good-man of Tours in the neighbourhood?' and having received his answer, say no more. Sup on the best and sleep softly, there will be no reckoning to pay. But in the morning a man, wearing a bunch of trefoil in his hat, will give you your next instructions. Follow these, but ask no questions. As you find it at Ouzay, so will it be straight through to Navarre. Everywhere you rest you will be expected, or, rather, not you, but the King's messenger, and everywhere you pass shot free."

"Then what is this for?" asked I, for while he was speaking he had filled a wallet with more gold coin than Solignac had ever seen in all my five-and-twenty years.

"For diplomacy," he answered laughing. "Where you cannot steal you must bribe. But there, I hear the horses in the courtyard, and since needs must when the King bids, the sooner you go south the sooner Solignac will give you a roof to your head. And who knows but the journey may find you a mistress for it! Brigitta? H'm, perhaps Brigitta, though I am no lover of swineherd wenches. Let me see the King's letter a moment."

I took it from the inner pocket where, half mechanically, I had placed it for safety, and handed it to Monsieur de Commines—an oblong envelope of crisp paper, a palm and a half in length by a palm wide, stout, substantial, close-fastened. He took it, and turned at once to the seal.

"My cypher and quarterings exactly, even to the flaw on the upper right hand corner of the collet; my shade of wax too, even to the perfume I commonly use. Men call me avaricious. It's a lie, de Helville; money is a good servant but the worst of masters. Yet I would give five hundred, yes a thousand livres to know what is written within, or even to see the writing.

Who knows but it may seem my very own? If I do nothing by halves, neither does the King my master, though how he procured the signet I cannot imagine." With a sigh and a shake of the head he raised his eyes from the seal. "No; truly things have not turned out as I desired."

In the courtyard he bade Martin follow with Roland and the pack-horse, and walked with me to the outer gate, his arm linked in mine. Neither spoke, for he was wrapped in deep thought, his face as dismal as if we followed a funeral. But as we passed along the outer fosse I saw his eyes lighten.

"Credentials! sneered the King," and he tapped the paper with his finger. "Perhaps he was more right than he supposed! That letter, without superscription though it is, may open a smooth way for you of which His Majesty never dreamed; though God forbid that I should judge how clear and deep are His Majesty's dreams. Keep it, friend Gaspard, and if you find a difficulty in making good your footing at—at—the end of your journey, Philip de Commines' forged signet, with his name across the corner of he knows not what, may clear away the opposition as no King's credentials would do."

By this time we were beyond the final drawbridge, with Martin, who had passed ahead, waiting for us, the bridles across his arm, and Roland's stirrup in his palm. Royal palace and all, Monsieur Gaspard must receive the humble service due to him, and so impress the loafers at the gate with his exalted rank!

"How can I thank you, Monseigneur!" I began. "Here was I, forlorn, helpless, a beggar, with neither hope nor prospect, not even a second suit to my back, and now, through you, I am an envoy on the King's service."

"For God's sake," he cried, "say nothing of the prospect till it is proved. Only remember this: first for your father's sake, and now for the sake of your father's son, Philip de Commines is your friend without reserve. That is a thing I say to few. If you tumble into a pitfall on this path of my choosing—what a fool I was to meddle with the King's affairs!—I'll pull you out, cost what it may; and oh, lad! lad! there's a huge cost to be paid by someone, of that I'm certain. And now, good-bye, and God keep you. Take care of him, Martin."

"To the death, Monseigneur; trust me. For what else was I born?"

"Farewell, Monseigneur, and again my thanks. How long do you give me to return?"

With a groan and an upward gesture of both hands, de Commines turned back towards the gate, now about to be shut.

"How can I tell? A month! Eternity! What I said at the first I say at the last—All is as the King wills"; and with that, which was at best a boding God-speed, we rode on our way.

So long as Plessis gates remained in sight Martin kept his distance, nor, though I reined Roland back to a walk, would he decrease the space between us by a yard. But once a turn of the path, following the river's curve, hid the towers, he drew up beside me.

"Oh, Monsieur Gaspard, Monsieur Gaspard, but this is good!"

"What is good?" answered I, holding out a hand to him, which he caught and gripped. I knew his meaning very well, but I knew, too, that it would please him to speak his thought.

"That we two should be out in the sweet air together, free from the rat-trap, free from the fox with the wolf's claws, free from—from—that accursed house in the Rue Trois Pucelles, and riding—God knows where! What does it matter!"

"Why, what was that house to you?" I asked, remembering a hint Monseigneur had let fall.

"It was very near being my last rise in the world, and having seen two poor souls travel by that upward road I had no heart to follow them. One was a common thief, a foul-mouthed gutter bully, and I daresay deserved his hanging. But the other was a miserable, white-faced wench who stole a loaf out of sheer hunger, and that she might keep her wretched soul one day longer in its starved body. They hung them together—for company, I suppose; and it made me sick to see a coarse, burly scoundrel climb out of that upper window and slide down the rope to the girl's shoulders and crouch there, tailor-fashion, laughing at some vile jest of his own making, while she—quite right, Monsieur Gaspard, I'll say no more about it. It's a filthy way by which to send even a sinner to God."

The picture Martin conjured up was a horrible one, and remembering Mademoiselle's grim suggestion as to what her fate would be if found in Tours, I had made an involuntary gesture of loathing. If it had sickened Martin to see an outcast of the streets—a nameless wretch haled from God knows what cellar of vice—suffer such foul indignity, how would the spirit not revolt to think of that pure, sweet face——

But even as I clenched my teeth and cursed at large, a new thought broadened upon me. What a spirit she must have had, what a courage, what a boldness, what an abnegation of self, to deliberately, and with open eyes, face so horrible an end in cold blood! It is curious how the little side winds of life fan the flame of love. Martin's chance words, and the shocking scene they forced upon the imagination, had turned my thoughts afresh in Mademoiselle's direction, warming my admiration to glowing point. But of that he knew nothing.

"And you?" I asked. "How did Tristan's brutal work touch you?"

"It was this way, Monsieur Gaspard. What had I to do with myself all alone in Tours? Nothing! So each day, yes, and twice a day, to keep Ninus in condition, I rode out as far as Plessis and walked him up and down where I could see the gates. You were inside, and they were always something to look at. For a time nothing happened. Then a fellow followed me out—a huge, pock-marked rascal on a raw-boned sorrel. Not a word did he speak, but as I sentried up and down he drew aside and sat watching me. Then he followed me back to the Cross of Saint Martin, and later on I saw him earwigging the landlord. What he learned I don't know. Possibly that robber of guests thought it his interest to remember what he told Monseigneur he had never heard, for next day and the next I was again followed. Then three more joined him, and before I caught their intention they had me on my back. 'I denounce him for a spy,' cried pock-pit. 'Lord! Lord! what a neck he has! He's so light it will take my weight to stretch it as I did the girl's last week. Three minutes on her shoulders, and—click! all was over!' But Monsieur de Commines met us on the road to Tours, and—and—here we are riding together in the cool of God's free air, riding to—— Where do we ride, Monsieur Gaspard?"

Stretching out my hand again, I caught his, squeezing it hard.

"I owe Monseigneur a good turn for that, and perhaps you and I may be able to pay him shortly." My idea was that the prompt success of de Commines' *protégé* would redound to de Commines' credit with the King, which was another reason against a too delicate squeamishness as to methods. "To-night we ride to Ouzay."

"And then?"

"God knows! Wherever a Jack-in-a-box of a fellow bids us."

"But surely, Monsieur Gaspard, you know the end of it all?"

"Navarre, I think."

"That's beyond my tether," said Martin, shaking his head doubtfully. "But there, the good God didn't open the rat-trap for us for nothing, that I'm sure."

CHAPTER XVIII
COUNT GASTON DE FOIX

The name of the inn at Ozauy must have been given in bitter irony, for house and host were alike unprepossessing. Custom seemed the last thing desired.

"Full," said he, opening the door an inch or two in reply to my third knock, though the blankness of the dark upper windows gave him the lie. "Go elsewhere, my fine fellow, and make less noise." And would have shut-to the door again, had I not thrust the end of my riding-whip through the crack.

"Tell me," I whispered, as he struggled to push it back, "is the good-man of Tours in the neighbourhood?"

On the instant the struggling ceased, and I heard a little whimper behind the door like the cry of a child too frightened of the dark to scream.

"Saints have mercy on a fool!" he said, flinging the door wide. "Come in, Monseigneur, come in! How was I to guess it was your Excellency at so late an hour? There are half a dozen louts drinking in the kitchen, some of them not too sober—we must live as we may these times. Shall I turn them out?"

"No, but prepare supper while we see to the horses, then make our rooms ready. But the good-man of Tours, what of him?"

"Certainly, your Excellency, in the morning; I shall see to that. To-night he is——"

But I remembered Commines' advice, and cut him short; besides, it was long past our usual hour for the meal, and we were half-starved.

"Is that your business? Bring supper."

"Again, certainly, Monseigneur, and a good one, though all Ouzay be scoured for it." Nor, when it came, had we any cause to complain.

What profession, beyond that of spy and jackal to the sick Lion of Plessis, the good-man of Tours followed I do not know, but at least he was diligent in his master's service. Before seven in the morning there was a knocking at our door, and when Martin slipped the bolt a fellow in peasant's dress entered, closing the door carefully behind him.

"Monsieur de Helville?" he said, looking from one to the other, but speaking not at all in a peasant's voice.

"I am de Helville."

"And I the good-man of Tours—or his shadow. Here are your orders. Go to the Red Cock in Poictiers, and ask the landlord the same question you asked last night, saying neither more nor less."

He had kept his hand on the latch while he spoke, and as he ended he opened the door and was gone before we could put in a word. Martin was for running after him, but I forbade it.

"To what purpose? We know as much as the King wants us to know. That masquerading peasant could tell us nothing more. It's my belief that, except Louis himself, not a man in France, not even either Monsieur de Commines or the Chancellor, knows the route we are to follow or the business we travel on."

"But, Monsieur Gaspard, why such caution?"

"For this reason, my friend; if we bungle our commission, the King can say, 'I never knew you,' and so leave us to our fate as wandering vagabonds."

As it was at Ouzay, so it was at Poictiers and for the rest of our journey. Poictiers sent us to Ruffec, Ruffec to Marthon, Marthon to Saint Gatien, Saint Gatien to Le Catelet, Le Catelet to Gabarnet, Gabarnet to Orthez, Orthez to La Voulle. Everywhere there was the same question, everywhere the same obsequious, frightened deference, with none seeing further into the King's purpose than the next post. Once our instructions came by way of a woman, and once through the inn-keeper himself.

This last was at The Good Queen in La Voulle, and there, for the first time, our orders varied.

"I am to tell you this," said he. "What you seek is at Morsigny. When you have found it, ride back here with all speed, and then, but not till then, open the sealed letter."

At the time I answered nothing, but next morning as we sat at breakfast, our host serving us, I asked, as if for gossip's sake, if he knew of such a place as Morsigny?

"The château, I suppose you mean, Monsieur?" he replied, playing up to my lead while he busied himself doing nothing with apparent zeal. "It is about three leagues to the south, and so not far from the hills. But you will not find the Count at home."

"Oh, the Count is not at home," I repeated vaguely, my information being of the weakest. I had not even remembered there was a Count.

"No, Excellency; he is with the court at Pamplona, though not altogether for love."

"Who, then, is at Morsigny?"

"Only the little Count and a small household. The life they live is of the quietest; few pass their way, and if you have news from Paris, or even from Bordeaux, Monsieur, you will be sure of a welcome."

"What?" said I doubtfully. The possible solution of an evident difficulty did not seem a good one. "A stranger? Hardly welcome, I think."

"That's just it, Monsieur, because you are a stranger, or no more than two. Were you fifty you would find the door shut so fast that fifty would not open it. Nor would you get a welcome if you came from Tours. We of the Little Kingdom do not love Louis. Jean Volran says it."

"Bold words," said Martin grimly. "But, my friend, here's advice to you: if you meet a certain Messire Tristan, keep your dislikes to yourself, for assuredly Jean Volran would never say it a second time."

"Bah!" replied he, shrugging his shoulders as he turned away. "I'm not afraid of your precious Messire Tristan."

No more passed, but as we rode on the way I had leisure to admire the skill with which His Majesty chose even the humblest of his tools. In three sentences Jean Volran had informed us of the position at Morsigny, had shown us a possible cause of welcome, and hinted a warning we would be fools to disregard.

It was curious, but it was not the seizing of the child that troubled my conscience, but the stealing through a friendly door under cover of a lie. But as I cast about how I might shift a downright lie to a seeming truth, and so cheat the devil in the dark, Martin could stand his uncertainty no longer, and so, for the tenth time since we had left Plessis, spurred Ninus up alongside of Roland that he might ease his curiosity.

"Are we at our journey's end, Monsieur Gaspard?"

"Nearly," answered I, finding safety in brevity.

"And what do we do next?"

"The King's business."

"Then it's turn about," said he, "for the King nearly did mine in Tours. But what is the King's business to us?"

"The restoration of the Hellewyl lands, the building of Solignac, and Jan Meert's life. Will that content you?"

But to my surprise, so far from showing the lively satisfaction I looked for, or even astonishment, his face grew grave.

"Is it as dangerous as all that? The old fox of Plessis never gives coin or life except at ten-fold usury. Who pays it, Monsieur Gaspard?"

"Are you a coward? Think of the gain, man."

"Ay! Coward! Think of the cost!" he answered dourly. "I say again, Who pays it? Pray God we don't!"

"That we may not," I answered, speaking more sharply than was just, for I had always encouraged Martin to be frank. "See well to Roland and Ninus, for when we ride from Morsigny we shall ride as if the devil or Tristan himself were after us. The pack-horse we shall leave behind."

"Morsigny!" said Martin. "I'd rather have Solignac, charred and roofless, than twenty Morsignys. God send us safe away!"

"God send us safe there," I retorted; "and that He may, do thou wait here till I ask our road. I hear voices across the break of whins yonder."

It is my belief that the sun, the rain, and the wind are at the bottom of half the workings of a man's spirit, nor, if nature be in a mothering mood, is it possible for wholesome five-and-twenty to withstand for long her comfortings. Never had Flanders shown me so blue a sky, rarely had such a kindly sun so warmed me. The very vigour of the trees, their depth of green, their splendid strength, their lavishment of southern foliage, was a beguiling and a delight. Long before I turned Roland out of the track my sourness had vanished, and in its place was the glorious exuberance and sweetness of youth, that thinks neither care nor evil. Care? To the back of to-morrow with care! All around me the world was sown with gold, the yellow of broom, the yellow of whin, the yellow of kingcups; and as the honey-sweet of the warm air smote my nostrils, my heart danced in time to the thud of Roland's hoofs. Over this bush we leaped, over that, zigzagging towards the sound of life.

"Ah dieu! me donc le joye d'amour!"

sang I, and landed Roland almost flat on the top of a fluttering skirt. With a jerk I pulled him to his haunches, and, bonnet in hand, sprang to the ground.

"Pardon, Madame," I began, but stopped short, my heart leaping again, but this time to the tune of my song. It was no Madame at all, but

Mademoiselle herself—Mademoiselle of the Star of Flanders and Tours Cathedral, and straddling in front of her was a little six or seven-year lad, his fists squared up at me.

It is another of my beliefs that, in the disadvantage of surprise, a woman's wits work more keenly than a man's. Certainly Mademoiselle found her tongue first, though that, perhaps, was yet more truly feminine.

"Welcome to Navarre, Monsieur Gaspard Hellewyl!" said she, sweeping me a curtsey so low that the exertion fired her cheeks ruddily. "Or is it Monsieur Martin? The changes are so confusing and the names so hard to remember."

"Gaspard Hellewyl, Mademoiselle," answered I; "Gaspard Hellewyl, and always at your service."

"Oh!" she exclaimed, curtseying a second time, "always at my service! That is very prettily said, Monsieur. And have you come all the way from Tours to kill a man to prove it? That was your way in Paris, and that was what you would have done in Tours, but here in Navarre I pray you prove it in some gentler fashion. We have so few men in Navarre, and"—the laughter died from her eyes as she paused an instant—"we may need them all to fight France."

"If all Navarre can double its fists as sturdily as your playfellow, Mademoiselle," answered I, giving her badinage for badinage, "then France had better call Spain to her help, or else cry quarter."

As we spoke she had folded her arms round the little lad in loving protection, but now she loosed him, and we stood for a moment in silence. Presently she shook her head, her mouth twitching, as if her gaiety was struggling back again.

"My playfellow! Ah, no, Monsieur Hellewyl, and I humbly pray you will pardon the freedom of my presumption in addressing you. I am Monsieur le Comte's *gouvernante* and nurse, but, to be frank, very much his nurse and very little his gouvernante, for I fear I teach him nothing but to love me. This, Monsieur, is Count Gaston de Foix, only son and heir to Monseigneur the Count de Narbonne. Monsieur Gaston, have I permission to present to you Monsieur Hellewyl?"

The child nodded gravely, acknowledging my bow with a quaint seriousness that moved my pity. It seemed a sorrowful thing that at six years old the ceremonies of court usage should already have been so deeply ingrained; but in an age when babes were betrothed in their very cradles, the prince knew even less of the joys of life than the peasant. Gaston de Foix! The lad to secure whom I was to turn child-stealer! Gaston! The troubler of France, and the bearer of peace to two nations if I could but succeed in my mission. Already I was drawn towards him, already I pitied him, for if court ways so cramped his life here in the freedom of the fields of Navarre, what would it be behind the walls of Plessis, or wherever the King might elect to quarter him?

"If Monsieur Hellewyl is your friend, Suzanne, then I am glad to see him," replied he, with all the sedateness of a councillor of state.

Suzanne! So that was her name! Somehow it pleased me that I should hear it for the first time from the lips of a child, and have my own conjoined with it as a friend. And yet, such is the discontent of mankind, I would have been yet better pleased if the child had put it that Mademoiselle Suzanne was friend to Gaspard Hellewyl.

With a gravity the equal of his own I returned the queer stiff little bow he gave me.

"Her friend always, that I can promise you, Monsieur le Comte, if she will but permit me the honour. And she has greater friends than I; Monseigneur the Prince de Talmont——"

With a sweep of her arm that should have been a revelation to me but was not, so intent was I watching her eyes, Mademoiselle unceremoniously put the boy aside.

"Commines!" she cried sharply, her face suddenly losing the freshness of its youth. "Monsieur de Commines has sent you! God's name, Monsieur Hellewyl, why did you not say so at once?"

"Because, Mademoiselle Suzanne, it is not quite as you put it."

"Oh, Monsieur, Monsieur, leave your precise niceness of orders aside, and come to the broad truth. It was Monsieur de Commines who told you where to find me, however cunningly he may have packed his meaning in doubtful words. I know his shifty ways. I mean him no offence. More than once he has shown himself my friend; but he is one of those who love to skirt the shadow of a hedge rather than cross a field in God's sunlight. He has ten several ways of saying Good-morning! and each has a different significance. Your message, Monsieur? Is it peace? What a fool I was to think—but no matter what I thought; is it peace? is it peace?"

For the second time I had unwittingly misled her. But though on this occasion the fault was certainly not mine, I was embarrassed how to answer.

It was not simply that to tell how, in blunt truth, I had stumbled on her by accident would have cost me the playful mischievous interest I had first awakened, but it must also have provoked enquiry. The woman who had cried of Villon, Is there no one to kill this infamous wretch? who had had the cool hardihood to ride under the very shadow of Tristan's gallows-house, because the greater safety lay in the greater danger, would promptly ask, If Gaspard Hellewyl does not come from Philip de Commines, what, then, is he doing in Navarre at all in these times of stress? It was the little Count who gave me sufficient breathing time to avoid the crime of a blundering lie. Naturally, he could not follow Mademoiselle's change of mood, and her pleading cry as she stood with outstretched arms seemed to him the cry of fear.

"What is it, Suzanne?" said he, running between us. "What has he done to you? If he hurts you, I'll kill him when I grow big—I will, I will! Go away, Monsieur Hellewyl, you are not a friend."

"No, my heart, no," answered she, again putting him aside, but gropingly, for her eyes were fixed on mine. "Monsieur Hellewyl, is truly our friend, or I hope he is, and am waiting to hear him prove it."

"Heart, head, and hand," replied I, not venturing to touch the white fingers, near though they were to mine. The brief interval had given my slow wit time to move, and I thought I saw my way clear. "As to Monsieur de Commines, his position is even more difficult than you credit. At times the path by the hedge is quicker than the straight road in the open sun. But this will prove that at least I am here with his full knowledge." Out of its inner pocket, and with a blessing on him for his crooked ways, I whipped the King's letter, turning first the false seal, and then the extorted endorsement towards her. "Do you recognise them?"

"I recognise them," she replied curtly, advancing her hand yet nearer. "Give it me, Monsieur; pray God you bring good news."

"From my heart I believe I bring peace, and yet I cannot give you the letter—cannot give it to-day," I added after a pause. "You see it has no address, and—oh! wait Mademoiselle, wait! Trust me, the best fruit ripens slowly."

"Wait!" she repeated, her arm sinking to her side; "that is always what men say to a woman! Wait! wait! as if to wait were not hardest of all; to wait, not knowing whether to hope or fear, or whether the new day brings a blessing or a curse. Wait! Ah, Monsieur, you cannot love your Flanders as we of the Little Kingdom love Navarre, or you would not say Wait! so easily."

Once more the little Count stood my friend.

"Come and play, Suzanne," he said impatiently. "Monsieur can find his way to Morsigny by himself."

"To Morsigny!" she cried, stooping to catch him in her arms so that I failed to see her face. "Yes, that is best. Why, what a clever boy you are, Gaston! Monsieur Hellewyl, the Count de Foix invites you to Morsigny. But oh! I fear that you will find it dull, for at Morsigny there are no men to be killed."

CHAPTER XIX
MADEMOISELLE SUZANNE, GOUVERNANTE

Now it will be understood why, for the sake of those who are to come after me, it is necessary to write this vindication. Men, not knowing the whole truth, have called me coward and traitor, because, said they, having a felon purpose in my mind, I crept into Morsigny behind a trusting woman's skirts.

That is not my view, and three times I have fought to maintain my opinion. You who have read so far, judge would I wilfully hurt Mademoiselle by so much as a finger prick? Judge, too, if Gaspard Hellewyl was the man to root his fortunes in his own dishonour? Nowhere have I laid claim to be more than a simple-hearted gentleman, and the King's scheme, as laid before me, seems to me now, as it seemed to me then, a not unreasonable solution of a grave, threatening political difficulty. That the wrench of the forced separation must give Mademoiselle pain I knew and lamented, but I judged her to be of too noble a mind to weigh selfishly the present brief sorrow, however sharp, against the peace, safety, and prosperity of a whole generation. At the court of France Gaston de Foix would certainly receive as honourable a care as in the wilds of Navarre, together with a more splendid education, and so be the better fitted to carry the responsibility of his station. True, that education would give his mind a particular bias, but what of that? We all more or less reflect that which lies nearest, and to a child that is neither a difficulty nor a hardship. Therefore from every point of view—from that of France, from that of Navarre, from that of Mademoiselle, even from that of the boy himself, I held, and hold to this day, that my action was justified. But slander holds otherwise, and it is easier to kill a plain-speaking and perhaps honest gentleman or two than choke a lie. But if at that time what men might say did not trouble me, Morsigny had its own perplexities.

By nature the South not simply suspects, but hates the North, and so the men of Morsigny gave us no welcome. Nor do I blame them. In race, language, and sympathies we were at variance, and Pamplona—the true Pamplona, not that which reflected Queen Catherine's Gallic sympathies—distrusted Paris even as the fox distrusts the wolf, or the pigeon the kite. At Morsigny there was courtesy, but it was the courtesy of silence and suspicion, so that in his twelve hours of the Louvre, Martin had learned more of the gossip of the kitchen than he did in as many days of Morsigny.

For one thing, we could not understand their tongue, nor they ours. Our northern guttural was to them a barbarism fit for fleering laughter, while their blend of Spanish, bastard French, and Basque sounded to us an unmeaning lisping prattle, pretty enough in a child's mouth, but a thing of derision for grown men.

Partly this isolation pleased me, for it threw me much with Mademoiselle Suzanne and the young Count, but only to find myself again fumbling with a doubt. The puzzle was Mademoiselle herself. In Paris she had stood for Narbonne and Navarre, pleading in the nation's stead as the very equal of Philip de Commines, while here, amongst her own folk, she was no more than body-servant to a child of six, his nurse, his playfellow, and at his wilful beck every hour of the day and night. It was true that Morsigny treated her with all respect, but her humility to the child Gaston was greater than the humility of Morsigny to Mademoiselle Suzanne D'Orfeuil.

To solve a puzzle the best course is to examine it closely and with persistent diligence. That is one obvious statement. Here is another: it is a pleasant thing when duty and desire run in pairs. So it was now with me, or so I persuaded myself. To solve the puzzle was my desire, to secure the person of the little Count was my duty, and the way to achieve both was to keep a close attendance on Mademoiselle—or so, and with great ease, again I persuaded myself.

Day by day, then, that I might the better fulfil my mission, we rode, we hawked, we hunted, we strolled, Count Gaston always one of three, and, what was much less satisfactory, a full-armed guard always where I did not desire them to be.

If we cooled ourselves in the woods, Anton and Pierre were prowling somewhere in the coverts; if we sunned ourselves in the garden, and played at the humanising passion of flower-culture, 'Tuco or Hugues glowered at me from unexpected corners. Was Mademoiselle doubtful of my loyalty? At the time I did not think so, but Navarre was unsleeping in its suspicions of France, and to Morsigny we stood for all that was hated in King Louis. It rather seemed to me as if their watchfulness drove us closer together, as if she would make up to the stranger for their surly want of confidence. For day by day she grew more frank, though never forgetting what was due from the nurse of Count Gaston to the friend of Philip de Commines.

That galled me, galled to shame everything that was best in me; for I knew well, however half-menial her place and service might be, that in pure devotion of spirit and singleness of heart she was as much above me as any saint in glory. Nor do I altogether mean a saint. Saints are too aloof from the mire of our world to give a true comparison; she was as much above as every true-souled, pure-thoughted, loving woman is above the man who splashes on along the bye-ways of life, not too careful where he sets his foot so that he be but one stride nearer to his goal. By that I think you will see that I was beginning to love Mademoiselle a little; and so, if you have some grasp of the complexities of the human mind, you can understand the half-conscious conflict that was in struggle between grieving the angel of my adoration and the shame lest, by omitting to cause that grief, certain white limbs should crack on the rack and certain lips I had kissed scream curses on the treachery of Gaspard Hellewyl. However soon a man may find other and sweeter lips to kiss, he can never, unless the beast of the field be the nobler brute, quite forget the touch of the mouth that has helped him to the dearer knowledge.

You see, then, the various cleft sticks that pinched me? And, if you are one of those having that grasp of which I have written, you will understand that Morsigny's cup of satisfaction was heavily drenched with bitters.

In the end I again persuaded myself to satisfy my inclination; that is, to save the lips I had ceased to love by so prolonging my stay at Morsigny that when the time came to ride north at a gallop Mademoiselle would say in her heart: I can trust and not be afraid. So would the lips I had learned to love not grow white for the loss of the child who lay so near her heart of hearts.

So, as I have said, day by day our intimacy grew franker, until, as we rode amongst the whins, I thought the hour had struck to loosen the knot of at least one perplexity. Little Gaston was on his pony, coursing in and out of the brakes like a rabbit at play, and we two pacing soberly alone. She had asked her daily question: Must I still wait, or has the time at last come to open Monsieur de Commines letter? and I had replied as usual: No, not yet, Mademoiselle; trust me, I beg—still trust me.

"Oh, Monsieur!" she answered, not petulantly, but as if out of a very sore and weary heart, "why must the faith be always on one side? Is there to be no trust in me?"

"No trust?" I echoed. "Why, all Navarre has trusted you, and to me it is a strange thing that a girl who is too humble to mount her horse at the Château gate should yet be chosen to speak for Navarre in Paris." For a moment she looked aside in silence, then drily, as if I presumed upon her, she replied: "In my station I am what God made me, Monsieur."

"For which God be thanked, Mademoiselle!" I answered, in a voice as sober as her own. "My mother taught me that what He does is well done, but none the less it was strange, and a very great trust. Is Navarre so poor that it must choose a frail girl and a—a—how am I to put it without offence?—must choose you, in a word, you who—who——"

"Am what I am! Do not be afraid to speak your mind, Monsieur. Honest service is no woman's shame. But I will answer your question with another: Is Hellewyl so great a name in France, or even in Flanders, that Louis—you come from Plessis, you know, and whoever comes from Plessis comes from the King—that Louis should choose Gaspard Hellewyl of all men to carry his message of peace to Navarre? Oh, Monsieur, Monsieur! because I speak plainly you are angry. Who is this child's nurse to scoff at a Hellewyl of Solignac! Can you give a thrust and not take one? A thrust? No, a whin scratch!"

"But a scratch that hurts, Mademoiselle."

"Yes, Monsieur, and hurts more than you; not even Gaston's nurse is pleased to be told she is insignificant. Have you the only thin skin in the world? But I forgive you, Monsieur. It is right that a man should have pride of race, and if it will heal your wound I will avow that you are the greatest name in Flanders, as"—she added softly—"you have shown yourself more than once to be the truest gentleman. But I will be even kinder; I will answer you your half-asked question: my insignificance was my safety. If Monsieur de Narbonne, Monsieur de Gourdon, Monsieur D'Arros, or any one of fifty who make the poverty of Navarre rich, had suddenly disappeared, your King's spies—do you know that he has spies, even in La Voulle? Would to God we could hang them!—would have traced him within a day, and all France have hummed like a tapped hive. But who would miss such an insignificance as Suzanne D'Orfeuil? Who would fear a couple of women travelling with a single servant? And yet, Monsieur Hellewyl, your Louis may find that a woman is not always altogether a fool. Oh, you men, you men! with your smug, complacent pride in your own proper wit, and your wisdom, and your courage! I tell you, Monsieur, a woman's heart is as big as yours, her soul as great, and the courage that dares fight for its life is not the greatest courage in the world! Oh, *Dieu-Merci*! Monsieur, I forget myself; but you see I love Navarre and Morsigny as dearly as you love Flanders and Solignac; and when a woman loves, she forgets everything, even herself, and remembers only that she loves."

"But she also forgives, Mademoiselle?"

"When a woman loves! You miss the context, Monsieur Hellewyl," she answered tartly.

"And am I not forgiven?"

"Oh, la, Monsieur! would you have me get down and curtsey? Who am I to forgive the friend of the Prince de Talmont and envoy of Louis of France! Surely you forget yourself, as you did a minute back, only now it is your dignity, while then it was—what it was! What would your King say to such an abasement in his representative?"

"No King of mine, Mademoiselle, as I have told you once before."

"He is our King whom we serve as King, Monsieur and I would to God it were any one on earth but Louis the Cunning; whosoever touches him touches shame," and with a vicious little cut of her riding switch she rode on.

That was ever the way with her—deep-hearted, shallow-hearted, bitter-tongued, and womanly sweet, gentle, wrathful, mischievous all by turns—till, for all our daily rides and nearness, I felt that she kept me as much at arm's-length as did any surly, suspicious, ill-conditioned Navarrois dog of them all. But a day came, though not till weeks had passed, when the little Count himself broke down the barrier.

From the first we two had drawn together. For myself, I have always loved children; their faults are mostly ours, their sweetness God's and their own. Their faith has no reserve, their love no limitation; and when Divine wisdom sought a standard by which men might measure themselves, He set a little child in their midst.

But apart from my general love for children, it was necessary, for the success of the King's scheme, that I should win the boy's confidence. Not simply that success or failure might hinge upon his willingness to travel with me, but that Mademoiselle, seeing how my heart had opened to the lad, would suffer less. So, playing to win him, I won him out and out, and soon Monsieur Gaspard rivalled even his beloved Suzanne as a playfellow.

But it was no play that broke down Mademoiselle's reserve.

As Jean Volran had said, Morsigny lay not far from the hills. First there was the green and gold of gorse and grass, then slopes of pinewood through which streams bickered and flashed in the sun, or angled through the groom like snow-wreaths blown by the wind. Beyond these were ruder hills, rock-strewn and sheer of face as they lifted shoulder by shoulder to the peaks in the blue distance. We have no such scene in Flanders, and for the novelty of its beauty I grew to love it almost as dearly as did Mademoiselle for old friendship's sake, or the boy Gaston, because there the healthy animal in him found full scope for play.

Did I say that in this companionship of ours little Gaston made one of three? That is a mistake. Except when within the precincts of the Château garden he made one of four. That I have hitherto forgotten Brother Paulus has but one reasonable excuse. Mademoiselle had pushed him from my thoughts. And is it a reasonable excuse? Brother Paulus would be the first to admit it—Brother Paulus of the grey withered face and shining eyes, the man's deep heart, the woman's tenderness, the child's direct simplicity and ignorance of the world. What wrongs, what sorrows, his youth had suffered, God and his own spirit alone knew. With him, as with the grapes of his own Provence, the crushing had but set free sweetness and strength, mellowed by age to a cordial whereby the weak grew strong, and they who fainted by the way took heart of grace to pack afresh their burdens on their backs and go cheerily forward.

So, at least, Mademoiselle Suzanne has said. I only know that a man's brave heart beat under the monk's black frock, and that in a time of trial Gaspard Hellewyl's perplexity of soul found frail Brother Paulus an unshaken rock of strength.

CHAPTER XX
WHAT HAPPENED AT THE GREY LEAP

There were four of us, then, who rode through the whin brakes, under the pines and out upon the rocks beyond. Indeed, there were six, for Hugues and the big Spanish fellow they called 'Tuco followed us, but that we did not know at the time.

Brother Paulus led the way with Gaston; Mademoiselle followed, and I, because the path was in places too narrow for two abreast, brought up the rear. Of us all, I think Brother Paul was the merriest; though, such is the alchemy of the hills, in us all the cares of life were transmuted into gaiety. Brother Paul forgot the weariness of age, Gaston the penalty of being born great, I that I was sworn to add to his penalties for his own good, Mademoiselle, the sorrows and dangers of Navarre. She went further, she even forgot that she was nothing more than Suzanne D'Orfeuil, nurse and *gouvernante* to the Count de Foix, forgot everything but that the skies were blue, the sun warm, the air thin and sweet. Care was behind us at Morsigny, and for that day the troubled woman entered afresh into her too early lost heritage of girlhood.

Woman! Man! We were neither one nor other. The horses had been left behind in charge of a goat-herd under the shadow of the last pines, and we were four children scrambling up the rocks with Gaston the oldest, because the most gravely serious, of the four. In a child, the joy and wonder of living are at times too great to find expression in laughter.

Up and up and up we climbed, a riot of life in our veins—up and up and up, not so fast as to lose breath for merry-making, nor so slow as to grow cold at the game—up and up and up, now by a goat-track, now by a dead watercourse, now by a tumbled scree of stones, the young Count as active as a kid, and Brother Paul, his black frock kilted to his knees, always near him in front. Up and up and up, and then from behind a jutted rock there came a cry, one only, but so fierce, so harsh, so edged with agony and despair, that Mademoiselle turning, caught my sleeve, gasping, "Jesu! What is that?" and we stood listening, but there was a great silence.

"Paul's voice," said I at last.

"Paul's voice," she answered; "yes, Paul's voice, but—God in heaven! what of Gaston?"

Loosening her hold she hastened on, I at her side, but below her lest she should fall, for her limbs were shaking. The nerves that were not afraid of Tristan for herself trembled at she knew not what for her charge.

"Paul has fallen," said I, steadying her with my hand.

"Then Gaston would have come back or cried to us. No, no; it is my boy, it is my boy."

The wail in her voice cut me to the heart. That she loved the lad I knew, but that she loved him with the yearning tenderness of a woman was new to me. Hitherto I had thought it was Navarre she loved in the person of the little Count, loved him because, as Louis had made clear, he stood for the peace and hope of her nation. That was greatness in her—a greatness, a loftiness of mind, a patriotism that led her to such heights of sacrifice as moved my admiration and worship. This was less great, but at once more human and more divine. For the common food of life we do not ask that our women shall be patriots, it is enough that their love flows out full and sweet and strong to husband, child, and kindred, and as this love of Suzanne's burst its bounds in that bitter wail, I knew that it had gulfed me. It was not that I loved her a little, I loved her as I had never dreamed it was possible to love, and at the suddenness of the revelation the blood roared in my ears with the roar of a winter's torrent thundering white into its basin. Under the hand that lay upon my shoulder as we plunged along the rocky slope I winced and trembled as if the fingers were a white heat.

Amongst I do not know how many others, two thoughts were clear cut in my mind; one, that not for my soul's salvation would I at that time have dared to touch that hand, the other an execration, a bitter loathing of myself that in a pretence of love I had ever kissed a woman's lips. Later—but let the later speak for itself. I pray God the divine measure of a man is what he is at his best, his highest; the sorrowful thing is that for every such hilltop of reverence, self-sacrifice, self-control, there is a valley, and the valleys burrow through the darkness further and fuller than the mountains stretch their pinnacles to the light.

Beyond the out-thrust of the cliff there was a shelving flat that seemed to fall away sheer to the air, and as we turned the angle, Mademoiselle ran forward with a cry. On the flat, breast down, lay Brother Paulus, his hands, on either side his chest, gripping the lip of the rock down which he peered. Stooping, Mademoiselle caught him by the shoulder, shaking him roughly.

"Gaston? Where is Gaston?"

Without shifting his hold the monk looked up, his grey face ashen-white, the mouth trembling like a frightened child.

"Oh!" he said, drawing a shivering sigh, "would to God it were I."

"Gaston?" repeated Mademoiselle, emphasizing her words with her nervous hands; "where is Gaston? Not there, oh God! not there!" and kneeling, she too peered down the cliff.

For answer, Brother Paulus stretched out a shaking hand.

"We were at play," he said hoarsely. "All day we were at play, and I forgot that this was the Grey Leap. There was a loose stone, and he slipped upon it. I think—I think—he is still alive."

What the fingers pointed at was plainly in sight, a little wisp of white caught upon a point of rock behind the shelter of which grew a stunted pine, but I readily comprehended how she had missed seeing him. A moment back, under the revelation of her cry and the touch of her hand, I, too, had gone blind as the sound as of many waters roared in my ears. And now, as love staggered her, she could not see the little bundle of white linen which might, as Brother Paul said, be alive, but which showed no life.

"Gaston!" she cried, her voice shrill and harsh by turns. "Gaston! Gaston!"

"I think he is alive," said Brother Paulus again, though what he founded his thought on God knows, unless it was on pure faith, for there was neither sound nor motion.

"Gaston! Gaston! Gaston!" she cried again, and then, rising, to my terror she set herself to find a way down the face of the rock.

Rising also, but only to his knees, Brother Paulus caught her by the skirt. He, too, had divined her intention, and saw its hopeless folly; no cliff amongst the many in the hills had so evil a repute as the Grey Leap.

"No, Suzanne, no," said he, "it is death; there is no way, I have searched, and there is none, none."

"You have searched, you, who let him fall! Stay on your knees and pray; that is your business; mine is to find a way down to my boy, or if there is none, to make a way."

"Let him fall?" said he, with a gasp, and wincing as if she had struck him with a whip. "How did I let him fall? Could I have helped it?"

"God knows," answered she; "but he was with you, and he fell."

I suppose love is cruel at heart, cruelly hard against whatever comes between it and the thing it loves. That the priest was nowise to blame

Mademoiselle knew as well as I, but she could not give him the comfort of saying so. That is why, I think, love is always feigned to be a child, for in its ignorant singleness of purpose there is nothing so ruthless. It was that same singleness of purpose that frightened me now. Matched against the lad, Gaspard Hellewyl counted for nothing, and never could count, and I dreaded lest, in seeking to hold her back, I should drive her by the nearest and most desperate path. To try a forced authority seemed the safest course; that, and a suggestion that she could help me from above, might keep her out of danger.

"You!" said I, with a rough contempt that must have hurt her had her heart not been in the bundle of linen twenty feet down the cliff. "What can you do, cumbered by your skirts as you are? Nothing but add to our trouble. Unless—yes! you may save us both by this, watch here and direct me how to climb."

"You!" The contempt was yet rougher than my own, so rough that the hurt she had escaped galled me bitterly. "We have trusted you so far, trusted you in part and because we could not help ourselves, but do you think we shall trust you there?" and with a sudden fierceness she pointed down the ledge. "Day by day you have said to me, Wait! Has your time come now, Monsieur the messenger of Louis of France? Has your time come now, Monsieur, it may be, his catspaw? Was it for this we have waited all these weeks? A touch of the foot by accident—by accident, you understand, one little slip for which no man could openly blame you—and the hope of Navarre would be where your master would have it be. Stand back, Monsieur! Stand back! If you dare to hinder me by so much as a finger, the monk and I, priest and woman though we are, will fling you after the boy."

So swift, so unexpected, so bitter was the attack that I had no answer ready, no exculpation, no assurance, no plea, and how the dead-lock would have ended I do not know had Hugues and the big Spaniard 'Tuco not come round the track at a panting trot. The group of but three where four should have been, Brother Paulus on his knees as if in prayer for a passing soul, Mademoiselle's white face blazing with accusation, her arms thrust out in defence or threat, none could say which, my own half-shrinking from the venom of her thought, not only told the truth, but with the truth linked so plausible a lie that I have never blamed them for their thought. I was of France, they of Navarre; and if Mademoiselle, into whose life I had grown daily these weeks past, could think so vilely of me, there was little wonder that their suspicion and ignorant hate out-leaped reality.

Their wits worked together. Waiting for neither explanation nor command they turned upon me, and I, taken unawares, was as a child in their hands, hardly even grasping their intent. But Mademoiselle understood, and it was not so much her shriek of No! No! No! as the grasp of her hands upon my shoulders as we overhung the very lip of descent that held us there, staggering. From the shoulders her hands slipped forwards, inwards, till her fingers knit themselves under my chin, drawing me back against her bosom; and there upon the edge we hung a moment, too breathless and shaken for words.

"Not his fault," she said at last, very hoarsely; "not his fault; tell them, Father Paul, for I cannot speak. Oh, Monsieur, Monsieur, forgive them, pray forgive them!"

CHAPTER XXI
"I TRUST YOU, COME WHAT MAY"

What the priest said I do not know, for he spoke in patois, but the grip on my wrists and arms relaxed—reluctantly, I thought, as if it was a pity to lose so excellent an opportunity of paying off old grudges. Very slowly all four drew back, breathing heavily, as men do who struggle to overmaster their breathlessness. So we stood for half a minute, then I moved aside to the upward face of the rock.

"Good!" said I, answering Mademoiselle's bitter mistrust, rather than her broken appeal upon the men's behalf. Against them I had no rancour; the fault was none of theirs, if their zeal lacked information. "Good! He is the Count de Foix! Let Foix and Navarre save him, only let them remember that there is fifty feet of a tumble below that bundle of linen there, and a bed of saw-toothed rocks to fall upon."

It is my belief that for these thirty seconds, and the minute or two of stress which preceded them, Mademoiselle had utterly forgotten the boy's danger. Instantly she turned, and, pointing downward, broke into passionate command. Her speech was that quaint mixture of slurred French, Spanish and Basque which passed for a language in Morsigny, and so was strange to me. But the clamour of the boy's need made her meaning clear, even had she spoken no word. Nudely, ruthlessly clear, and a grim gladness warmed me to see that Hugues and the Spaniard grew cold as she waxed more and more passionate, her brief authority lost at the last in a pleading almost choked by tears.

A word or two of the slurred French I understood, such as peace, Navarre, their duty, then Navarre again, and yet again Navarre. But to more than fifty feet of a fall left them cold. Peace? The peace of a loosened grip was too profound a peace for their taste! Duty? Surely the soul's first duty is to its own body! Navarre? They looked at one another; Navarre would have battles to fight, and dead men, even dead in duty, make no war. So they argued, speaking no word; and so, with my back against the cliff, I read their reasoning and laughed aloud.

But the laughter died in my mouth.

If it failed to shame them, being coarse-grained peasants, it moved Mademoiselle to an unendurable despair. With a last indignant word, some acid, biting phrase of scorn, she knelt to renew her folly of descent. But to do Hugues and the other justice, if they were careful of themselves they were careful also of her, for even before I could reach her they held her back.

"Leave me go, you cowards, leave me go!" she cried, struggling, her face wet with unconscious tears of rage and shame. "My God! is there not one man amongst you!"

"It is for Navarre," said I, giving my bitter mood rein, now she was safe. "It is for Foix and Navarre; let me beg you both to fall down fifty feet for the glory of Foix and Navarre. The thought will comfort you—till you hit the stones at the bottom."

It was not a very manly gibe, but in the best of us, and I do not claim to be that, there is a beast who only needs rousing, and at that moment the man in me was not uppermost. From the hilltop I had sunk to the valley. My new found and newer trampled love was too raw in its wounds to be just. Had not Mademoiselle, in her very last words, called me a coward with the rest? And yet it was she whose scorn and contumely forbade me to climb.

"Oh, that I were a man!" she said, swallowing her sobs till they choked her; "then would I sooner lie dead with the child."

While she was speaking, Brother Paulus had risen and stripped himself of his clinging frock. Now, flinging it aside, he turned to me.

"So would I; she is right, Monsieur Hellewyl; the shame of it is not to be borne."

"A man," said I, answering Mademoiselle, but laying the flat of my hand on the priest's breast, that he might do nothing useless. The spirit within him was strong to dare, but the flesh was weak. Had there been ten Father Pauls, they must have followed one another to the bottom of the cliff. "A man—that is, a true man—one trusts. Do you trust me, Mademoiselle?"

"Oh, you are cruel!" she cried, but the sobs were softer. "Would you let the child die because of a girl's——?" she paused, searching for an adjective, but finding none that fitted her thought went on—"Must I ask your pardon, Monsieur? Must I humble myself to you? I'll do it, I'll do it gladly."

"I would have you say: I trust you. Come what may, I trust you, now and always."

As a child repeats its lesson she answered me, her face all drawn by pain, the tears still shining in her eyes. "I trust you, Monsieur, now and always, come what may."

Of what followed I have no desire to say much. Of neither the manner nor the motive of the exploit have I any reason to be proud. For the one, I am a man of the flats, and with no skill for such a piece of work. To every crevice, every cranny, every boss of rock I clung as a drowning cat clings to a crumbling bank when a swishing current tears at her flanks; and if I did not howl in my terror like the same cat, it was because I grit my teeth and whimpered inwardly, for there is no denying I was horribly afraid. Fifty feet of air hung from my ancles, dragging me down like so many pounds of lead. As to the motive, it was compounded of as many diversities as go to the mixing of an apothecary's potion. There was a little pity, a little pride, a little love, some contempt, some braggadocio, Jan Meert's throat, and a new roof to Solignac all blent through it. But most of these I left on the ledge or dropped into the void at the first touch of despair, and thenceforward pride and a dogged love of dear life were motive enough.

Blunderer as I was, and hampered by Brother Paul's frock knotted loosely across my shoulders, I must inevitably have followed the bulk of my influencing ingredients, had not Mademoiselle directed every move.

"There is a knob of rock to the right; no, more to the right—more yet—yes, that is it; but, oh, Monsieur, try it first before you trust your weight upon it, lest it crumble. It holds? Thank God for that! Now a foot below there is a crevice, and then to the left an open seam for your fingers. You have it? That is splendid, splendid! Remember, always to the right, little by little, the—the—boy lies there, and—oh, God! he is stirring. Gaston! Gaston! do not move! Jesu! Jesu! that he may not move! Lie still, Gaston, lie still, *mon gars*; the brave Monsieur Gaspard is going down to you, and there is nothing to fear, nothing—do you hear me?—nothing at all."

For which sore straining of the truth may she be forgiven! Nothing to fear? If there was nothing to fear, why was the sweat pouring down my back, or that sob rattling in my throat? And why was the brave Monsieur Gaspard realising fully for the first time how good a thing is life?

How long the boy had recovered consciousness I do not know, but the bewilderment of the shock had passed away, and now the courage that had squared his fists in the whin brake saved him. From the silence which followed Mademoiselle's passionate adjuration, a thin voice piped out: "I'm not afraid, Suzanne. I hear you, and I will be quiet."

"*Mon brave*! Thou art not afraid, no, not thou; but do not stir, my heart, no, not a finger. Monsieur Hellewyl, are you rested? There is a ledge below you sloping to the right. It must be four inches broad—good! that is it. Only a moment now Gaston, and the rest is easy." For which second straining of the truth, I say again, may she be forgiven! Later, long after, I learned that this time the lie was on my account. In the brief pause I had glanced up, and from the agony of soul stamped on my white face, Mademoiselle for the first time truly recognised the risk I ran. The Paris rabble had taught her it was no common danger that made Gaspard Hellewyl go in frank terror for his life—I use her own words—and with a quick wit she set herself to put heart in me, and at a time when there was least heart in her own hope. But I believed her, and the lie steadied my nerve. Believing the rest to be easier made it easier, for there is no courage like the courage of faith; that of manhood or despair alike pales before its forces.

Nor was the upward journey so difficult, even with the child upon my back in the monk's frock, knapsack fashion. Every foot climbed was a year or more of life gained, and Mademoiselle's face, still white, but with the tears dried from the eyes, turned down to mine, drew me. Not a word was spoken, hardly a breath except my own seemed to stir; but God, He knows what prayers went up through the silence. Then came the end. Down from the top 'Tuco stretched his long arms, grasping my wrists. With a heave, Hugues helping, I was breast high; another, and we rolled forward on the ledge, four pairs of hands holding us, with Mademoiselle sobbing and crying as she had neither sobbed nor cried while the fear of death was cold upon her.

"Let come what may, Mademoiselle?" said I, when I could command my breath.

"Let come what may," she answered, and this time it was not the tears that shone in the eyes, but the eyes behind the tears.

Thenceforward, not even 'Tuco the Spaniard held us in doubt, and as we rode into Morsigny I knew that my bleeding finger-tips had drawn nearer three such differing rewards as Mademoiselle's friendship, Jan Meert's throat, and the building again of Solignac.

CHAPTER XXII
THE MESSAGE OF A FOOT OF STRING

Yes, the barriers were broken down, or were breaking.

That very night, when Mademoiselle came to announce that the child Gaston was more shaken than hurt, she turned at the door with one of those humble curtseys that were to me so like a blow on the face.

"When one tells a lie and is sorry, Monsieur Gaspard, should she go to her priest or—or—to the one she has lied to?"

The question was grave and the voice was grave, but there was a tender demure look on her face, and had her eyes been raised, I am sure there would have been that spirit of laughter in them which I had come to know so well.

"A lie, Mademoiselle?"

"A lie, Monsieur, a lie that hurts me to remember, for truly I am not accustomed to lie. There, on the Grey Leap, I was desperate, and—it was not quite the truth."

"That you trusted me?"

"Yes, Monsieur."

"And yet you told me once that I had shown myself true?"

"Ah, Monsieur! do you not know there is a faith of head and a faith of heart? In my heart I trusted you, even from the first, but my head said, 'Nothing good can come out of Plessis'; and so, because there was no other way, I—I—Monsieur, those cowards of a Hugues and a 'Tuco drove me to it."

"And now?"

Letting slip the latch she came forward a little.

"Now? The head followed the heart even at the Grey Leap. But lest you should think that was the lie emotional instead of the lie desperate, I repeat it again. It was like this. Once you looked up—oh! it was horrible to see you hanging there on an inch of rock with all that swimming void below. Your face—Monsieur, what am I to say? A man can be brave and yet love life, and the grandest courage of all is the courage that knows and resents the desperate risk, but still goes forward. You might have come back, and yet, knowing all, and clinging hungrily to life, you went forward. Since then, Monsieur, it was no lie; since then—though what a foolish girl thinks can matter nothing to a spirit like yours—since then I—I—do you think you understand, Monsieur Hellewyl?" Her eyes were shining, but there were tears between the lashes, and the fingers of the hands clasped upon the breast twisted round and round each other in and out. "We who love and serve Navarre, who serve even as humbly as I serve, pray, God bless you, Monsieur Hellewyl."

It was my opportunity perhaps, to have passed beyond the broken barrier a little nearer to her heart, but I dared not use it. That day I had found myself to be something of a coward, but I was not coward enough to trade upon a grateful woman's generous emotion, and under cover of a newly stirred gratitude try to steal more than her sober sense would be ready to give. So, instead of reaching forward and taking those shaking hands, I folded my own behind my back and forced myself to a cold answer.

"Then at last you trust me, Mademoiselle, and will trust, come what may?"

"Oh, yes, Monsieur! I and all Morsigny. And to prove it, I shall never again ask you, 'Has Monsieur de Commines' time come yet?'"

"In that, too, you may trust me; so soon as I may, I shall speak."

"I know it well, Monsieur," and with a little grave curtsey, she left me.

I am not so stockish a man but that what followed was all very sweet—Mademoiselle's new gaiety, a gaiety of both heart and head, the boy Gaston's childish adoration, Brother Paul's thanksgiving overflowing in affection. Of Brother Paul's part in the final scene on the Grey Leap I have said nothing, and only now say this lest that kindly, gentle-hearted servant of love and mercy should be thought cold or callous. There on the ledge he had patted and fondled me with his withered hands, his heart too full to say more than, "Ah, my son, my son! God be thanked for His mercy, God be thanked! God be thanked!" And since then he had petted me like one who was a son indeed, a son long lost and newly found.

Sweet? It was blessedly, perilously sweet to a lonely man at hourly odds with his conscience, so perilously sweet that the days slipped on, and though ten times the child was mine for the taking, I persuaded myself that to wait yet a little longer was wisest. Solignac, Jan Meert, Babette, old hate and old love, were alike forgotten, and I lived on through the glorious days of early August as if there was no such shadow across the sunshine as the power and vengeance of Louis of France.

But as once on a day of feasting there came a hand upon the wall and wrote, so now, when my heart was a nest of song-birds, that sang of peace and love till my little world was full of the harmony, there came a warning which crashed the music to a discord with a curt, Thou fool! It is hate, and there is no peace.

It was always Martin's custom to meet me at the gate on the return from our daily rides, partly that all Morsigny might see I was well served, but partly, and as I love to believe, chiefly that he might the sooner see his beloved Master Gaspard. On the day of which I write he was there as usual—Brother Paul was in Pan, and Mademoiselle would neither mount nor dismount at the Château gate—but he was there with a difference. His bow was deeper, his swagger had a larger pride, and instead of himself leading Roland to the stables, he handed him over to a groom's care with an unwonted air of authority. Then with a "This way, Monsieur, it you please," he led the way to my sleeping-room, and shot the bolt behind me.

"These with haste," said he, drawing a letter from an inner pocket; "and, my faith! but they must truly be in a hurry to send all the way to Morsigny after us. *To Monsieur Gaspard de Helaville, at Morsigny, in Navarre. These in haste.*"

At the sight of it my heart went sick as sick as when I had hung upon the sheer face of the Grey Leap. And well it might. The solid earth, and that which is so much sweeter, and, at times, so much more real, the world of my own imagining, had crumbled suddenly under my feet, and the abyss below was as deep as all eternity.

"These with haste," repeated Martin, rolling the words in his mouth with a relish. "All Morsigny knows of it; I took care of that. The seal is Monseigneur the Prince's quarterings, and that, too, I took care to tell them. These louts will better understand now what is due to a Hellewyl of Solignac, who has letters sent him a week's journey. These with haste!"

Commines' quarterings; yes, I had seen that from the first. Even the flaw in the collet was there; but what did that prove? Commines' quarterings, Commines' colour of wax, Commines' handwriting in the address, even a faint lingering of the perfume Commines most affected, and yet all, so far as Commines was concerned, might be as gross a lie as that which frayed its edges upon my heart.

"These with haste," said Martin again, but this time testily, for his curiosity was at bursting point. "What is the use of a man foundering a horse, as I'll wager he who brought this foundered his, if you don't open it, and see what's inside?"

"Brought it?" said I. "Who brought it, and where is he?"

"God knows," and Martin's face fell, the pride dying out of him like the wind from a ripped bladder. "It was pushed in at the porter's window, and yet the guard at the gate swear that no one but a goatherd or two passed Morsigny all day. But," he added, brightening up, "there it is, all the same; there it is, 'These with haste,' and with Monseigneur's seal to back it."

"And all Morsigny knows of it? A messenger comes in secret to your master, comes like a thief, and all Morsigny knows of it? You fool! oh, you fool! Remember, if harm comes of this, it is your doing."

"Oh! Monsieur Gaspard, Monsieur Gaspard! I never thought— —"

"There, the mischief's done," said I, softening as I saw the rueful sorrow on his face. After all, it was the zeal of his love that had been indiscreet. He had thought to glorify his Monsieur Gaspard in the eyes of Morsigny, never looking to the consequences. "We shall see what Monseigneur has to say," and tearing off the silk that, running through the wax, bound the packet, I ripped open the outer cover.

The enclosure was both thick and crisp, as if of several folds, and across the face of the paper this was written, the writing being undoubtedly that of Monseigneur.

I am bid send you what is within. What it is I know not, but, dear lad, for God's sake see to yourself. To say so much does the King no wrong.

The folded paper was again fast sealed, as was that within it, but in each of these latter cases with a plain device. Inside the third wrapping was a foot of thin cord, and at the end of the cord a noose. Across the paper was written, *So saith Tristan.*

Taking out the cord by its end I thrust a finger-tip through the noose, and dangled it in Martin's face.

"These with haste, so saith Tristan," said I, and laughed in a grim contempt of my own helplessness.

"Tristan of the House of Nails?"

"Tristan of the House of Nails," I answered, and laughed again. Through the laughter there came a knocking at the door. "See who is there."

Screwing his neck as a man does who swallows his spittle to moisten a dry throat, Martin shot back the bolt, opening the door an inch or two, and peering through the crack as if behind whoever knocked he looked to find Tristan himself, with a dangle of ropes in his hand.

"It is Mademoiselle Suzanne."

Mademoiselle Suzanne! Already she had heard of the letter, already she knew that it came from Commines, and that knowledge forced a crisis. In these few seconds thought travelled fast. Should I trust her? Should I say: Here, in the yielding of the boy, is the peace of Navarre, here is France turned friend; Louis, Gaston's protector. Give him to me, and there is a final end to your fear. But swift on the heels of the question came the reply: That is to throw your responsibility on to her. She is accountable to Jean de Narbonne. Before she dared say yes, she must send to Pamplona. That meant negotiations, *pour-parlers*, and above all, publicity, and what publicity stood for; a warning to the adverse party in Navarre, a threat to Spain, even a confession of France's weakness. And would Louis wait? Unconsciously I tightened the noose upon my finger, and in the pain of the pinch found an answer—Louis would neither wait nor forgive. What then? Our only safety, the boy's, my own, Mademoiselle's even, lay in instant action, and crumpling the letter out of sight, I motioned to Martin to fling open the door.

As the light broke upon her, Mademoiselle shrunk still further from it across the passage.

"Monsieur, they said—Oh! I know I promised, and indeed, I trust you—but they said there was a letter, and that Monsieur de Commines had written. Have you—that is, is it good news, Monsieur?"

"Have no fear; good news, Mademoiselle," lied I, with the string swinging from my finger. "I was just about to search for you, and—oh, yes, good news, good news indeed, only all is not yet quite clear."

"Must we still wait, Monsieur?"

At the disappointment in her tone I winced, but there was nothing for it but to brazen out my part as best I could.

"That is just it, we must wait. But this time, not for long, and to shorten the waiting I think that to-morrow I shall ride into La Voulle, perhaps with Gaston?"

"To La Voulle with Gaston? That is a long ride for the child."

"Long? Surely not. He rides as far every day, but he rides as a dog runs, up and down, here and there, so that we lose count of distance. I thought it would please Brother Paul to meet him in La Voulle. You know he returns to-morrow from Pau."

"But,"—and in the shadow I saw a touch of colour flush her cheeks—"I do not think I can go to La Voulle, at least not to-morrow. Once all is clear between us, and Brother Paul is home, it will be different."

"Is not all clear now, Mademoiselle?"

"Oh, Monsieur!" she replied, dropping me the curtsey I so hated; "I mean between France and Navarre."

How I cursed Martin in my heart for a tactless, blundering booby. Here was my chance to say: And must it be always and only France and Navarre? May it never be Suzanne D'Orfeuil and Gaspard Hellewyl? Always Kingdom and Kingdom, and never man and maid as lover and lover? The peace of one's country is very well, very splendid and much to be desired; but we are men and women as well as patriots, and the heart has a peace of its own that is sweeter and dearer and yet more to be desired than that of France and Navarre. But with that leathern-faced idiot standing at my elbow, staring open-mouthed, how could I say all that, or any part of it? Ten chances to one, if I had, he would have reminded me of Brigitta under the beech tree, and poured his contempt upon Mademoiselle Suzanne as he had upon her.

"For a Hellewyl of Solignac, you have a strange taste," he would have said. "First it was a swineherd's daughter you chose for your philandering, and now it is——" and he would have blown out his cheeks with an exploding puff that left the suggestion worse than plain words.

And how would Mademoiselle have looked at such a tale? I did not dare consider that point, so answered soberly:

"To-morrow will make all clear, Mademoiselle; I can promise you that."

CHAPTER XXIII
A ROSE OF PROMISE

Next morning it was easy to find an excuse for taking Martin with us: Ninus needed exercise; it might be necessary to send a messenger to Monsieur de Commines—any tale was sufficient. Of the little Count's willingness to ride so far there never was a question. Had I said to him: Monsieur Gaston, let us ride to Plessis; he would have answered: At what time shall I order the horses, Monsieur Gaspard?

To avoid the great heat of the day, and that at the first we might spare our horses, we left Morsigny early. How far or how fast we might have to travel beyond La Voulle I could not tell. It was there the King's letter was to be opened, and where it bade us ride, however great the distance, there ride we must.

Naturally of this second reason Mademoiselle knew nothing as she set us on our way. At first she walked beside Gaston's pony, the fingers of one hand twisted in its mane. The sleeve of her linen bodice had slipped back to the elbow, leaving the arm bare and whiter than marble against the dark hide of the shaggy beast. Riding behind, I saw that though the boy in his eager excitement was full of childish words, she answered nothing to his many questions, and at the last her farewell was brief.

"Kiss me, my heart," she said, looking up suddenly.

Without checking his pony, Gaston stooped aside, and as their lips met, she clipped him in her arms.

"Ah, Suzanne! you will have me down!" he cried petulantly, and loosening her clasp, she loitered back to where I followed.

"Monsieur," she began, laying her hand on my bridle hand, but with so much unconsciousness in the act that I could no more have covered it with my right than I could have covered a man's, "you will remember how anxious I am, and how hard it is to wait? It is always worse for us women than for you. You act, you men; you work, you forget yourselves in danger, lose yourselves in the thing to be done; while we can but wait at home and hope and—yes, thank God, we can always pray. Ah, Monsieur, how I shall pray until you return!"

"Was Paris waiting?"

"That was once in a lifetime, and was easier than this. You will remember?"

"Oh! be sure I shall remember; my fear is lest you forget."

"I, Monsieur? Forget what?"

"Gaspard Hellewyl; when there is no more need for him, and Gaspard Hellewyl is—elsewhere. Will you remember then, Mademoiselle Suzanne?"

For the first time that morning a little pucker of a smile caught up the corners of her mouth, and her eyes lightened; nor, I remembered afterwards, did she lift her hand from where it rested, though her fingers shook; neither, let me say, was there any pressure; no, not the faintest.

"Oh, Monsieur! be sure I shall remember Paris."

"Mademoiselle, what do I care for Paris?"

"Tours, then, and how eager you were to kill a man—only there was none to kill."

"No, nor Tours either."

"The Grey Leap? Ah, Monsieur! surely you do not think I can ever forget the Grey Leap?"

"Not even the Grey Leap; I said Gaspard Hellewyl."

The smile deepened a little. With downcast eyes and hands now clasped demurely before her, she dropped back a pace.

"Now, Monsieur, it is you who forget. You forget you are a great gentleman of Flanders, the friend of the Prince de Talmont, the envoy of the King of France; you forget you are Monsieur Gaspard de Helville! the bearer of a great name—did we not agree that it was a great name? While I—— You will bring Gaston safe home to his nurse, will you not, Monsieur de Helville?"

She spoke so softly, with such a hesitating depreciation, that I could not tell if it was in raillery or in earnest, but it seemed to me that the glance flashed into my eyes at the last was not all mischief, "You are—Mademoiselle Suzanne. I dare not trust myself to say what more you are, but God be thanked for you. My prayer is that some day I may speak plainer, to-day I must not. As I sit here I am a poor gentleman of Flanders, so poor that I have not even a roof to offer the woman I would dare to love as wife. But it is my hope this peace to Navarre may change all that, may roof over Solignac and give me enough of my father's lands to make that wife, not a great lady of Flanders, but the happiest, the most reverenced, the best beloved. It is in that hope I ride to-day to—to—La Voulle, to end that which is begun; and but for that hope, I swear to you I would never call Louis King even by service. Ah, Mademoiselle Suzanne, Mademoiselle Suzanne! trust me, I pray; not a little, but trust me much until I dare to ask to be trusted all in all. God keep you, Mademoiselle."

"God keep you, Monsieur," she answered softly, again raising her drooped eyes, and this time there was no mockery in them, not even mischief—a wistfulness rather, a pathos almost the beginning of tears. "Believe me, I truly trust you. Once already I have said I have ever found you the truest gentleman, and, Monsieur, I do not see any reason to change, nor, I am sure, will you give me reason."

"Then, adieu, Mademoiselle!"

"No, no; adieu is a long word! But, lest you should forget me in La Voulle, keep that to remind you of—Morsigny!"

Reaching up, she dropped a half-blown rose on the saddle before me, gave Roland two or three little dainty pats on the neck, then, before I could take her hand, she stepped aside between the whins, now no longer in their glory of gold, and so left me.

Perhaps it was best so. The witchery of that last upward glance had so moved me, tingling every nerve to the finger-tips, that had I once touched her hand as man to maid, I must have blurted out more than was wise or even honourable in one who had work to do for Louis of France. But if that sweet folly was denied me, the rose at my lips and her last clear look, so grave, so shy, so almost tender, set my heart dancing; and slow as was our ride to La Voulle, the little Count had no cause to complain of my gaiety.

Had I dared, I would have avoided not only The Good Queen inn, but La Voulle itself. But balanced against the risk of interference from the townsfolk was that of disobedience to the King's orders, and of the two I feared the wrath of Louis more than all La Voulle howling beyond the door. If he said, Return to the inn, he had his reasons, and the man who dared question them was a fool to his own hurt.

Riding up to the door, with its swinging, half-effaced sign of I do not know what Queen of Navarre's portrait, I enquired boldly for Brother Paulus. Boldness was our safety, and for that day, unknown to himself, Brother Paulus was to guarantee our good faith. If the person of the little Count was well known in La Voulle, so was that of the chaplain to Morsigny, and my plan was to ride out with the priest in company as if we returned home by the shortest way. It was all so simple, so natural, who would raise a question? Once clear of the town I would give Paul a letter to Mademoiselle, and, with or without his consent, seize Gaston and gallop for the King's tryst. Let that be where it might, Louis could be trusted to have smoothed the road for us.

"Brother Paulus?"

"Certainly, Monsieur. He arrived from Pau late last night, and being tired, keeps his room."

"Good! Monsieur le Comte and I will go to him. Do you see to the horses, Martin, and come up for instructions in an hour, for I think we shall leave early. Tell me," I went on, to the servant who led the way, "is Volran in the house? Yes? Then let him know that the Count de Foix and Monsieur de Helville dine here to-day."

So far Martin had not been taken into my confidence, but I calculated that in the time named I should have read the King's letter and so be in a position to arrange our plans. In the carrying out of these Martin's cunning and experience would help me. Volran too, who might have later orders for us, would be warned by our presence.

As I spoke, a door facing the stair-head opened, and Brother Paul in his black frock appeared on the landing.

"Ah! my two sons, is it you? Whose kind thought was it that you should come so far to meet so poor and lonely an old man? Mademoiselle Suzanne's?"

"No, it was my Monsieur Gaspard's," shouted little Gaston, rushing forward, and flinging his arms round the monk's knees. "Isn't Monsieur Gaspard good to me, *mon père*?"

"But better still to me, *petit fils*. We please ourselves in pleasing the young, but few give a thought to please the old, and yet there are times when the old sadly need comforting." Reaching out above the little lad's head he caught my hand in his and held it. "In a good day for us he came to Navarre; we must try and keep our Monsieur Gaspard, we two."

"He shall marry Suzanne, *mon père*, and when I am Count de Narbonne I shall give him an estate."

"Not Suzanne, I think," answered Brother Paul, looking me smilingly in the face as one who would say, Be tolerant to his ignorance. "I do not think that would do, but we shall find some one else."

"And while you are looking for her," said I laughing, "I shall go and see that there is dinner enough, lest I starve while I wait."

Not Suzanne! said Brother Paulus, and how well I understood the significance of his indulgent smile. Gentle as a Saint John, tolerant as a Saint Francis, he was aristocrat to his finger-tips. A Hellewyl of Solignac marry Gaston de Foix's nurse! No wonder he smiled and said, Not Suzanne! It was all of a piece with the generous little lad's foolish talk of granting estates. A Hellewyl of Solignac would naturally be courteous to one in Suzanne's position, but more than courteous, no! and it was with a sudden flush of discomfort that I remembered Brigitta, and what Martin had called the philandering under the beech trees. Thank God there had been no thought of philandering with Suzanne D'Orfeuil.

CHAPTER XXIV
JEAN VOLRAN, TAPSTER, AND TRANSLATOR OF LATIN

My intention was to ask Jean Volran for an empty room in which to examine the King's letter, and at the foot of the stair I found him waiting. But it was not the Jean Volran I had known for a night and morning. The obsequious smile, the almost servile cringing, were no longer there; there was no deferential welcome for the great, no fawning upon the happy man who bore the King's letter and was the King's will in the flesh.

Then, had I said, Set La Voulle ablaze and thrust your hand into the fire, *Le Roy le veult,* he would have done it and made no protest. Now his back was as straight as my own, his mien as distant, his eye as supercilious. He eyen outstared me, as if he were Gaspard Hellewyl and I Jean Volran.

"You have kept me waiting, Monsieur," said he, pushing a door open and leading the way into just such a room as I desired.

"I? I have kept you waiting? What insolence is this?"

"Tut, tut!" he retorted, turning his back on me while he closed the door carefully. "Did you really think that for such a post as this his Majesty had chosen a man with no better brains than to fill wine pots for fools to empty? You have not only kept me waiting, but, what is worse, you have wasted your time with your dilly-dallying, and made the King to wait also. I would have had what was wanted here inside of a week. Why the King chose to employ you at all is a mystery, unless it was that if his plan miscarried it would please him better to see a Flanders man hang for it. The King did not send you to Morsigny to gather roses," he went on with a sneer and a nod at the flower I carried buckled to my bonnet, "but I guessed the message I brought you yesterday would put another thought than girls and girls' love tokens into your head."

"You? None but goatherds passed Morsigny yesterday."

"And I was one of them, as I have been many things in his Majesty's service. Now, Monsieur, the King's letter, if you please."

But there I had him at a disadvantage, and was in no mood to abate a jot of it.

"Be what you like, goatherd, scullion, tapster," I answered, with as brusque an incivility as his own, "that is between you and the King, and no odds to me, but the letter is my affair."

"Why, man," he cried, too astounded at my opposition to take offence, "don't you know you are but a catspaw, and I am here to finish the affair? Come, come, you have cackled your little crow over me, and we are quits—the letter, and waste no time."

"Even allowing for the goatherd and scullion," I answered, "I take you for a kind of a gentleman, and so do not say you lie, only, I heard nothing of this at Plessis. On the contrary, His Majesty was quite clear, that which I began I was to finish. Show me your warrant, but I warn you, nothing less than the King's signet and sign manual will move me."

For a moment he stood clenching and unclenching his hands before him, too full of passion to find words. Had he not been in his innkeeper's dress, and so without a sword, he would have tried force, so mad with rage was he. Then he turned aside to the window, and stared between the bars into the court where Martin was rubbing down Roland.

"You play your game with a high hand, Monsieur," he said at last; "but if you think I have sweated here in the grime all these weeks while you were feasting at Morsigny, just to see you pocket the profits, you don't know your man."

But when, with another turn of his heel, he would have stridden past me, I stepped between him and the door.

"Monsieur, who shall pay you your wages I do not know, but you are not coming back to stab me unawares and rob me of what the King has committed to my trust. Since you have brought me here to this room, in this room you shall stay until I have read his Majesty's letter. Nor do I see why we should quarrel. If the end of this affair has indeed been committed to you, show me some token? God knows I have no love for the work. You have no token? No warrant? Nothing but your bare word? Then, since you profess to know so much, tell me at least what steps I am next to take, something, anything to prove you are in the King's confidence, and that your bare word is not a bare lie? You cannot? Then tell me this: if you were Gaspard Hellewyl, and I you, how far would you trust the man who came with nothing but a blustering wheedle of words in his mouth? Not a foot! Not an inch! Nor will I. It is my life, Monsieur Tapster-goatherd, it is my honour, and by God! I'll give neither the one nor the other to your keeping.

Stand there by the window, Monsieur, and if the King bids me give you the letter, or—or anything else I control except these two, then, on the faith of a gentleman, you shall have it, but not unless."

Three times while I spoke I saw No! in his face, though he answered nothing; but as I ended, he half laughed, shrugged his shoulders, and did as he was bidden with a swagger that matched his clothing badly. Who he was, or what his rank, I never knew, but clothes so much make the man that not even the Prince de Talmont himself would in like circumstances have looked anything else than that very ridiculous object—a country inn-keeper in a rage.

Partly to gain time for thought, but partly, I confess, that his helplessness might gall him deeper, I played with the King's letter, examining silk, seal, and superscription as if all were strange, instead of as familiar as the bottom of my own pocket. The situation was growing clearer to me with every passing minute, and it will have been noticed that I do not think rapidly.

No doubt the fellow glowering at me from the window shutter was not alone in La Voulle; no doubt, too, his ten-crowns-a-month-cut-throats would be this, that, or the other about the inn—groom, drawer, even cook. Three or four of these there might be, but not more. Where there is a secret, there is no safety in numbers. Against these I had only Martin, unless, indeed, I played the bold game of raising La Voulle to defend its young Count, and as a climax carried him off myself! My scheme would have to be recast, which was a pity; its very simplicity had guaranteed success. But the nature and extent of the change must depend on the King's wishes, so with a smiling nod of encouragement in patience to my host at the window, I broke the seal.

Either the crackle of the paper or the polite impertinence roused him. Setting his foot against the angle of the wall, he stiffened himself for a spring. Once he had me on my back, circumstances would lead him. If his own fellows came in just then, there was an end to Gaspard Hellewyl; if La Voulle heard the scuffle, he would cry Treachery! and trust for justification to the King's letter found in my hands. But I saw the move, and hitched the handle of my sword forward a foot. It was a parry to his thrust, and back he lounged again against the shutters.

Tearing the outer wrappings to small pieces, I scattered them on the floor. The next sheet was a blank, nor, though I held it up to the light, could I trace a mark of any kind. Not so the third sheet, for eight or ten words were sprawled across it in short sentences. But at the first line the exultation of triumph over my enemy by the window fell cold and flat; the letter was in Latin, and never a word of Latin had I learned in my five-and-twenty years of life.

Latin! Why the plague Latin? No doubt it was part of the old Plessis fox's scheme for hiding his identity. Neither Jacob's voice nor Esau's hand must show the truth, though the supplanter and the Ishmaelite, he whose hand was against every man's, joined in him their cunning. Suppose the letter was seized upon me, what then? Outside the seal was Commines', the writing Commines'. Inside was a tag of monkish Latin scrawled as if an earwig had scratched its tail across the paper; who could connect either with Louis in Plessis if Louis chose to say No! with a sneer, and let Navarre's vengeance on the man who carried the letter pass unrequited? No one; and let it so pass he would, if, indeed, his virtuous indignation did not itself call aloud for vengeance. Louis had no mercy on failures.

But Latin! Why the plague Latin? Then I began to see. The cover once destroyed, Latin might come from Spain, from the Empire, from England—anywhere! And behind it France lay hidden in safety. More than that, and at the thought I ground my teeth, it was perhaps a tongue that brute grinning from the window at my perplexity could translate. If so, it was his turn to smile, and as I met his eye there was little of politeness in his ridicule. No doubt dismay was stamped across my face easier to be read than the words on the paper, and my need was his opportunity.

Not to give him the satisfaction of sarcastically offering his services, I spoke first.

"Do you read Latin, Monsieur?"

"Latin?" he returned, a scowl wrinkling his face. "What new nonsense is this?" Then an inspiration broke upon him, and he came briskly forward, his hand outstretched. "Ah! now I understand. You wish me to translate the King's letter? Certainly, Monsieur, certainly."

But tapping my sword hilt, I motioned him off. "Keep your distance, my good fellow. The writing is large enough to be read from where you are."

Reversing the paper, so that the light fell full upon it, I watched his face, and if ever a man was blankly puzzled it was my friend the goatherd-tapster. That he was as innocent of Latin as myself I guessed, but with the King's tools as with himself it was not wise to assume overmuch. What he had hoped was that I would put the letter into his hands, and once there he would have risked his skin to keep it.

"Well?"

"It is difficult," said he, playing to gain time. "I wonder why his Maj——ah! ah! ah! I begin to see. A man grows rusty in his learning; you find it so, do you not? But now I have it; yes, yes, just what I expected. You know no Latin, Monsieur de Helville?"

"Not a word. French and Flemish, nothing more."

From the paper he glanced up at me cunningly, his eyes narrowed, but with a malicious smile peeping through the lids, then back to the paper. Out went a forefinger, and nodding his head he passed from letter to letter, picking out the words as a child might spell his way through a hornbook. This he did twice, till, thinking he wanted to commit them to memory, I snatched the paper away.

"If you can translate, translate and have done with it."

"But I wish to have it exact," he protested. "Well, then, here it is," and again there was the cunning upward glance. "'*That which you have brought give to him who waits; return then whence you came until the King writes a third time.*' It is as plain as day, now that I have mastered the translation. I am he who waits; so now, Monsieur, give it to me and let me go."

Before he spoke I knew he was playing with me, and had no more Latinity in him than I had. For whatever quality the King had chosen him, it was not for that of a good liar. But the splendid audacity of the lie filled me with admiration, and that I might draw him to a greater fall I led him on a little.

"But what are your orders, or have you, too, a letter?"

"That," he answered, with just such a little smiling nod as I had given him, "is my affair, and between me and the King. Your own words! Come, Monsieur, give it to me, and let me go."

"It!" said I banteringly, for I was fool enough to play him further. "Is your Latin not rusty? And if it is rusty, may it not be wrong? Should your 'it' not be 'him'?"

"Him?" he repeated. "Him? What do you mean? By God! I have it! It's the boy upstairs—it's the little Count himself! Monsieur, Monsieur, you fly at high game, and I offer you my apologies; in some things you are not such a fool as I took you to be. To lead him like a pet lamb with a ribbon, and into his own town, too! No violence, no noise, nothing indiscreet! Monsieur, I could not have done as well myself. Can a man say more?"

"But the Latin?" said I. "What of the It, Master Scholar?"

"Who said It? Not I. *That which you have brought*, was what I said; *That, That*, not It, and *That* is the Count de Foix!"

"And I am to return whence I came?"

"So it seems, Monsieur, and I wish you joy when they find the boy does not return with you. I fear they'll hang you, faith of a gentleman! I fear they will."

"Stop a minute, I'm not there yet. I was to wait the King's third letter, was I not?"

"Yes, yes," he said impatiently. "You have had two already, and so the next must be the third—any fool can see that!"

"Just so, dear Monsieur Volran; and it was a fool who saw it. Since when was his Majesty among the prophets? Yesterday the second letter came, came because the King was kept waiting, and yet this, written two months ago, foresaw it, and so the next will be the third. How, two months ago, could the King know, there would be need for a second and so promise a third? My compliments on your imagination, but you do not lie well."

"Lie, Monsieur, lie?"

"Bah! Never bluster with your sheath empty; bare hands cannot bully hard steel. God forgive us! but we all lie at times. I did awhile back when I said I knew no Latin. I know one tag—a worthy monk taught it to me a month ago, when, out hawking, the kite missed its stoop. How is this it ran? *Laqueo*—let me see; *laqueo Venantium*—ah! I forget. Like you, I am rusty. But I remember its meaning. Shall I translate, Monsieur scholar-tapster? It has something to do with an escape from the snare of the fowler."

"Oh," he cried, stamping, "you shall pay for this!"

With my hand upon the door I turned upon him.

"Dare so much as lift a finger, dare so much as breathe a threat, and King's man though you are, bound up in the same bundle as me though you are, you'll find the Morsigny gallows waiting for you here at La Voulle; nor will Louis say more than, Curse him for a blundering ass! It is I who hold the King's orders, not you; cross me in my obedience at your peril!" and passing out, I struck the door noisily with the letter.

The crackle of the paper was a louder voiced threat than my own, and as such the man I left swearing behind me understood it.

CHAPTER XXV
IN WHAT WAY THE KING SOUGHT THE PEACE OF NAVARRE

Of the many thoughts that danced across the darkness of my mind, thoughts as impotent of light as fireflies flashing through a summer's gloom, one alone brought any satisfaction—Brother Paulus could make clear the King's instructions. Nor was I afraid that through seeking his aid would come any premature disclosure of our scheme for securing the peace of Navarre. The choice of Latin was now finally clear to me. It was not simply that it concealed the writer's identity, but it readily lent itself to translation. Thanks be to God! the ministrations of the Church are always to be found in this Christian country of ours, and where the Church is, there is learning. Louis could be trusted not to betray his purposes. Through fear of death he was the Church's humble son and servant in all things spiritual, but woe to the priest who, presuming on his office, meddled in things temporal to the detriment of France. At the door Brother Paul met me, his finger on his lip.

"He is asleep," he whispered, beckoning me to be quiet. "The early rising and the ride have tired him. A noble-hearted boy, Monsieur—loving, brave, unselfish. I think he will grow to be a good man, a hard thing for one born great. Some day Navarre will bless Gaston de Foix. Speak softly, though indeed a thunderclap would hardly waken him now, he sleeps so sound."

"So much the better, he has still far to ride. All the better, too, for now we can talk more freely. Father Paul, what does this say?"

It was wonderful how his eyes lightened. At Morsigny he had made no parade of learning, but, hiding it out of sight, had lowered his talk to the level of our ignorance. But the scrawl of Latin was to him as the face of his mistress to a devout lover, and it was with a kind of quaint reverence that he took the crumpled paper, smoothing out the creases tenderly.

"This, my son? Where did this come from?"

"I found it a while back. It is Basque, is it not?"

"Basque! No, no, Latin, and, I think, better in the letter than in the spirit."

"Latin! and that I should have taken it for Basque! I shall have to go to school again. What does it say, Father? Curiosity always has an itch for the unknown."

"That, too, is the gift of God, or how would learning grow? But this—this is foolish, or worse. *Numquid vivet? Non vivet. Morte morietur, sed statim interficies*. Oh, my son, that is not good! Either it is part of some horoscope, a sinful wresting of their secrets from the stars, or else an unhappy soul has sold himself to Satan for a necromantic prophesy, and such a prophesy!"

"But, Father," I cried, almost forgetting both love and reverence in impatience, "what, is it?—what is it?"

"Hush!" he whispered, shaking a warning finger at me. "Remember the child; we must not disturb his sleep. This is the meaning: '*Shall he live? He shall not live! Let him die the death, thou shalt surely kill him.*' Either a foolish jest," he went on, stooping over the paper, "or a spark from Hell, and at times the one is not far from being the other. The Latin is sound enough as Latin goes in these degenerate days; that is what I meant by saying the letter was better than the spirit. It is the reverse of the text. The letter killeth, but the Spirit giveth life. Here it is the letter that is sound and wholesome, but the spirit killeth. Note the terseness of it. Either the necromantic or the devil, his master, was—oh! my son, my son, what is the matter? Art thou ill? Faint? The sun this morning? Jesu! What is it?"

How could I answer? How could I do more than stand aghast? What a plot it was! What a damnable, cunning plot! What a playing on the passions—love, greed, vengeance, and what passed with the King for piety! What an interweaving of life and death and the powers of Hell! Oh, what cunning, what damnable cunning! If a bribe will buy this houseless, ragged wretch, this friendless outcast from his class, then there is Solignac and the old lands of his house waiting for him in Flanders. If love will hold him obedient, here is his mistress hostage to my mercy, the mercy of Louis of France! the mercy of the rack in Plessis and Tristan's House of the Great Nails, that all may know this is the King's vengeance for a duty unfulfilled! Or perhaps hate will move him! Then take Jan Meert, take my own ancient tool, who has never known a scruple to trip him in my service—take him, and do as you list by him. Or if these fail, if Navarre outbribes me, if a new love quenches the old, if revenge grows cold, there still remains the Cross of Saint Lo whereon who swears falsely perishes both in this world and the next. Remember the child! said Brother Paul, his finger on his lips. Remember him? Would God I could forget him!

Something of this was in my face, but not to be read aright by the gentle heart beside me, for Brother Paul took me in his arms, fearing I would fall, and how could a priest of God knowingly so hold one sworn to shed innocent blood? But I put him aside.

"The paper, quick!" and snatching it from his hand, I tore it into fragments too small to be pieced together again. I do not pretend I had any clear plan in my head; a blind instinct often moves us, and it is only later we understand why we did thus and thus.

But what Brother Paul failed to read in my face he gathered from the sudden violence of the act, though dimly. What mind as innocent as his could, on the instant, plumb to such an infamy? Again, being his Master's servant, he took me in his arms, laying his hands upon my shoulders, his grey face all lined with sorrow.

"You, Son Gaspard? Ah! I see, I see! Satan hath desired to sift thee as wheat, but I have prayed to the Father for thee. There, on the Grey Leap, I prayed; He has ventured his life to repair my fault, give me his life, O Father, spare him and give me his Greater Life. And so it shall be. I know it by faith, and if we could not know by faith, how could we live at all? Tell me your trouble, my son. Am I not Father Paul, God's Priest, and your friend? Confess yourself, and remember you speak not to me, but in the secret ear of God."

And I spoke. Kneeling between his knees as he sat upon a settle, I told him all from the beginning. What passed between us at the first is for no man's curiosity. Then, that being done with, and we back in the world again, the world in which men must use their lame wits and feeble understandings as best they can, I, tramping up and down the room, cried,

"But what next? I cannot see what next; it is all dark."

"No, no," said Paul, "not all dark, never all dark. No, my son, no; the Lord God never leaves a soul in the All Dark. Somewhere, somewhere, there is a gleam, and that gleam is an inspiration. Is it love? Follow it, my son, follow it. Duty? Then follow duty. A clean conscience? In God's name, follow it wherever it leads. Who am I to say more? The gleam is the one divine thing in us, therefore follow the gleam, follow it, follow it."

"It is easy for you, sitting there, to say so," and pausing in my walk, I stood over him; "but the arm of that cunning devil in Plessis can reach, as he told me, from Arragon to England, and from the verge of the Empire to the sea in the west. Gleam? There is no gleam."

"There is your oath, my son."

"My oath? An oath taken in blindness is no oath."

But Brother Paul shook his head.

"A Christian man's oath is the honour of his soul. When you swore your oath at Plessis there was always an alternative you could follow."

"To return?"

"To return," he repeated.

"But—that is death?"

"I said it was the honour of the soul. The ancient tongue has a motto, *Prius mori quam fidem fallere*. Sooner die than break faith—faith with God and all that is best in ourselves, faith with that unhappy woman who for no fault of hers, for no cause but that she loved you, stands to-day in your place. Were you Paulus and I Son Gaspard, I would go back to Plessis—and die. Not that I dare to judge for you."

"I cannot see it," I cried, the love of life and the love of Suzanne both strong within me. Was her rose not buckled to my bonnet? "Father! Father! Is there a God at all that we men are put to such straits?"

Priest though he was, he did not so much as utter a rebuke, but, rising, he laid his hands upon my shoulders as he had done almost at the first.

"I am not afraid of your doubt, for listen to this, my son: the man who has never greatly doubted will never greatly believe, never greatly love, never, even, greatly live. Every doubt a man puts under him is a step nearer to perfect faith, perfect love, and perfect life. Again I say, I cannot judge for you. But because doubt is a devil who must be fought alone and in the desert of solitude, I will go outside the door—outside the door, but never outside your life. The Lord bless thee, and keep thee! the Lord——" and then he slipped off into his beloved Latin, ending in *det tibi pacem*.

Softly lifting the latch and softly closing it, he was gone.

Pacem! That was peace. But where was I to find peace? Unless such a peace as lay so coldly at the foot of the Grey Leap that it had chilled 'Tuco's courage. From Arragon to England, from the Empire to the sea, Louis would find me out. Return to Plessis? I knew what that meant. Peace! It was easy for a priest to say Peace, peace! easy for the man who ran no risks to say Follow the gleam! but for me not so easy.

Just then Gaston turned on the bed, drawing a deep sigh of placid rest and contentment; Gaston, the child of whom Louis had written, Thou shalt surely kill him! Gaston, helpless and asleep. He shall die and not live, said Louis of France; his life for yours! Yet Paul had left him in my charge without a plea, without a pledge, without even the tremor of a troubled doubt. That moved me to my very depths.

To be thought capable of a great action, of a great sacrifice, makes both possible. I do not mean the sparing of the child. Thank God, that was never in doubt! But the fulness of Brother Paul's faith meant this to me: I trust you to do that which is highest, let come what may. That meant, return to Morsigny, put the child in safety, and humble yourself in the eyes of the woman you love; ride then to Plessis, and say: Here am I, let the woman I have ceased to love—no! the woman I have never loved—let her go her way. That meant—God knows what next, but nothing that a man could think upon without a shiver. If the woman who had done no wrong would writhe and scream and curse for what the King would call my treachery, what might not the traitor expect? And yet, that way shone the gleam, and another's faith in me gave me faith in myself.

But it was a relief to have the excuses of voices outside the door to put thought aside and find refuge in activity. It was Martin, come for orders as I had bidden him. Back to Morsigny, and with as little delay as possible, seemed the best plan. Once the boy was again safe behind its walls my responsibility ended. Yes, Morsigny first, and for that day it was my wisdom to look no further, lest I should see too much and be afraid.

But while I debated how best to avoid an altercation with the man who called himself Jean Volran, Volran's voice came from the stairhead with Martin answering loudly, roughly, as if in altercation; then followed a scuffle, the sound of a fall, and again Martin's voice:

"Monsieur Gaspard! Monsieur Gaspard! Quick! quick!"

He was standing at the stairhead, his back to me, his shoulders crouched, his knees bent, the right foot advanced, and both elbows hugging his ribs. I could not see it, but from his attitude I knew his sword was out, hidden by the bulk of his body. Back against the wall, where the well of the stairs made an angle, was Brother Paul, his arms raised in astonished protest; above the line of the topmost step jean Volran was rising to his knees where Martin had flung him.

"There is some roguery, Monsieur Gaspard," said Martin, but though he heard the latch click he was too wary of fence to turn his head. "This fellow, who an hour ago was a thieving inn-keeper, has now a sword at his hip——"

"You blundering fool!" said Volran, rising and shaking himself. "You took me unawares, but you shall pay me as fully as if you did it aforethought. Monsieur de Helville, there are only two of you, but I have four, and we seven can laugh at La Voulle."

"This fellow," went on Martin, as if Volran had never spoken, "this fellow came up here three at a stride, and was told by Father Paul you were busy. He would not take No for an answer, but tried to bustle us, so I tipped him downstairs to teach him patience."

"Monsieur de Helville, it is the King's business, and there is no time to waste," cut in Volran. "Bid this chattering idiot of yours be silent. You two can never hold the boy, and you know it. But we will help you. Come, sir, finish what brought you to La Voulle."

Putting Martin aside, I took his place on the top step.

"Have no fear, Jean Volran, or whoever you are, we two can hold the boy safe as far as Morsigny."

"Morsigny?"

"I said Morsigny."

"Morsigny? Then for what have I wasted three months in this rat-hole of a La Voulle? That you might march the Count de Foix into the town, and then march him home again? Was it for that the King sent you to Navarre?"

"That is between myself and the King, as I told you once already to-day, but the Count de Foix goes back to Morsigny."

"Mad!" said he. "Stark mad!" In his eagerness he came up a step or two, one hand stretched out before him as if to grip my attention and hold it. "Do you know who it is you deride? Whose face you slap? It is Louis'—Louis'. Why, man, he will crush you as I would a fly."

"Keep your distance," answered I; "you are five and we are two, but we have the vantage, and in narrow stairs two are as good as twenty. Come up but one step more, and Father Paul will shout A Rescue! from the window behind, and then you will be the flies."

"Better do it without waiting," said Martin. "Rouse the town, Father, or they may attack us on the road."

But I held the priest back.

"Not yet; I have a use for Monsieur Volran's life, and, liar though he is, I will trust his word. In spite of the trade he follows, there is enough of the gentleman in him for that. You see how it is, Monsieur Jean Volran? Let Father Paul put his head out o' window and shout, and there's an end to you and your four; with the townsfolk below and us above, it's a choice of rope or steel. Swear that neither you nor any of your four will molest us on the road, and, for aught I care, you may all go to the devil."

"Or to Plessis," said Martin.

"I mean to Plessis; that is my use for him. Do you swear, Monsieur Volran?"

For a moment he hesitated, glancing down the lower flight of stairs to the hall below. That his four transformed scullions were waiting him there, I knew, for they could not keep their clumsy feet quiet on the flagging, and he was calculating chances.

"Be ready, Father," said I softly. "If he stirs even an inch upward, shout Murder! Navarre to the rescue! Navarre! Navarre!"

But there was no need. With a snarl and a stamp of the foot he stepped back to the landing.

"Do you think this ends it?" he cried, shaking both fists up at us, his face all twisted with passion. "By God! No!"

"Do you swear, Monsieur Volran?"

"Swear?" he frothed. "What can I do but swear? Yes; Louis can pay to-day's debt better than I can, and so I swear. Oh, what a payment that will be! What a payment! What a payment! God send me there to hear you curse the bribe that has bought to-day's treachery."

"No bribe," answered I a little huskily, for the venom of his exultation shook my nerve more than any threat could have done. "But tell the King this: Gaspard Hellewyl has failed to fulfil his mission, and according to his oath returns to Plessis by the road of his Majesty's choosing."

"To Plessis!" answered Volran incredulously. "Bah! Why add a lie to treason? To Plessis!" and in his contempt he laughed.

But from behind, Brother Paul laid his hands upon my shoulders, drawing me back into his embrace until I felt the throb of his heart.

"It is the gleam, my son; God be praised, who never leaves us in the dark."

"It is my oath, Father; and you, Monsieur, do you carry your message to the King."

For a moment Jean Volran stood watching me curiously; then he drew himself up and raised his sword to the salute.

"Till we meet in Plessis, Monsieur."

CHAPTER XXVI
THE JUSTICE HALL IN MORSIGNY

But let it not be supposed that we trusted entirely to Jean Volran's oath; those who served Louis' court of honour too easily found absolution for vows broken in the King's interest. From the watch-tower in the steeple of Saint Suzanna the band of five were seen to ride northward, and when, having dined, we left La Voulle, it was with an armed company of the townfolk, to do honour, as Brother Paul said, to Monseigneur the Count de Foix.

These we dismissed as soon as Morsigny was in sight; nor did we lose time on our way. It was little Gaston's first forced march, and hugely he enjoyed it. But we elders were silent; when the heart is troubled, the tongue commonly takes holiday. Once only did Brother Paul speak.

"From the bottom of my heart I pity him," he said, turning to me suddenly.

"Pity whom? Jean Volran?"

"That most unhappy man, Louis of France. I sometimes think—though it is heresy, from which God deliver us all!—I sometimes think we make our own hell, people it with devils of our own creating, and by dwelling with them become like them."

"If by hell you mean our own follies," I began bitterly, but Brother Paul stopped me, and his voice was infinitely gentle.

"No, my son, no—not that; such pains truly are stripes of healing. But Louis! What a mind he must have to think that every man is such another as himself, and—oh, for poor human nature!—how often he must have found it true. To every man his price! But it is a lie, a lie, and to-day proves it a lie. I am glad, though, that you go back with us first to Morsigny. Mademoiselle de Narbonne has a shrewder head than I, though I am thrice her age. She may help us in our straits. I have great faith in Mademoiselle de Narbonne."

"Mademoiselle de Narbonne?"

"Yes, Suzanne."

"But I thought she was Mademoiselle D'Orfeuil?"

Brother Paul smiled and shook his head.

"That was some jest, some whim of hers, and yet, perhaps, with a purpose behind it. Suzanne is no light-of-mind to jest just for jesting's sake. Perhaps she thought you would be more at ease at Morsigny. Nor was it an untruth. She is Suzanne D'Orfeuil de Narbonne, Monseigneur's cousin. Because of your ignorance of our tongue she had only Gaston and me to reckon with. To Gaston she was always Suzanne, and I humoured her, as why should I not? She can always make me do as she wills."

"But now?" said I blankly, and feeling as if again the bottom of my world were dropping out.

"The time for such toys is past," answered Brother Paul gravely. "It does not become my office to countenance the prolonging of a jest in the face of such issues as lie before us."

I made no reply; and he, perhaps in contemplation of these same issues, he too fell silent.

Mademoiselle D'Orfeuil de Narbonne! What a fool I had been in my condescension. How she must have laughed as she played her part from day to day; laughed at my simplicity in swallowing her mock humility, laughed at my clownish setting her at her ease, she who miscalled herself, lest Gaspard Hellewyl, the broken-fortuned country lout of Flanders, should be overawed by her greatness! Who is there has not been wise after the event when he might have been wise before? And who is there has not cursed the puppy-blindness in him that could not see what was plain before his face? Not a day had passed but the gilding of the Narbonne had shone through the homespun of the Orfeuil, and yet the glint taught me nothing.

But it might have been worse. I might have spoken more boldly, more openly, and so have given myself more frankly to her laughter. I owed her some thanks that I had not, for even my bitter heart set this to her credit, that she had never beckoned me to a fall. Her jest had not been that cruellest of jests that spoils a life for a pastime. Yes, it might have been worse, though that is cold comfort when might have been worse is elbow-neighbour to as bad as can be, and there was a kind of grim satisfaction in the knowledge that Louis would soon give me other things to think of.

Never, by day or night, was Morsigny left unsentinelled, and Mademoiselle, being warned of our coming, met us at the gate.

"Welcome home, *mon coeur*!" she said, having dropped, and for the last time, her little curtsey. "Hast thou had a good day? How red thy cheeks are! Monsieur Gaspard must have—oh! Monsieur, Monsieur, is the news bad? Is there to be no peace for Navarre that you are so grave? What has happened, Monsieur? Tell me, tell me!"

"Much, Mademoiselle de Narbonne, but not what you think."

"Thank God for that! And Narbonne! Ah," and frank laughter chased away the sudden seriousness. "But you are not angry at my poor little pretence? You should not be, for it was you who taught it to me. Remember how I took you for Martin."

"Mademoiselle, if I have deceived myself, I have deceived you also."

"What?" and she looked me imperiously in the eyes, "are you, after all, Martin the servant, and is the other the Gaspard Hellewyl Monsieur de Commines called friend? If that is your meaning——"

"No, no; worse than that, much worse. I am, most unhappily, that Gaspard Hellewyl, and so it is much worse than that."

As may be supposed, the grooms had led away the horses, and we four were alone, the little Count being clasped in her arms. Before she could reply, Brother Paulus intervened.

"Run to thy Marie, Gaston, *mon gars*; she will give thee thy bread and milk for to-night."

"Yes," said Mademoiselle, kissing him, and letting him slip to the ground. "Run away, *p'tit*, I shall come to thee presently."

"I think you are angry with my Monsieur Gaspard," said he; "but you must not be angry, Suzanne; he took such care of me all day. From the time you gave him the rose he has in his bonnet until now he has never let me out of reach of his arm. Kiss me, Monsieur Gaspard," and, forgetting he was a prince, with a rush he hugged me round the knees.

As I stooped over him, I thought a touch of colour rose to Mademoiselle's face, and I know it was a relief to hide my own; it is not easy at all times to keep the heart from showing through the eyes.

"Sleep sound, *p'tit ami*," said I, kissing him on the forehead.

When, with a bend of the knee to Brother Paul, he had gone, Mademoiselle turned to the priest.

"It is serious, then?"

"It might have been," he answered. "With anyone else than Monsieur de Helville it might have been serious beyond words, but he has saved us."

"Saved you?" I echoed. "Do you call that saving? Mademoiselle de Narbonne, I have a story to tell, and afterwards, if you will give me a night to rest the horses, Martin and I will go."

"Go? Go where?" she asked blankly.

"Whence we came."

"Yes," said Brother Paul, "to God's keeping."

"So I think," said I significantly, "to God's keeping."

Without a further question Mademoiselle led the way to the main door of Morsigny, through the great hall, and into a broad, timber-roofed chamber. It was the Justice Hall of the Count of Narbonne, and, facing the east, was already gloomy, though the sun still shone yellow on the grass.

Seating herself on the carved chair that faced the top of the table, Mademoiselle pointed to a bench beyond its angle and looked round her. From the almost black walls of dull oak glimmered in steel the wordless history of her race. Lance and sword, shield and casque, glaive and morion, told their story in dint and notch how the House of Narbonne had risen, fighting; had thriven, fighting; and fighting, held its own. Many a Gaston, many a Phoebus, many an Antony, had gone to its building, laying himself down as a foundation stone on which the fortunes of his race might rise. And never had it risen higher than at that day. No wonder Paulus had smiled at little Gaston's promise that I should marry his Suzanne. A D'Orfeuil of Narbonne, comparatively remote though she was from the direct line, was not for a homeless Hellewyl, and I, like the blind fool for which I still cursed myself, had inverted the pyramid of his thought.

Was it for that, I wondered, was it to point this difference between our fortunes that she had brought us to this room of all rooms in Morsigny? Or, more significant still, was it to say, It is here that Narbonne judges and condemns?

Mademoiselle must have understood something of what was passing in my mind, for her first words brushed aside the alternative.

"Here we can be undisturbed," she said to Paul; "and here, you know, we take counsel together. Monsieur Hellewyl, you said you had a story to tell; but before you begin, I wish to say this: I do not retract a single word spoken on the Grey Leap."

"That was your ignorance, Mademoiselle," said I; "wait, and hear me out."

"I am not afraid," she answered, "and—will you believe me?—though I am a woman, I am not curious. Tell me no more than you wish to tell."

"And that is everything."

Already she knew the story in part—how that a landless, penniless gentleman had been driven from his home like a smoked rat, how he had found a friend in Philip de Commines, and how he had come to Navarre on secret service. But I went back to the beginning and told it all over afresh, hoping vaguely that my forlorn helplessness might plead an extenuation for me.

From Plessis the story differed from what I had allowed her to believe, and stooping upon her crossed arms, she leaned towards me over the table, losing no word. Slowly, simply, I told it all, palliating nothing, and hiding one thing only; it did not seem necessary to mention Brigitta. She belonged to Solignac, and had no interest for Morsigny; but all the rest I laid bare. Once she interrupted me. It was as I told of the King's commission, the sealed letter, and how that, through little Gaston was to come that peace to Navarre for which she had so fervently prayed in the chapel in Saint Gatien.

"And you really believed him?"

"Yes, the scheme was plausible."

"Plausible!" she echoed, with a laugh that was the nearest to a sneer I ever heard from her mouth. "Truly, Monsieur Hellewyl, Plessis must be very remote from Solignac."

"I believe," said Paul. "I remember the Grey Leap, and I believe."

"I, too, believe, but now Monsieur Hellewyl will understand why at the Grey Leap I doubted. Go on, Monsieur."

Thenceforward the story, being chiefly what had happened at Morsigny, was shortened. The error Mademoiselle had fallen into because of Commines' writing; the second letter, which I passed over as simply a warning to make haste; the inn at La Voulle—none of these called for any detail; nor did she again speak until I ended—"And so, no harm being done, I pray God, but good rather, since you are warned and on your guard, we shall go to-morrow if you give us leave to rest the horses until then."

"We shall think of that presently," she answered, but speaking as if her thoughts were elsewhere. "Monsieur, a while ago I said that though a woman I was not curious. That was a mistake. Have you told me everything?"

"A full confession, Mademoiselle."

"Confession? But at times there are other things besides confession. What was the warning Monsieur de Commines sent you?"

Thoughtlessly, or rather with the thought that she was suspicious of my entire good faith, I handed her Monseigneur's letter, which, holding it slanting to the light, she read through twice before handing it on to Paul.

"What was within it?"

"Within it, Mademoiselle?"

"Yes; he says, I am bid send you what is within."

Then I saw what a fool I had been. The story of the King's full-handed bribes, his promise of a new Solignac, of restored lands, and of a blood for blood vengeance on Jan Meert I had told her in full detail, but of the blunt threat sprawled across the other side of the account I had said nothing.

"Well, Monsieur, what was within it?" Then, as I still hesitated, "A full confession, Monsieur Hellewyl."

"This," and upon the table between us I laid the piece of cord, the noose still looped at the end. "This, and the message, So saith Tristan!"

She leaned, as I have said, across the table, resting on her folded arms; now she drew back, shrinking into the capacious hollow of her rounded chair as if the foot of innocent string had been a death-adder at the least. Of its symbolism there could be no mistake.

"That? You had that in your pocket to-day at La Voulle? You had that while Gaston lay asleep, and you faced Jean Volran on the stairway? Jean Volran? Not him alone; Jean Volran had four others, with him. Five against two are great odds?"

"No, Mademoiselle, not really great odds. We held the upper stairs, and Father Paul would have raised La Voulle behind them."

"Five against two are great odds," she persisted, "odds that no man need be ashamed to find too great—compellingly great—when he carries that in his pocket. Nor need Father Paul have raised La Voulle; that thought was yours? You had your chance there to save your honour, Monsieur Hellewyl—and your life," she added, tapping the table an inch away from the noosed cord.

"Should I have taken the chance?" said I; "or do you think that only frail, gentle-nurtured girls should ride into the shadow of the House of Nails?"

"It was for my nation, Monsieur?"

"It was for my honour, Mademoiselle; for though the world might say I had saved it, my own heart would give the world the lie daily, until I died. Besides, you make too much of it. The King is in Plessis, and I——"

"You are safe in Morsigny, and Morsigny can hold you safe; yes, thank God for that!"

But I shook my head, unwillingly enough, though I trust the unwillingness to be hanged did not show too plainly in my face.

"No, Mademoiselle de Narbonne, that cannot be. Why! the King would rake Navarre as with a wool-carder's comb until he found me. Martin and I go hence to-morrow."

"Where?"

"Does that matter? Anywhere."

"I can tell you where," said Paul, breaking in for the first time. "He rides straight to Plessis. I heard him tell Jean Volran; to Plessis by the road of the King's choosing."

"To Plessis!" cried Mademoiselle, bringing down her clenched hand upon the noose. "To Plessis, with that before you? Never!"

"My oath, Mademoiselle, my oath by the Cross of Saint Lo, whereon who swears falsely dies here and hereafter."

"For the dying in this world I can answer," said she; "Louis will see to that. As to the hereafter, Christ who died upon the Cross is above the cross. The keeping of such an oath is the sacrilege, not the breaking. Promise me, Monsieur; not to Plessis? Think what we owe you—Navarre, Narbonne, Morsigny, I myself. Oh, Monsieur, Monsieur! do not put your blood upon our heads for such a blind oath as that. Promise me, promise me."

But again I shook my head. This was the bitterest moment of all that bitter humiliation, and yet, knowing that it was not altogether my oath that drew me, I could not leave her to sorrow over a seeming useless sacrifice.

"There is another reason, Mademoiselle; the King holds a hostage for my return."

"Oh!" said she blankly, the fire dying from her eyes; "a hostage? Who is he?"

"It is a woman, Mademoiselle."

"Oh!" said she again, but this time with a subtle sharpening of the emphasis; "a woman? As I said at the first, tell me no more than you wish to tell."

"Then you trust me, Mademoiselle?" I asked, but doubtfully, for if her mouth said, Tell nothing, her eyes said, I, too, am a woman; tell all.

"Why not?" she answered, her voice prim and hard, until her eyes, which had been looking proudly into mine, fell, I don't know why, and rested on the cord, then it grew gentle again. "Say nothing, or—everything."

"Everything, then. She is a peasant of Flanders, a herdsman's daughter. The story is common enough——"

"Too common, Monsieur," she broke in, her eyes blazing, her hands clenched in her lap as again she shrank back as far as the hollows of the chair would let her. "Oh, you honourable gentlemen! Do you think that because I am Suzanne de Narbonne and she a peasant I care nothing for her womanhood? Shame, Monsieur Hellewyl, shame; she is my sister."

"I thought you trusted me, Mademoiselle?" I retorted, not sorry she had put herself in the wrong.

"I said so, Monsieur, but this common story of yours——"

"Is it not common that a man should think himself in love with the one pretty face he has ever seen in his life? that he should dress her coarse mind with the graces he knew later had never touched her, no, not for an hour? that he should hold her sacred for her very womanhood, and worship as God's fine gold what, when his knowledge wakened, he knew to be at its best but honest potters' clay? Is it——"

"Yes, Monsieur," she interrupted softly, and stretching her open hand across the angle of the table, "that last at least is so uncommon from a Seigneur of where you will to a peasant born in his woods, that I may be forgiven if for a minute I doubted. Am I forgiven, Monsieur Gaspard?"

It was a return of the old Suzanne D'Orfeuil, and resting her hand on mine, I kissed it as I might have kissed a Queen's, or no, not quite: if the kiss was reverent and carefully passionless, the touch of the lips lingered a moment or two beyond the nice allotment of ceremony.

"No woods of mine, for I owned not one rood of the land nor stick of the timber."

"Never mind that," she answered, withdrawing her hand; "you understand my meaning, and I think I need hear no more of the woods of Flanders. What of the hostage in Plessis?"

The rest was easy; not even when the King put the construction he did on the mention of Brigitta's name did the softness wither from her face. Only at the grim picture of how other limbs would writhe in my default, and a tortured woman scream her curse of Gaspard Hellewyl, she drew in her breath with a shudder, covering her eyes with her hand as if to shut out the sight. Nor, when I had ended, did she say more than—"Yes, you are right, and Father Paul was right; there is nothing for it but Plessis and the King's mercy."

The King's mercy! I had it in my heart to copy her bitter phrase: Morsigny must indeed be remote from Plessis when you talk of the King's mercy! But her white face restrained me. And why recall the only reproach she ever uttered?

CHAPTER XXVII
"GOD KEEP YOU, NOW AND ALWAYS"

But the next day Mademoiselle de Narbonne would not let us go.

"There is no need for haste," said she. "Consider for yourself; truly there is no haste. Jean Volran, once his blood is cool, will kill no horses riding to tell his master your plot has failed. This time bad news will bait by the way. Even then that woman is in no danger. The King is not wanton in his wickedness. With him evil has a purpose, and he is ruthless rather than cruel. The woman will be safe for at least a week."

She was right, and in the reaction which followed the high-strung tension of the conflict at La Voulle, judge if I did not catch greedily at the procrastination. But not for a week; the risk every way was too great; two days perhaps.

"Two days?" she repeated, glancing at Paul. "What do you say to that, *mon père*?"

"Sufficient, I think," he answered thoughtfully. "Yes, more than sufficient, for we had last night."

"Good! On Tuesday, then," said she, and the two left me.

More than sufficient! That was a hard saying, and not like Father Paul. Yet even to me the hard saying was a true one. These two days were more than sufficient to weary me of Morsigny, for in them I was left to isolation, except for a half hour thrice a day when we came together to break our fast. Now that her nurse's masquerade was over, Mademoiselle de Narbonne appeared to be burdened with affairs, and it may be that there were letters to write, for couriers were sent away thrice, once to Pau, and twice to Pamplona.

I suppose Paul guided her in these, for not even he was visible, until at last, having haunted Morsigny all that Sunday for a glimpse of his kindly sorrowful face, I shut myself up in my own chamber at sunset, an ill-used, ill-tempered man. Of what use was it to say, Wait two days, if in them I was shut up to my own thoughts for company? Not even Mademoiselle's rose, nodding towards me across a rim of glass, was any comfort.

I do not think there ever yet was a man who never repented of making a great sacrifice. In his soul he knows he was right, but the baser part of him repents, and there never was a man yet whose baser part did not get the upper hand at times, while with most of us it sits astride on top.

I was five-and-twenty, and loved life with the natural, wholesome, riotous love of any healthy animal. Of death or the judgment to follow I had no conscious fear, but the life I lived was sweet and good and satisfying. It suited the flesh of my manhood's robust strength as no other life could, suited it exactly as the Lord God meant it should; and so, as I stared, chin on palm, above the blown rose at the blue of the far-off hills, I asked myself if I had not been a fool?

My oath? Oaths comfort no dead men, and Mademoiselle had herself torn the figment of my oath to tatters. Brigitta? Again I called Mademoiselle to witness; had she not said the King had a method in his wickedness? His cruelty was not the lust to kill for killing's sake. With a fright, a whipping perhaps, he would let her go. Her healthy flesh would heal, her peasant's mind would take no shame. In six months' time she would be none the worse except for a scar or two on the back, none the worse body or soul, while I——? Clenching my fist I struck it against the table. Instantly a small soft voice answered me, a voice without words. Mademoiselle's rose had fallen, and the heavy petals whispered as they toppled on the polished wood; one, two, a dozen; those left, trembling at the shock of loss, nodding a farewell before they, too, lost their hold on life.

"See, old friend of yesterday," they said, "see what comes to all of us. We do our little work in the world, and then—we go. We give a little of sweetness, a little of perfume to the dry, dull air of the world, we breathe a little of love, a little of promise, our best and all we have, and then, having done our work in the world—we go!"

Ay! we go! But we do not go utterly. Even my rose had left something of its sweetness behind. From the petals gathered in my palm the breath of yesterday flowed upwards, perfumed and delicious. My rose was gone, yes, but it was not utterly gone. Its memory lived, fragrant and undying. Surely, surely, I could at least leave as sweet a name behind me as a rose of yesterday!

"We go, old friend," said I, nodding back at the shaking petals. "Yes, we go; but if truly we have done our work in the world, and if our memory lives in fragrance after us, what does it greatly matter?" And—will it be believed?—I drew strength and comfort from the withering petals flattened in my palm.

There was much need for both. Monday was as the Sunday had been. Mademoiselle and Brother Paul were busied everywhere but where Gaspard Hellewyl looked for them, nor did we meet till supper. Then Mademoiselle was restrained, preoccupied, eating little and talking less; her only reference to the next day's departure being a cold enquiry as to when I desired the horses. Had we been going for one of our rides, as in the blessed days of July, she would have shown more animation.

"Eight o'clock," I answered, steeling myself to an equal coldness. "We must ride to Orthez; the King's post at La Voulle is temporarily closed. May I suggest, Mademoiselle, that you should keep a watchful eye on the next tenant?"

"Orthez!" repeated she thoughtfully. "Yes, eight o'clock should do."

"Oh, Mademoiselle!" said I, with an elaborate show of courtesy to cover my bitterness, "if the hour is inconvenient we can always leave—earlier! But I do not think you need be afraid for Morsigny. The King knows you are warned. Shut your door upon our backs and you are safe."

She looked aside abruptly before replying, and when she turned to face me again her eyes were brimming, though her mouth was hard set.

"You think us ungrateful, Monsieur, you think us callous, you think us cold; but you think wrong in all three. But there is, I pray God, a life to be saved, if to save it is possible, and there is much to be thought of, much to be planned. You will excuse me for to-night? To me the danger is greater than you admit—I cannot bear to speak of it. I am more truly a woman than you credit, and—and—God keep you, Monsieur, now and always!"

Before I could reply she had gone, still half mumbling the words between her shut teeth, leaving me touched to the heart with self-reproach. Not that I believed the danger to the boy was serious. Now that his scheme was laid bare, Louis would resort to no impolitic violence; but love, given unreservedly as Mademoiselle's love was given to little Gaston, is never calmly rational, but, over-anxious, measures danger by its own depth.

The next morning Brother Paulus and I broke our fast alone, nor did I see Mademoiselle until the horses stood by the mounting-blocks. That she had rested badly, sleeping little or none at all, was plain from the black hollows which underlay her eyes. Even Gaston saw the change.

"Suzanne is ugly to-day, Monsieur Gaspard," said he, running forward to feed Roland with a morsel of bread. "I think she has been crying. That is silly, Suzanne, for if people go away they always come back."

"Let him think so," said she, trying to smile as she shook a finger at him. "To me it seems a sin to make a child sorrowful. Come and say good-bye to Monsieur Gaspard, Gaston."

It was strange, almost grotesque, certainly pathetic, how the child in him froze to the dignity of the Count of Foix.

"Goodbye, Monsieur," said he, coming forward sedately, but with a back-turned glance of regret at Roland whinnying after him. "My father, the Count de Narbonne, will be sorry—oh, you have a new kind of spurs on, Monsieur Gaspard! Suzanne! do you see? Is that because you have so far to ride."

"Goodbye, Monsieur Gaston," said I, smiling in spite of my heavy heart at his struggle to be two such incongruities at the one minute as a dignified prince and a wholesome-natured child of six. "When next we ride together we must have just such another famous gallop as we had on Saturday."

"Shall we? Shall we?" he cried, gleefully clapping his hands, the prince all flung to the wind. "Oh, but it was grand, that ride from La Voulle! Suzanne, you would have thought the King of France was after us, we rode so fast."

But Mademoiselle had me by the hand, and was biting her lip, so that I said my farewells hastily.

"God bless you, Mademoiselle! Only He knows what you have been to me in my weakness," and stooping, I kissed her hand as I had kissed it once before. "It is not so very hard; never believe that it has been very hard. Father Paul——"

But Father Paul was fairly crying, and when I saw the tears running unrestrained down his cheeks, I judged it time to be in the saddle, lest I should disgrace my manhood. To weep at a friend's grave is no shame, but a man who rides in his own funeral should keep back his tears that others may not suffer with him.

What benediction was in Father Paul's heart I do not know, for his tongue turned traitor and would not speak, but I have no doubt that He to Whom it was addressed heard and recorded it.

Almost in silence I left the great door of Morsigny, but not the outer gate. There waited Hugues, 'Tuco, Antony, and the rest, all who had so rightly mistrusted me. They were in two lines, between which we rode bareheaded as they. At first they were dumb, and stood to arms as soldiers stand when a fellow soldier goes where a soldier may look to go in the fulfilment of his duty. But as we passed beneath the teeth of the portcullis a roar followed us, a cheer, a hoarse shout like the rumble of thunder, "Vive Hellewyl! Vive Solignac! Vive Flanders!"

At the shout I turned in the saddle, my heart beating fast, my eyes wet, and the last I saw of Morsigny was not Mademoiselle's white face, nor Brother Paul's tears, but a forest of bare steel shaken in the air, and quivering like fire as the sun caught the flat of the friendly blades. Truly it was something of a triumph that Navarre should cheer a man of Flanders who came by way of Plessis-les-Tours!

But the mockery of it. Vive Hellewyl! Vive Solignac! Long live the man who dies within two weeks! Long live the man who rides in his own funeral! Long live Solignac of the burnt roof-tree! Solignac, the harbour for owls and bats! They might as well cry, Long live Death and Destruction! And yet at the ring of the hoarse roar my blood warmed, my eyes lightened, and my heart leaped. Gaspard Hellewyl would pass as the over-blown rose had passed, but his memory would live, and Morsigny would hold it fragrant. There was some comfort in that to the man who so dearly and without hope loved the mistress of Morsigny.

But such comfort soon passes; the spirit needs stronger meat than a windy cheer, however well meant, to keep it in health, and as my pulses calmed I saw facts in their true proportions. So long as I was at Morsigny, so long as I was in touch with Mademoiselle, she was the prism at which I looked at life and the hours shone red or blue at her mood's pleasure. Now that was finally done with, and thenceforward if there was a light at all it was cold and passionless. In that glamour of interweaving reds and blues I could play the stoic and say, It is not so very hard. And at the time it was true. We all have a high note in us, though all too soon it dies away in a quaver.

Nor was Martin helpful. Sour and disconsolate he rode behind, whistling a *Dies irae, Dies illa* of his own composing, until Morsigny was no longer in sight. Then, according to custom, he spurred up Ninus until his muzzle was a foot or two ahead of my girth.

"I don't understand it at all, Monsieur Gaspard. We come to a place where we plainly were not wanted, stay there two months playing ourselves, then ride back where plainly we do not want to go. Why is all that? Do you remember, we were to roof over Solignac, redeem the old lands, and catch Jan Meert, and when we rode from Morsigny we were to ride as if the devil or Tristan were after us. But here we are, pricking along leisurely, as if——"

"Tristan was before us, which he is. Cannot you see that we have failed?"

"And Solignac?"

"My poor Martin, there is no more a Solignac."

"And the lands?"

"Never again will a Hellewyl have lands in Flanders."

"Jan Meert?"

"Perhaps," said I, grimly, "perhaps Jan Meert. The King has promised we shall meet, and when it suits him to do so he keeps his word."

"The King?" a spasm had poor Martin by the throat, just as in my room at Morsigny when the noosed cord was dangled in his face.

"For me," said I, "but not for you. I go to Plessis, but you—to Solignac, I think, will be safest."

His only answer was the reproach in his eyes, and a "God forgive you, Monsieur Gaspard," as he reined back again. Of course, he meant that where I went there would he go also: nor, so complete was his faith that what I did was the one and only thing that could be done, did he attempt remonstrance or persuasion.

But ten minutes later I heard the sober trot of the hoofs behind me quicken to a clatter, and again Martin pricked up alongside, but this time he was smiling.

"I have it, Monsieur Gaspard! We have failed"—he never stopped to ask in what, or to say the failure was none of his, since he did not even know the scheme—"we failed, but that was because they were too many for us. And what is more, we did our best, did all that men could do, for they killed you, and as you lay a-dying, with your last breath you bade me ride to Plessis and tell the King all that had happened. Meanwhile, you will go to Solignac by way of Auvergne, Burgundy, and Lorraine, and I, when—when—the King has rewarded me, as of course, he will," he went on, whimpering in spite of the gay prospect, the excessive brightness of which made his eyes water, and his mouth to tremble with a queer smile, "I'll join you there, and—and—; there, that's settled, but I think you need not go to Orthez."

"And tell me, how does King Louis reward failures?"

For a moment he blinked in silence, but though the shadow on his face deepened, his voice was brave as he answered—"This was no common failure."

"You are right, old friend," said I, grimly twisting his meaning. "It was, indeed, no common failure, and what is more, news of it is already on the way, so that the King will have ample time to prepare the reward. What shall we do with it when we get it, you and I?"

"Don't laugh at me, Master Gaspard, for I can't bear it," he answered gruffly. "And why should I not go to Plessis? Why should I not die for you?

What use is a man's love if it can't do a—a—little thing like that? Why can't I go to Plessis, Monsieur Gaspard?"

"Because, old friend, there are some debts a man must pay for himself; because, too, in your heart of hearts, you would not have the last Hellewyl of Solignac turn coward, even to save his life."

For a moment he looked me straight in the face, saying nothing; then, raising his hand to a salute, he turned Ninus back, and thenceforward we rode apart. Even at Saint Laurent, where, by Mademoiselle's suggestion, we halted to bait, he kept his distance. His only explanation was a gruff, "A man who isn't good enough to die for another isn't good enough to live with him, or eat or drink with him either, Monsieur Gaspard."

So, also, was it through the afternoon. He trailed a dozen lengths behind me, the packhorse dragging uncursed from his hooked elbow, and it was with a dreary sense of isolation, of being outcast from all love and sympathy in the world, that I rode into the court of the inn at Orthez, to see Mademoiselle's face smiling at me from the doorway.

CHAPTER XXVIII
A LIE FOR A LIFE

"Mademoiselle Suzanne!" I cried, and at what she read in my face the white in her cheeks went to the pink of a shell. "Why! what does this mean?"

"That there are more roads than one to Orthez, Monsieur; and that Father Paulus, who is within, will tell you the rest."

"But, Mademoiselle— —"

"But, Monsieur, the roads are free to all; only," and turning on the midway landing of the stairs up which I followed her, leaving Martin and the landlord to care for the horses, she went on, lowering her voice, "remember that henceforward there is no longer a Mademoiselle de Narbonne, only Suzanne D'Orfeuil. Father Paulus is here, Monsieur de Helville."

Thenceforward? What thenceforward did she mean? And why, in a chief city of Navarre, should a Narbonne of Morsigny deny her name? Taking my two hands in both his at the top of the stairs, Father Paul answered my second question as directly as if I had spoken aloud.

"Though it is Orthez, it is also a post of the King of France, and to travel as Suzanne D'Orfeuil is less risk."

"To travel? To travel where?"

"To Plessis, my son."

"Did you think," broke in Mademoiselle through my dismayed protest, the door being shut behind us, "did you really think us so cold, so callous, so ungrateful? If so, then we have not taught you much in our two months, Monsieur."

"Not taught me much? Suzanne D'Orfeuil has taught me more than can ever be told to Mademoiselle de Narbonne. Not taught me much? From a man I have learned faith; from a woman—ah! Mademoiselle, I dare not say one half— —"

"Then do not try, Monsieur," she began, with one of her little old-time curtseys. But her forced gaiety ended in a sigh. "All that is past, and where we go there is little love and no faith," which showed that, though she stopped my mouth, she caught my meaning.

"Plessis? Father Paul, that must never be."

"Why not, Son Gaspard?"

"Our Suzanne at Plessis? Our Suzanne in the power of that cold, cruel devil, Louis of France? It is monstrous; it is infamous! Yes, I will speak!" for with her hand upon my arm she tried to silence me, not understanding that her very nearness, the mere touch of her fingers, was a spur to protest. "Why should I not? You are Suzanne D'Orfeuil, and Mademoiselle de Narbonne is at home in Morsigny; why should I not speak? By what right, Brother Paulus, do you risk a life not your own?"

It was Mademoiselle who answered.

"Then if you must speak, speak to me if you please, Monsieur, not to Brother Paul. I love him like a father, I reverence him as my guide spiritual, but if you think Brother Paul would keep Suzanne D'Orfeuil from doing that which Suzanne de Narbonne has bidden her, then, I say again, we have not taught you much in our two months at Morsigny."

"Then, Mademoiselle, I ask you. By what right do you risk a life not your own?"

"Not my own? Then whose is my life, Monsieur, if you please? and when you answer, take care you do not presume too far. Whose, Monsieur, whose?"

"Navarre's."

"Has a nation no honour, even as a man has?"

"Its honour is dishonoured if it saves its honour at a woman's cost. Oh! Mademoiselle, you know not what you do. You have not heard the King's threats as I have, the rack, the cord, infamy not to be named in words; no, no, you know not what you do. For God's sake return to Morsigny, that your blood be not on my head."

"And would there be none on mine?" she answered vehemently, and with a passion the equal of my own. "Would I be blood-guiltless if, with a *Good-day, and merci, Monsieur*! I curtsied a good-bye on the steps at Morsigny, and gave no second thought why you rode away and where? Or for whose sake you carried a foot of King Louis' cord in your pocket? His Most Christian Majesty's new-founded Order of Noble Faith!"

"Oh! that?" said I lamely, for I remembered that the ease with which she sent me to my death had hurt me sorely; "that was not a woman's business."

"A man's, then? Brother Paul taught you a man's faith, did he? Fie, fie, Monsieur! Is it a man's faith to pray in safety to the good God to do for us what we should do for ourselves? And did Brother Paul not teach you, bad theologian that he is! that faith without works is little worth? There, Monsieur, the man and the woman are both accounted for; are you content?"

Content? Desperate, rather, and in despair I turned upon the priest who stood by in silence, the lines upon his face those of perplexity rather than doubt or anxious care.

"Do you consent to this worse than madness?"

"Is it madness?" said he, taking Mademoiselle's hand in his to comfort and hearten her. "Then, my son, and I say it in all reverence, then was Christ mad. He came— —"

"To die for the sinful and unworthy," I cried in bitterness of heart; "you need not tell me I am that, I know it already."

"Because there was no other way; and who knows but Louis will hearken," said Paul gently, his eyes growing wistful, "though, indeed, Monsieur Hellewyl, even while my heart said she was right, I gave faith the lie and urged her all I knew not to go."

"Louis hearken!" I answered scornfully. "What can she say to move him? I tell you, Paul, Louis will wring the rights and freedom of Navarre out of her woman's flesh."

"No, no, you mistake; Suzanne will not appear at all, Louis will know nothing of Suzanne. She will move Monsieur de Commines, and Monsieur de Commines will move the King to mercy. We have thought it all over. It was settled the night we returned from La Voule."

"By me it was settled as we sat at the table in the Justice Hall," said Mademoiselle. "Could you give yourself up to save a peasant woman who was nothing to you, nothing at all—remember, Monsieur, I understand she was nothing at all to you—while we, to whom you—you—are so much, raised no finger to aid you? There and then I settled my plan, and we have had two days to think it over, Brother Paul and I."

Oh, the irony of it! the unconscious, sardonic irony! yes, and the pathos, too. They had thought it all over, these two—the gentle unworldly priest and the generous, tender-hearted, too grateful woman, they had thought it all over, and now in their swerveless cleaving to what they held to be right, they were as inflexible, as inexorable, as stonily determined as Louis himself.

But if argument and pleading failed, there at least remained protest.

"Remember, this is not done with my consent."

In an instant she was Suzanne D'Orfeuil de Narbonne, and turned to freeze me with a stare.

"Consent! Monsieur, consent? You forget yourself surely? When I desire either your consent or your approval, I shall ask for it; till then I take leave to decide and act for myself."

There was no more to be said. With such a bow as a Mademoiselle de Narbonne had a right to claim from a Gaspard Hellewyl I withdrew.

Men and women, liars all, have whispered that, having crept like a traitor into Morsigny under cover of a woman's skirts, I now tried to purchase my own safety by the sacrifice of Mademoiselle de Narbonne. The men have not repeated the lie but the women knew they were safe. It has been openly alleged that, knowing her loftiness of mind, her generous-hearted impulsiveness, I so played upon her sense of gratitude that she took the desperate step of substituting herself in my place, and that I, a traitor to the King and to my salt, accepted the sacrifice like a coward and a cur. More lies! the only truth being that the loftiness of spirit is there, and the generous loyal heart is there. But that is the way of the liar: even the devil himself would not be believed if he did not mix some truth with his falsehood. But of every fair mind, of every one who reads this record for the first time, I ask, in the face of such a withering rebuke as she gave me at the last, Was there room for further protest?

But if there was no more to be said, there was more to be done—there was the saving her from herself in spite of herself. To this end I sounded Brother Paul when presently he joined me, his mouth full of excuses for the sharpness of her rebuff.

"Do not be vexed with her, my son, she is nerve-weary, over-wrought, and fretted by care. For three nights she has not slept, for two days she has laboured and planned that no harm may come to Morsigny in our absence, and all that time she has not eaten as much as would keep a bird alive. Her spirit alone keeps her up."

"And yet you send her to Plessis?"

"Let us not speak of that, but rather how good may come out of evil."

"Tell me your plan."

"It is Suzanne's, not mine, and nothing could be simpler. We will ride together, all four of us, till we come to Poictiers, following the King's stages day by day. No doubt from each stage he will be warned that Gaspard de Helville is keeping faith, and so the woman will be safe. At Poictiers we part. You and Martin remain behind, while Suzanne and I ride on to gain the ear of Monsieur de Commines. He is pledged to you and to her, and through him there will be a respite. That will give us time, and with time——" He stopped short, rubbing his chin. Even to his guilelessness it was plain there was a strained link in the chain. "With time," he went on lamely,—"oh! all the world knows that with time anything can be done."

"Ay!" I answered, "and much more, I pray God, with Eternity! for once you reach Plessis there'll be little time left to any one of us. How is it that so many men who are wise for the next world are fools for this? Do you think that already Louis has not been warned how a priest and a woman met Gaspard Hellewyl at Orthez? Do you think that henceforth that priest and that woman will not be traced step by step, wherever they go? Do you think that when Mademoiselle knocks on Plessis gate the first to hear of it will not be Louis himself? What, then, will follow? She is Suzanne D'Orfeuil, a kind of serving-wench at Morsigny, and the purpose of this serving-wench is to come between the King of France and his vengeance. Will the King believe her account of herself? Not for an instant. Serving-wenches do not mix themselves up in State affairs. You he will hang, and I do not think the knowledge will hold you back for an hour. But what of Mademoiselle de Narbonne?" Leaning forward, I caught him by the shoulder, shaking him. "Father Paul, have you ever seen a woman racked? The white limbs stretched naked on the frame, and strained and strained until the joints crack, until the muscles tear from the ribs and the writhing mouth screams, frothing?"

"God forbid!" he said, stammering. "God forbid!"

"God forbid!" I retorted hotly, "Do your own work in the world, Father Paul, and do not ask God to do it for you. Is the Lord God a lackey to do that for a man which he should do himself? God forbid? No! but do you forbid!"

"How?" he answered, swaying as I shook him in my passion. "I forbade it at Morsigny, and she put me aside. How can I forbid it?"

"By seeming to consent until Poictiers is reached. There we will reverse the parts. That night I shall ride on, and next morning, when she asks for Gaspard Hellewyl, do you say, He is at Plessis."

"She will follow."

"I think not," I answered slowly, striving hard to marshall my thoughts in order. With such a nature to deal with as that of Suzanne de Narbonne, it would not do to leave any emergency unprovided for.

But just because hers was such a nature—loyal, pure of spirit, faithful, hard as steel in her sense of honour—I thought I saw my way clear. It was not a pleasant way, it was a way that bade good-bye for ever to my dream of a rose-leaf, fragrant memory. But what would the shattering of even so dear a dream as that matter, if only I saved her from herself?

"Did you guess," I went on at length, "that I love Suzanne D'Orfeuil, and that she knows I love her?"

"Mademoiselle de Narbonne?"

"No! Not Mademoiselle de Narbonne, with estates in Bigorre and Bearn, but Suzanne D'Orfeuil, nurse to Monsieur Gaston de Foix."

"Suzanne D'Orfeuil? Yes, I understand now what you mean. Oh! my friend, I am sorry, very, very sorry."

"You need not be; no man is the worse for loving a good woman. Love is a fire, and when it does not consume it purifies; so do not be sorry. But she was not the only one, nor the first. You remember?"

"Brigitta?"

"Brigitta. You saw how Mademoiselle blazed out at Morsigny when she supposed—you know what she supposed well enough?"

"But she was wrong, you told her she was wrong."

"Suppose," said I slowly, "suppose I leave a letter at Poictiers telling her that she was right, and that I had lied? Suppose I tell her that the woman Brigitta has a claim upon me which none but a wife should have upon a man, a claim which not even such a scoundrel as I can deny? I am not all bad, you see; if I were, Mademoiselle would have found me out; and being not all bad, I admit the claim. Suppose the letter goes further, and says that all through it is Brigitta I have loved, but that being at Morsigny I passed my time pleasantly—would she follow me then?"

"I understand," he repeated, his brows wrinkled in the effort to follow not alone the meaning of the words, but the full extent of the lie they told. "I am not good at—at—tricks of speech, but I think I understand. No, Suzanne de Narbonne would not follow you then. And you could say that to the woman you love?"

"I could say it because I love her!"

A bitter draught is none the less bitter for being of our own mixing, and what I drank in that hour is past telling. I suppose my torment of spirit showed in my face, for he laid his hand on mine holding me fast.

"Did I not rightly say that those who greatly doubt can greatly love? And greater love has no man than this, that a man lay down his life for his friend."

Some will say, Why not have told your lie to Mademoiselle there in Orthez? But that would have spoiled all. In her then mood, and coming so quickly on the heels of my past urging, she would have seen through the subterfuge, scoffing it for the clumsy falsehood it was. Let a week pass, let her emotions cool, let her healthy youth regain its dominance, and the clumsy lie of Orthez would seem a scoundrel truth in Poictiers.

So day by day that week passed, and not so very gloomily. Wholesome youth is not long melancholy. If I had Mademoiselle for company and so was happy through the warm August hours, she had faith and enthusiasm to comfort her. That there was life and movement also counted for much. Blessed be activity! Cabernet succeeded Orthez, Le Gatelet Cabernet, Saint Gatien, Marthon, Ruffec, night by night with but two exceptions: once we were barred by a swollen river—the Dordogne was in flood—and on Sunday we rested. But our days of peace came to their end, and on the 28th, the last Thursday in the month, we entered Poictiers.

CHAPTER XXIX
HOW MARTIN WON HIS HEART'S DESIRE

And now I come to what has saddened all my life since, and still must sadden it.

In Poictiers, it will be remembered, much was to happen. There Mademoiselle de Narbonne was to leave me behind in hiding while she rode on to Plessis to gain the King's ear through Philip de Commines. There, too, I was to forestall her useless sacrifice and, in a triple sense, disappear into the dark, into the night, into her scorn and contempt, into the valley of the shadow, from which none ride out at the hither end.

And yet none of these things came to pass. We reckoned without the King's energy of will to strike, and the swiftness of his wrath.

Once only she referred to the part she proposed that I should play. It was on the morning of that last Thursday in August, and the great silence of the deep heart of the wood through which we rode had fallen upon us.

"Father Paulus has told you that we part at Poictiers?" she said, looking straight forward between her horse's twitching ears.

"Yes; it is all arranged between us."

Then silence fell again, but she gave her reins a little impatient shake as if she asked in her heart what manner of man was this who had no word of gratitude or even of plain thanks to offer her. But it was better so; the graceless boor would easier seem the lying scoundrel.

"What will you do, Monsieur, while you are waiting for news?" she went on at last.

"Rather let us ask, what will you do? How, for instance, do you propose to pass the gates of Plessis?"

"I have thought of that; by the King's signet which you hold."

"The King's signet?"

"Yes; when Lesellè refused you admission to the presence the afternoon you left Plessis, Monsieur de Commines passed you the King's ring, and in the haste that followed it was overlooked. You have it still?"

"Mademoiselle," I cried, shaken out of my enforced coldness, "you astonish me. I had forgotten the King's ring."

"You had less need to remember than I," she answered, glancing at me for the first time. "When those we—we—esteem are in danger—but this is no danger, Monsieur? All will go well, will it not?"

There was a little catch in her throat as she ended, and my own was not free from a significant parchedness as I replied, giving the lie as light an appearance of careless truth as I could—"Surely not; Monsieur de Commines will protect you."

"I was not thinking of myself," said she, "but for fear the ring should be forgotten in to-morrow's haste, as it was when you left Plessis, you had better give it to me now."

For a moment I hesitated. Since she was to remain behind in Poictiers she required no token to open the gates of Plessis. But, on the other hand, neither did I! No fear but by day or by night the drawbridge would swing down that the traitor Gaspard Hellewyl might pass over! Then a new thought decided me, and drawing the signet from the inner pocket where it had lain forgotten, I handed it to her. In the doubtful days to come, the days that lay between Poictiers and Navarre upon her return journey, the King's ring boldly used might hold her safe. There was comfort in that.

"See how you make all smooth for me," said she, smiling up at me as she took the ring; and partly because she was Suzanne de Narbonne and I nothing better than Gaspard Hellewyl, but partly also because of the lie she was so shortly to be told, I dared not answer her back, dared not say, Would God I could make all smooth till the mound of the grave makes all rough for the one left behind.

At the Coq Rouge, the inn of the King's choosing, we parted without formality. Some trivial excuse appeared reason enough, but the truth was I did not dare trust myself to drift into a farewell that was for her a Good-night until the morrow, but for me until the great morrow of the Eternal dawn. I had my letter to write, and how, having the one moment kissed her hand, could I the next coldly set myself down a liar and a scoundrel?

But an hour passed, and the letter was still unwritten. Then, as I tore up my sixth draft, the door opened without a knock, and Martin slipped quietly in.

"Mademoiselle wants you, and I think there is trouble," he said in a whisper.

"Mademoiselle de Narbonne?"

"Mademoiselle Suzanne."

"It is all one."

"Maybe, but she bade me say Mademoiselle Suzanne sent me; Mademoiselle Suzanne, I was to make no mistake about that."

"Where is she, and why do you think there is trouble?" For the moment the only trouble I feared was that I would forget myself, and being a lover, fail to play the man.

"In Father Paul's room. There is a woman with her, and nine times in ten when trouble comes, it comes by way of a woman."

"Tell me what you know, but quickly, for Mademoiselle is waiting."

"Let her wait," he grumbled; "we waited long enough at Morsigny, and for no good. That is always the way, let a woman come, and poof! a man's love of a lifetime is forgotten. All right, Monsieur Gaspard, I'll go on, but you'll allow it's hard to be put aside for a stranger. As I was sitting in the court below, one of the house servants came to me saying there was a woman wanting the lady who travelled with us. Naturally I came first to tell you, the woman following all smothered in a hooded cloak, though the air outside is like a furnace. But as I turned to the left, the fool of a man cried out that Madame's room was to the right, and what could I do but take her there? Mademoiselle came at my knock, and I think she must have lain down in her clothes, for though she was fully dressed, her hair was all tumbled about her shoulders. But she had not rested much, her face was so black and white, and her eyes like the eyes of a fever."

"I know all that, get to the end," I said harshly. It cut me to the heart, angering me almost beyond bearing, to hear him catalogue her weariness so bluntly, and know how bitterly I must still make her suffer.

"You said, Tell all you know," he answered. "But as to the end, the end was that, telling me to stand aside, she spoke a minute or two to the woman, shrinking from her first, then catching her in her arms as if she was her sister, and a bouncing armful she is—she'd make two of Mademoiselle. She took her to Father Paul's room, which was empty, and bade me tell you that Mademoiselle Suzanne wanted you. 'Remember,' said she, 'remember to say Mademoiselle Suzanne wants him.'"

"Come, then, but wait outside the door. If Father Paul should return, tell him what you have told me, but let no one else in."

The room was long and narrow. In three of the corners there were beds, and in the fourth a bench; a table carrying a lighted lamp stood in the centre. At the further end a window overlooked the roof of an outhouse with a walled lane beyond. The casement was open, and through it came the clear sound of voices from the lane's-folk taking the air in the slowly cooling August heat. The two women were by the table, Mademoiselle de Narbonne at its side and facing the door, her companion at the end nearest the window, which she fronted. The hood of her cloak hung back upon her shoulders, and as I closed the door she turned.

"Brigitta!"

"Brigitta, M'sieu," and with a giggling laugh she dipped an awkward curtsey. Then I knew why I had hated to see Mademoiselle so salute me in the old days of her masquerade at Morsigny; it seemed to lower her to the level of this Flanders peasant.

From Brigitta I looked with anxious apprehension to Mademoiselle de Narbonne, but to my relief she was smiling through a twinkle of tears, and the look of heavy care which had oppressed her these ten days was entirely lifted.

"Brigitta! I thought you were in Plessis?"

"So I was, Monsieur Gaspard, but four days ago the King gave me to Jan Meert and sent us here."

"To Jan Meert?"

"Oh, not for the first time!" said she, tossing her head, but though it was to me she spoke her eyes were on Mademoiselle's face as if, being a woman, she feared the woman's judgment rather than the man's, "and I'm not ashamed either. What do we dogs of peasants who love one another need with a priest?"

"I rated you higher than that," said I.

"I know you did, Monsieur Gaspard," and the defiance in her eyes softened. "It was the one thing I loved in you, that, and that you were a gentleman who could make me mistress of Solignac, but I thought you a fool all the time. Then Jan Meert came and burnt Solignac for my sake, and that settled it. I'm no owl to roost on charred sticks, even to be called Madame."

"Jan Meert burnt Solignac for your sake?"

Again she laughed, but this time with a fuller heartiness, as if she were on surer ground and better pleased with herself.

"It's not every woman has her man do such a thing for her."

"He did more than that, he killed Babette?"

"Babette was a cat with claws in her tongue, many a time they've scratched me to the bone. Babette's no loss. But I let no harm come to you, Monsieur Gaspard. Remember how I lured you to me that day and kept you safe; you owe me thanks for that."

"Then you knew?"

"Not for certain, though I better than guessed. But you had always treated me *en gentilhomme*, and so——"

"Have we time for all this?" broke in Mademoiselle, speaking for the first time. "Tell him why Jan Meert is in Plessis."

"There is no need," answered I, remembering the King's promise that, fail or succeed, I should meet the man who had made me homeless. It was truly a genially humoursome way of flinging his old tools to the rubbish heap. "He is there by the grace of God and Saint Louis of Plessis! What I do not understand is why she is here."

"That you may escape! Do you not see?" cried Mademoiselle, half laughing, half in sobs, "Do you not see that there is no need for me to go to Plessis at all now she is safe?"

"Why," said Brigitta, "was it to save me—me, old Pieter the herdsman's daughter, that you came back? Mademoiselle! did I not say he played his part *en gentilhomme*? Oh, Monsieur Gaspard, you may not own a rood of land worth the having, but you are a Grand Seigneur for all that. To save me! and I burnt Solignac."

"I did not know that."

"You would have come all the same, you know you would."

"I know he would," repeated Mademoiselle, her face all aglow; "but now, thank God! there is no need for either to go."

"No," answered I; "after I have met Jan Meert there will be no need to go on to Plessis. But since she came to warn me, why is she here with you?"

"I'll answer that," said Brigitta, and as she spoke, a flush reddened Mademoiselle's cheeks. "Peasant or Grand Madame, we women are all one flesh. If Mademoiselle had come a-visiting my man in the dusk I'd ask the reason why, and ask it sharply, so to make no mischief I came straight to her."

"It was well meant," said I, "but——"

"But it was not needed," said Mademoiselle, her face still rosy. "I can trust my Grand Seigneur."

"Oh, Mademoiselle! Hush! hush!"

"True, Monsieur, it was you who were to speak plainer, was it not? At least, so you told me one morning at Morsigny."

"Suzanne! Suzanne! do not try me too far, lest I forget myself, my poverty, my broken hopes, everything but——"

"But the one thing I pray God you may never forget," said she, finishing my sentence for me a second time, but not as I would have dared. "Do you think I do not know what you are? Whether would you have a woman love a man or a county in Flanders? There in Paris you risked your life to save an unknown woman's honour, there in Tours"—and she laughed a little, not loudly, but the merriest, happiest laugh I had heard for two weeks—"in Tours you were ready to kill a man or two for the same woman's sake, though the wrath of the King was only a mile away in Plessis. Hush! sir, hush! I shall speak. I cannot, I will not, risk the spoiling of my life by a mock modesty. These things are the truth, and my justification. The King hoodwinked you to a folly that was a crime. Oh, Monsieur!" and again she laughed, "who ever denied your simplicity, and even there, in the being hoodwinked, there was that living by ideals which women love—at least in others. Thinking no dishonour you saw none, and so rode to Morsigny to do the King's work. There in Morsigny the serving girl wore to you the crown of womanhood——"

"You are Mademoiselle de Narbonne," said I hoarsely.

"I was Suzanne D'Orfeuil to you, Monsieur Gaspard de Helville," she retorted, "and you, the friend of the Prince de Talmont, with the building of your fortunes, as you believed, made certain, were not ashamed to stoop. Now I am Suzanne de Narbonne, and you—you are the man who climbed the Grey Leap for my sake, who carried Tristan's halter back to Tristan for my sake, who laid his life at the feet of Louis——"

"For my sake!" cried Brigitta.

"No!" said Mademoiselle, "but for mine! For mine, because he would not seem little in my eyes. And now he says, You are Mademoiselle de Narbonne! all because of certain acres in Bearn and Bigorre, acres that I love dearly enough, but not so dearly—"

"Suzanne! Suzanne!" I cried, drawing her to me inch by inch, drawing her slowly for the bare pleasure of feeling how she hung against my strength, and yet was not loth to come; slowly, slowly, till she was in my arms and I bending over her. "Suzanne, is it true? is it true? Oh! why, why is there a Jan Meert in Poictiers?"

With a wrench, just as our lips touched, she twisted herself free from my clasp.

"Jan Meert? Gaspard, I had forgotten Jan Meert; in my happiness I had forgotten Jan Meert. He is coming, coming to-night, and I had forgotten everything but you. Do not go by the door lest you meet him. By the window, Gaspard, and—yes—there is Father Paul's cloak, take that and muffle your face. Kiss me once, Gaspard, and go."

The first half of her commands I obeyed, and not once only, but the second——

"When I am done with Jan Meert, *ma mie*! he owes me a life—Babette's."

"Babette's?"

"Yes."

"And I, am I owed nothing? Oh, my dear! it is not because of Jan Meert that I am afraid, but because of the King who stands behind him. For my sake, Gaspard, yes, for love's sake——ah! what is a dead hate compared to a living love? Think what I was ready to give for you. And Brigitta, do you owe her nothing? She loves this Jan Meert even as—as—I love you."

"And Justice?"

"God has all eternity for Justice, yes, and all time too. I have only you and now. Go for to-night."

"They will call me coward, and how could so brave a heart love a coward?"

"A coward? You? They dare not!" she answered, her pride defiant in her eyes. "It is I who am afraid."

"Yet you would go to Plessis?"

"For you, and all the time, coward that I am, I was horribly afraid, as I am now. Go, Gaspard, go for to-night."

And I went; what else could a man do but go? But not far; feeling my way along the outhouse roof I hid myself in the shadows and watched for what should happen.

Closing the window behind me, Suzanne returned to the table, and there the two stood talking, Brigitta, I surmised, explaining much that was uncertain. It was like a living picture. By the light of the lamp I saw everything, but from where I crouched no sound reached me through the shut window. But in the midst of their talk I saw Brigitta touch Suzanne's arm and hold up a hand for silence. So they waited for a breath or two, their faces turned from me; then the door opened a foot, and Martin backed into the room, his drawn sword pointing straight before him. This way and that the blade flashed, half hidden, half in sight, as he fenced in the narrow space till the door opened with a burst and he staggered back.

Of the five men who followed him, I knew but one, and he, when I had last seen him, called himself Jean Volran. The corridor where I had left Martin was dark, and I take it they had only then recognised him, for I saw Volran's mouth open in a laugh, and shaking a hand in the air, he waved the others back; there was a certain fall in the inn of La Voulle to be avenged.

But that did not please the rest. They had other ends to serve than that one of their number should satisfy a private quarrel. Motioning Volran to be quiet, their leader turned to the two women, who had drawn together at the window end of the table. He was a well-built fellow, fresh-faced, fair-bearded, his eyes frank and bold, his mouth stern but not unkindly; Jan Meert, I judged, for I had never yet seen him, and thus the King kept his word.

What passed was dumb show, but there was no excitement; the pot that had boiled so fiercely a minute before was for the moment off the fire, and simmering. One thing reassured me, Brigitta seemed in no danger through the warning she had given us. It was she who did most of the answering, even laughing as if she jested, Suzanne contenting herself with a shake of the head from time to time. Then Volran pointed to the window, threatening Martin with his fist, and instantly the pot bubbled.

Backward to the window sidled Martin, covering himself with his point, all five pressing him. As they came nearer, the rasp of steel rang out. Through the play of heads and flash of blades I saw the door open and Father Paul stand framed in its hollow, but only for a moment. Seizing the lamp, Suzanne flung it on the floor, and immediately the room was black dark.

But the rasp of steel continued, and as my sight cleared I saw Martin's back, a shadow pressed almost against the tiny diamond panes. Five against one for my sake, while I crouched without in safety? That was indeed to be a coward, and creeping back along the roof I flung myself through the casement, carrying with me the flimsy network of rotten wood. With a crash I was in the room, but the impulse staggered me, nullifying the gain of the surprise; worse than that, I slipped, stumbling on the broken casement. Before I could recover, and while still upon my knees, a shadow from the hollow of the room sprang forward, and I saw the dull glimmer of steel as once before I had seen it in the Star of Flanders.

"Dead or alive!" cried Jean Volran's voice. "The King's orders, dead or alive!"

Making no effort to parry the thrust Martin flung himself before me, lunging into the dark as he did so. In the same instant both strokes went home, and with a gasp he fell across me in a last effort at protection.

"One—less—Monsieur Gaspard—my Monsieur Gaspard," he whispered, gritting his teeth that he might not groan as his arms gathered me to his breast. "I did—the best—I knew—but—it is waste—waste——"

In upon us crowded those who remained. My sword was wrenched from me unused, thrice Martin winced as they stabbed him, but his clasp never loosened. Then they flung him aside as so much lumber, and I was dragged to my feet, pinioned fast. So we stood, one blood-drunken minute, panting in the darkness, then lights were brought, and when they saw I could by no means escape they let me stoop over Martin.

Martin? No, there was no more a Martin. Martin had followed and found the gleam, and a flicker of its glory still played in the smile on his dead face. In the end the Lord God gave him his heart's desire, to die for his Monsieur Gaspard. "Waste" was his last word, "waste! waste!" But it was not his own life he mourned for. That he gave without a grudge. But the gift seemed to him as nothing because it failed in its purpose. Waste? God who has mercy on our failures forbid the thought! How can love go waste?

Kissing him on the forehead, I laid him gently back upon the floor, and looking round the room, rose to my feet.

"I am ready, gentlemen."

Father Paul stood beside the overturned table, Brigitta was on her knees lamenting over Jan Meert, but Suzanne was nowhere to be seen.

CHAPTER XXX
MADEMOISELLE SPEAKS

To decide where my part of the story begins is the difficulty. A chain swung across a gulf from a staple fixed into a rock has a strain put upon it at a certain link; does the strain begin at that link or at the staple?

Of the chain of my knowledge of Gaspard Hellewyl, one end is fixed in a sordid Paris inn, the other—I think the Eternal Himself holds it, for God is Love. Upon many of the links of that chain a special strain falls; the link of Tours, of the Grey Leap, of the morning he rode to La Voulle with my rose in his bonnet, of the day he left Morsigny between the lines of foes turned friends, of the August night in the *Coq Rouge*.

At any one of these my story might begin, and though it paralleled what he has already written, it would be no twice-told tale, for a woman does not read motives with the eyes of a man. All through he saw poverty, shame, failure; while I know there were riches, clear honour, and achievement; a wealth that to me outweighed Narbonne, a humble seeking after that which was highest, and a winning of a greater glory than any gift from a King's hand.

But because it has been told already I let it pass, and slip out of the darkened room into the yet darker passage beyond the door. Of Martin's death I knew nothing. Events, hopes, despairs, fears, yes, and joys too, had so crowded one upon the other that my brain was in a whirl. One thing only was clear: Gaspard was so far safe, and would be until the King's pleasure was known; that much the woman Brigitta had told me. Instantly upon his arrest an express was to be sent to Plessis. There the King lay sick, three-parts dead some whispered, and it was her belief that my dear one's life hung upon Louis' mood of the moment. So had it been with her. While she looked for nothing less than death the King had repented, turning her over to Jan Meert and life at a caprice. That gave me hope for Gaspard.

In the rumour of his sickness I had no belief. It was Louis' policy to make all things serve him, even death itself, and twice by a rumour of death he had sifted his covert enemies to their confusion. But he who made all ambitions subject to his own was in turn subject to his moods, and Monsieur de Commines, seizing the softer moment before the blunt story of the arrest spurred his malice, might move him to mercy.

If the express was to be instant in its departure, so must I, and slipping past Father Paul in the darkness, I stole out into the passage. It was empty. When the fox of Plessis went a-hunting, meaner beasts—if meaner there could be—kept out of sight. But a hissing whisper came up the stairs, and that I might pass unnoticed I paused a moment to recoif my hair.

In the hall below all was dark, perhaps by Jan Meert's orders, perhaps by reason of the closeness of the August heat, and gathering up my skirts, I raced down. The passages were full of excited groups, and once, passing through these, I was challenged. But with a frightened whimper and the curtsey I had so long practised at Morsigny, I fled on; that a serving maid, upstairs upon her duties, should be in terror of the clash of swords was reasonable enough, and no one gave me a second thought.

First I blundered into the empty kitchen, then into a store closet hung with flitches, smoked hams, and branches of dried potherbs, but once in the grey of the yard, a rattle of manger-chains guided me. Like the kitchen, the stable was empty except for the horses in the stalls. In one corner stood a filthy horn lantern. The *Coq Rouge* had few guests, and the Morsigny horses filled a row of stalls apart. By each, upon a great wooden nail, hung bridle and saddle, and that night I thanked God and my father that I had not only strength, but knowledge how to use it. There never was a girl Narbonne but could bit and saddle a horse for herself.

Then came the question, a man's saddle or a woman's riding chair? I could use either; that, too, my father had taught me, but for seven years I had never backed a horse man-fashion. It was the speedier, but after all I was a woman with no more than a woman's frail strength; in seeking more haste my woman's weakness might make the worse speed. My dress? That would have been no hindrance. It was for Gaspard's life. If I saved that, a world's jeer or a world's laugh would matter little, and if I failed they would matter nothing at all.

Leading Anita out, I mounted her from the square raised stone set across the kennel, and turned her head the way we had entered. I knew the road through the city, and when presently Jan Meert's express went thundering northwards, none would say as he passed the walls, There is a woman before you!

At the Angoulême gate I met my first check. That it should be fast closed and guarded was to be expected, and that the guard should be an insolent, ribald crew was nothing strange. Those who served Louis earned their wages more by licence than as lawful pay. There were some half dozen of them, and I could hear their laughter long before I drew rein, crying peremptorily, though my teeth were almost chattering—

"On the King's business, open, and quickly! On each of the round towers flanking the gateway there hung a lantern, so smoke-grimed as to give light nowhere but where it was least wanted, that is, upwards to the sky. Lifting one of these down a guard flashed the glare into my face.

"The King, my pretty?" said he, laying a hand upon my knee and shaking me. "Won't a simpler man do you?"

"Learn manners, brute!" said I, slashing him with my riding whip as he leered up into my face. "Learn manners, and be thankful I have no time to wait to see you flogged. Fetch your master; this is the King's business of life and death."

Half to my surprise he obeyed, and presently returned with the officer of the night.

"By the King's command, Monsieur," said I, holding the ring so that the light fell full upon the collet.

"It is against orders, and who, Mademoiselle, are you?"

"The King is above your orders, and I, Monsieur, am the King's messenger. That is my passport." And I pushed the ring fairly into his face. "Do you know the King's cypher, or do you refuse to honour it?"

"I know it well enough," he answered civilly. "Twice I have served at Clery when his Majesty was in residence; but this is against all rule."

"Have it so," said I, gathering up the reins. "I can return the way I came, and say to those who sent me that Monsieur the King's officer of the Angoulême gate rates his captain higher than his King. May I suggest, Monsieur the King's officer, that it will be wise of you not to be found in Poictiers at daybreak to-morrow! But I give you one more chance. In the King's name and by the King's authority, I bid you open the gate."

With a shrug, and "It can do no harm," he unhooked a bunch of huge keys from his girdle, and drew aside one leaf of the great gate.

"It is your wisdom," said I curtly, and spurred through. Nor, so long as the *pa-lop pa-lop* of her hoofs could be heard did I ease Anita from her gallop. Then by such faint light as the stars gave through a misty sky I fumbled my way round the city towards the north.

Once only, and then by day and in the reverse direction, had I before travelled the road. What wonder I blundered and went astray, rousing up sleepy villagers too stupid to set me right? What wonder I despaired, and flinging the reins on Anita's neck, left her to pick her own path? What wonder that, being a woman and weak, I wept myself into helplessness, and then, being a woman who loved, prayed myself back into strength and courage again?

Through shallow fords we splashed, fords mercifully low in the August drought, else must we have been swept away in the darkness; under overarching woods of denser, solemn night; past the stubble of new-reaped cornfields, a golden glimmer even in the mirk, through villages silent and evil-smelling in the dank heat of the night; now by a hill, now by a valley, now by a flat wilderness of whin-brakes, until the east lightened and a coolness rose with a wind before the sun. Then, when I was no further than Ligueil, the dawn came.

The dawn, and Plessis ten leagues away. Doggedly, despairingly, I pushed forward at little better than a walk. How could Anita, poor beast, go faster? The day before she had made a march of forty miles, and the nine hours struggle to keep her feet in the darkness had worn her out. A walk! The impatience of my heart burned like fire roaring down the wind. Stiff though I was, it was a relief to dismount and plod through the dust, a relief to feel the stones rough and cutting under my feet.

Let those who have sat by the last awful struggle of one they love judge how bitter were my five hours' agony with the sun upon my back. I had failed, and the price of failure was a holiday-spectacle in the market-place of Poictiers. Jan Meert's express was hours ahead of me, and I was too wise or too weary to hope for the King's mercy.

As the day broadened life crept out to its labour; peasants in the fields, women by the village wells, children in the doorways, stood and stared as I passed. On the roads, especially as I drew near Tours, the trickle of travel thickened, forcing a march in the cool of the morning. Merchants with their bales, men-at-arms, a noble and his train of hired bullies; and though these did more than stare, their coarse jests failed to penetrate the armour of my despair. The whiteness of my face, and perhaps the fire in my eyes, saved me from any insult worse than words; for once, when one who would have called himself a gentleman seized my rein, I had but to throw back my hair and look him in the eyes. With a "Curse her, she's mad!" he snatched back his hand, and I rode on unmolested.

But even these five hours came to an end. At the gates of Plessis there was an astonishing disorder. Had I been coifed, court clad, and dainty as a lady fresh from Tours, I might have passed without notice in the confusion. But the dust-sown woman on the broken horse, her riding chair awry, her skirts rent, her hair in straggled wisps below her shoulders, could not go unchallenged.

"Monsieur de Commines, take me to Monsieur de Commines; on the King's service!" and I held out the ring. "Oh, sirs, sirs! for the love of God, make haste!"

At first I thought they would refuse me, for they drew aside and talked in whispers. Then one in authority said, "Better take her; who can tell what will happen next, or which way the wheel will turn." So they led me in through the triple gates, Anita with her nose between her knees for weariness, and the fellow who held the rein cursing her slowness, while he looked back at the entrance as if his heart lay there. Midway, down a quadrangle, he pointed to a door. "Commines' lodgings," he said curtly, and returned, running, the way he came.

Leaving Anita where she stood, I pushed the door open and called aloud—

"Monsieur de Commines! Monsieur de Commines!"

"He is with the King," answered a voice from the floor above, and leisurely feet moved towards the stairs. "Who wants Monseigneur?"

"Gaspard de Helville," said I; "and oh! Monsieur, whoever you are; if you have any pity, will you make haste!"

"Gaspard de Helville!" The leisurely tread quickened to a run, and a well-grown page lad came flying downstairs almost at a leap. "De Helville? How can that be? De Helville is—Madame—Mademoiselle—"

"Monsieur de Commines? Bring me to him. Oh, Monsieur! can you not see the haste and trouble I am in?"

"But he is with the King."

"Then he must leave the King."

"But the King is ill, some say dying——"

"Other men die as well as kings, and are we all to go a-mourning because the King is ill? I must—do you hear?—I must see Monsieur de Commines." Then I tried a woman's wile upon him. Smoothing back my hair, so that he could see my face, the weary whiteness of it, and the great black hollows circling the eyes, I touched him timidly. "See, Monsieur, I have ridden all night from Poictiers to save Gaspard de Helville's life—I, a woman, and alone. I know there is a risk to you in this thing I ask——"

"I'll do it," he said curtly, too much of a man not to be moved, and too much of a boy not to be wounded in his pride; "that is, I'll put a message through, but I don't believe Monseigneur can come!"

"Ah, Monsieur!" I cried, "your heart does justice to your kindly face," which made him redden, for it was his susceptibility that was touched rather than his heart, and he was still too much of a boy to relish a compliment. "Fetch pen, ink, and wax, that I may write the message."

For this very purpose I had brought with me the letter Monsieur de Commines had written to Navarre months before, and which was the cause of my journey to Paris. As may be supposed, it was not one to compromise the writer, no matter into whose hands it fell. Across it I wrote—*Suzanne de Narbonne. The Cross of Flanders. Paris*; and, reversing it so that the letter and address were inside, sealed it with the King's seal as a warrant for any importunity at the door of the sick room.

"Is anything known of Monsieur de Helville?" I asked, tying a strand of silk through the wax with hands that shook as much from dread of the answer as with fatigue.

"Jan Meert, the Fleming, left Plessis on Monday——"

"I know all that, but since then?"

"Nothing. Monseigneur has not quitted the King's side all night. When I heard your voice I thought Monsieur de Helville had changed his route, and so evaded capture."

"How could he?"

"Second thoughts, Mademoiselle."

"When he had passed his word? I see you do not know Gaspard de Helville. Do gentlemen in Plessis break their word on second thoughts? There is the letter, Monsieur, and oh, I pray you, make haste back!"

CHAPTER XXXI
THERE IS HOPE—TILL DAWN ON SUNDAY

And so he did, and with him came Monseigneur, though not so quickly but I had time to lessen the disorder of my dress.

"Go thou upstairs and wait, boy," he said curtly; then, closing the door, came forward with both hands outstretched, but in appeal rather than welcome. "Mademoiselle de Narbonne! Mademoiselle de Narbonne! What does this madness mean? Would you ruin us all?"

"Monsieur de Helville—what of him? Oh, Monseigneur, what has happened?"

"De Helville!" and he drew in his breath with a prolonged hiss like a man who receives a hurt. "I feared it, from the first I feared it; poor de Helville! Mademoiselle, it is no fault of mine."

"Oh, Monseigneur!" I answered bitterly, for this excusing of himself before he was blamed angered me, "when were you ever at fault; you who are so clever, so cautious—of yourself! But what of Monsieur de Helville? who is too honest to be clever at court, too single of heart to think of himself. Is anything decided?"

For a moment he stood looking down upon me, his hard, keen eyes piercing me through and through; never have I met a man with harder, keener, bolder eyes than Monsieur de Commines. Then a softening pity broke across his face.

"Mademoiselle de Narbonne, what is de Helville to you?" said he, but with a gentleness, a commiseration, that took the offence out of the blunt question.

"Everything, for I love him," I replied, trying hard not to sob. "Oh, Monseigneur! cannot you see how this waiting tears my heart to pieces?"

"The King is implacable," he answered, "inexorable; there is no hope."

No hope! I could not speak, I could only put a hand to my throat and fight for breath.

"On Monday Jan Meert was sent to Poictiers——"

"Oh, Monseigneur, I know that; come to to-day."

"But," he persisted, "at least you cannot know that after nightfall yesterday Monsieur de Helville was arrested?"

"I saw it done, God help me, I saw it done."

"You, Mademoiselle? But it was at Poictiers!"

"At Poictiers," I echoed. "And all night I rode to catch your ear first. But I failed, unhappy woman that I am, I failed."

"All night?" he said, throwing his arms up. "A girl like you? Oh, poor child, poor child! We must try to save him yet."

"Is there time? Ah, Monseigneur, believe me, the worst truth is the truest mercy. Is there possible time?"

"Till dawn on Sunday," he answered, and for a minute we looked into one another's face in silence. What his thoughts were I do not know, but I struggled hard to count the hours that lay before the breaking of that dawn. But I could not; my brain was dumb of thought, and I could not. At last I caught at the one word—Sunday! and over and over again I said it as they say birds repeat a word when taught to speak. Sunday! Sunday! Sunday! and with as little understanding as they.

"The King fixed the day. All through he has taken a marvellous interest in this mission of de Helville's. I trust, Mademoiselle de Narbonne, that you know I am ignorant of its purposes, entirely ignorant?"

"Oh, Monseigneur!" answered I, "what do you or I matter? Or our ignorance or our knowledge either? Tell me of—of—Gaspard."

Perhaps I spoke more sharply than was just, for his face hardened, and his keen eyes grew stormy. But only for an instant, and it is much to Monsieur de Commines' credit that he bore so temperately with the captiousness of a petulant girl.

"I say the King was marvellously interested in de Helville's mission to Navarre," he went on quietly. "I think he knew it was his last blow for France, and that it should succeed was very near his heart. As time passed without news from de Helville he grew impatient, fretful, hotly passionate. For hours he would sit in the sunshine with not even his dogs near him, sit staring into vacancy while he mumbled his finger-tips like a dog a bone. Then in a flash, and for no cause, a storm of rage would shake him to so violent a mood that not even Coctier himself dared cross its course. Crooking his fingers he shook them in the air, cursing whatever crossed his mind, his son

Charles, Rochfort, Navarre, de Helville, the Saints themselves, but chiefly Navarre and de Helville. At last, three weeks ago, he wrote again. What he said I do not know, though my seal closed the letter."

"I know," said I. "It was a truly Kingly warning, and of a noble dignity. Go on, Monseigneur, if you please."

"Then—I was absent in Tours that day—there came a post from the south, and for the first time I saw the depths of the King's rage. Mademoiselle, I am his servant and his friend, and I cannot speak of it. But the fierce mood was gone, and in its place there was an ice-cold, hungry, unemotional hate; an itching, craving lust for de Helville's death, infinitely more hopeless than the outbursts of his boisterous anger."

"And yet he let the woman go free?"

Monsieur de Commines searched my face anxiously.

"You have heard of her?"

"From Monsieur de Helville, at Morsigny. Monsieur de Helville had nothing to hide. How did your friend and master come to let the woman go?"

"That was Francis of Paulo's doing. Louis would have—I do not know what he would have done. But the friar stood over him, just these two alone, and the King, falling back into one of his dour, silent moods, gave way."

"Then there is hope yet!" I cried. "Surely surely, he will move the King to mercy——"

But Monseigneur, holding up his hand, waved away the hope.

"He has tried already, tried time and again, and failed. He even threatened to withhold absolution, and the King turned on him like a beast rather than a man. 'Away with you! away! away!' he cried. 'Your prayers were to prolong my life, and yet what am I? Is this—miserable that I am!—is this all your prayer can wring out of the Lord God? If you cannot save the lesser thing of the body, how can you damn the greater soul? Curse, if you must curse, but this Hellewyl dies.'"

"And yet," said I dully, "he moved the King to spare the woman."

"Louis has his own code of law. By it de Helville's return absolved the woman, and so in that case the monk prevailed. But no power can move him for de Helville. I pled with him, knelt to him, almost wept; prayed that if ever he owed me anything for all my eleven years of labour to pay it now in this one man's life. His only answer was a scoff, and that as I had betrayed Burgundy for pay eleven years ago, so now I would betray France. 'It was you,' he added, 'who put this milk-souled boor of a Fleming into my head, and by God! I have a mind to hang you alongside him as a warning to all fools as well as rogues.' Move him! Not Gabriel, not Michael, not the whole hierarchy of heaven would move him. He cries it is but Justice—Justice, and de Helville was arrested in Poictiers last night."

"I know, I know, but what came next?"

"At daybreak this morning the express reached Plessis, and by Louis' orders the news was at once brought to him. I was with him at the time; all night I have never left him. But when I would have spoken he shook his finger at me, and laid his hand upon the collar with the Cross of Saint Lo. 'Dawn on Sunday,' he whispered to Lesellè. He is so weak, Mademoiselle, pitiably weak in the flesh, but the will and the spirit are as strong as ever. 'Dawn on Sunday. That day the saints draw nearer to us, and I would not kill the soul with the body. Hang him at dawn, Lesellè.'"

"And this man is himself dying!" I cried.

"Dying, Mademoiselle?" said Commines. "Who said he was dying? I know that even in Plessis there are those who waver, and would fly to Charles if they dared; but—dying? No! no! It would be the ruin of France."

"Oh, Monseigneur! what do I care for the ruin of France? Dawn on Sunday! Gaspard! Gaspard! not two days! Monsieur de Commines, I must see the King."

"The King? You?" he answered brusquely. "No, no; how could you see him?"

"Your King is not so great but Suzanne de Narbonne might be received."

"I know, Mademoiselle, I know; but it is precisely because you are Suzanne de Narbonne. Why destroy yourself? Your very name is fatal."

"Do you think, Monsieur, that if I were afraid for myself I would have ridden from Poictiers last night? He need not know my name."

"But I dare not risk it," and again he shook his head.

"Risk what, Monseigneur? Risk me, yourself, or the King?"

"All three," he answered—"all three. You cannot understand."

"Then what you dare not I will dare. In spite of you, Monsieur de Commines, I will force my way to the King, and if all three perish, they perish."

For a moment he stood and stared angrily at me, then, as once before, his face softened.

"Oh, you poor child! There are six separate guards, and you could not pass the first of them."

"What! Not with that?" and I held the signet up towards him.

"That?" He bent forward uncomprehendingly. But a single glance was enough, and as he understood, I saw him wince.

"The ring de Helville carried away? I remember now. When the King asked for it I said I had given it to him that there might be no delay on his return. He was so eager for news that he held me excused."

"Then you are beaten, Monseigneur?"

"Yes and No," he answered. "I will tell you the whole truth, Mademoiselle. The King is too ill; this time I fear he is dying."

"And yet I shall see him. Monsieur de Helville is more to me than any King living or dying."

"Mademoiselle, you force me to say more than is safe. Alas! it is you who are beaten. You might as well cry to a log upon the bed. The King is unconscious. Had that not been so, I could not have left him. The express from Poictiers sapped his strength."

"The news of Gaspard's arrest? That is the finger of God, Monseigneur."

"Perhaps so," he answered moodily. "But remember, Mademoiselle de Narbonne, in spite of all, he is my King and my friend."

There was a silence between us while I tried to tear a way out of the net that bound me, then, in desperation, I cried out—

"Monsieur de Commines, you are a subtle, supple courtier-politician, playing your own game through the hand of the King. Is all this true?"

"True, God so judge me," he replied solemnly. "But, Mademoiselle, I do not say there is no hope; I believe the stupor will pass. I promise you this, so soon as the King's brain is clear you shall see him. I owe de Helville too much not to make the effort, and even though my debt was less, your courage and your love would compel me."

At the time I thought that my holding the King's signet had much to do with the compulsion, but I curbed my tongue. For the present I was helpless, and the future was in the hands of his good-will. Therefore I only said—

"I hold your promise, Monseigneur; on the faith of a Christian gentleman?"

"You hold it, Mademoiselle," answered he, earnestly; "and now, while I return to the King, you must eat, drink, and rest. Oh! not for your own sake," he went on, as I shook my head in protest, "but for Monsieur de Helville's. If you are to move the King at all, you must have strength to command your every word and act, no matter under what provocation."

The sound sense of that was plain, though I could see that Monseigneur spoke more out of a perfunctoriness and kindness of heart rather than any real expectation that I should have cause to put a tax upon my powers. So, while he was absent, Blaise, his page, served me, and I made it my steadfast duty to force down bite and sup, resting on a couch as I ate. And, indeed, I was not only very weary, but in much pain, though more of spirit than body. Think what the waiting in inaction was to me, and judge if each minute did not creep through my thought slowly, slowly, and yet searing as if it was red hot.

CHAPTER XXXII
THE MERCY OF LOUIS THE ELEVENTH

At last, late in the afternoon, the lad Blaise came for me in great haste.

"Mademoiselle, the King is asking for you."

"For me? How can that be?"

"I only know what I am told," he answered, fumbling at his bonnet.

"Is that all Monsieur de Commines' message?"

I have studied boys as well as men, and from his confusion I guessed his mind was burdened by more than he had delivered. At the question, his face flushed red in the sunlight, and he broke out—

"Mademoiselle, I hate the court, and court ways. God made me for a plain soldier, and not to truckle in mud."

"Wait," said I; "presently you will find that mud is your surest stepping-place to fortune. What more had you to say?"

"Monsieur de Commines beseeches you not to be angry if the King thinks evil of you; if he even puts a vile construction on your friendship for Monsieur de Helville."

"The King can think no more vilely of me than I of him," I answered hotly. Then my heart leaped into my mouth. Not for myself; for me the bitterness of fear was long past: but with that illumination which they say the drowning have at the last, I suddenly realised that Gaspard's life hung not alone on my powers of pleading, but on my self-control. All my grown years I had hated, loathed, and despised Louis of Valois, not only as the merciless enemy of Navarre, but as the vilest, meanest cunning spirit that ever made flesh contemptible. What if that loathing and despisal crept into my pleading and pled against me? What if that hatred, which to me was almost a religion, flashed through my prayer and blasted the King's mercy? What if they hardened Louis' softer mood, and so left me all my life guilty of Gaspard's blood? What if——

"Mademoiselle! Mademoiselle!" cried Blaise, half piteously, half in indignation. "Do not look so horrified, so troubled. It was a lie, we all know it was a lie."

"Did Monsieur de Commines say, It is a lie?"

"For policy's sake, Mademoiselle— —"

"Policy! policy! policy! That is Monsieur de Commines all over. Truth? There is no truth, there is only policy. A woman's honour? her reputation? her good name? To his slippery, pliant policy all these are nothing. There, there, Monsieur Blaise, it is my turn to say, do not look so horrified! Monsieur de Commines is his master's mirror."

At the first door a red-haired youth whom Blaise called Dâvidd was waiting for us, and with him as surety we passed through guard after guard unchallenged. Up what stairs, along what corridors, through what anterooms we were led I do not know; nor could I tell whether the furnishings of Plessis were those of the palace or the prison. If the hanging, were of silk I did not see them; if there were carvings, gildings, fretwork, my eyes passed them blindly by. Only there were men everywhere, men who whispered eagerly together in groups of threes and fours, and who turned to watch us curiously as we left them behind.

Before an open door, guarded as every other door had been through which we had come, Monsieur de Commines was waiting for us.

"Come!" said he, brusquely, almost dragging me after him, while Blaise and Dâvidd stood aside, "and remember, no matter what he may say, remember more than de Helville's life hangs on the turn of a word."

"I am not afraid," I began.

"But I am," he interrupted, "horribly, horribly afraid."

"Hey! Is that de Helville's woman, d'Argenton?" said a weak, whispering voice from the end of the room. It was the King, pipingly thin and harshly raucous by turns as weakness of flesh or strength of spirit got the upper hand. "Get out of the light, and let me look at her. Heh! heh! heh!" and he laughed a little snickering laugh through his nose. "What a lover he was, that de Helville! Bloused as a poppy or peaked and pale, they were all as one to him. What is your name, girl?"

From where he stood, a little in advance of me, I saw Monsieur de Commines start. He even opened his mouth as if to speak, but though he kept silence, his side-long glance was at once an entreaty and a repetition of his warning.

"Ah! Sire," said I, "might I not be spared that?"

"You can understand, your Majesty," said Monseigneur, his voice hard and jerky as if in bad control, "that under the circumstances Mademoiselle would prefer— —"

"Of course," broke in Louis, though how can I give the cutting contempt of his sneer? "Modest retirement at all times becomes a woman. Meek virtue that consorts with this Hellewyl from Navarre to Poictiers, and heaven knows how long before, is shocked at the bare whispering of its name! Heh! heh! heh! What do they call you, girl?"

"It is not that, Sire," said Monsieur de Commines hastily, waving a monitory hand at me behind his back that I should keep silence. It was a hard thing to ask a woman at such a time and under such an imputation; but it was Gaspard's life I played for, and so I controlled myself. "Not that, ah, no! such brazen bashfulness would truly be absurd—in such a woman as your Majesty describes. But Hellewyl is unhappily in disgrace— —"

"Disgrace!" cried Louis, his voice strengthening to a screech. "God's name! man, have you no better word than that? A damned treacherous cur who has cost France a province, and you sweetly lisp he is unhappily in disgrace! If to hang like a common thief is disgrace, and no more than disgrace, then, yes, yes, you are right, your Monsieur de Helville is in disgrace. But he was always a friend of yours, Monsieur le prince?" Flinging back the scarlet cape that covered his meagre shoulders, Louis tore open his cambric vest at the throat and lay back on his high pillows, gasping. "Coctier! Coctier! Come to me, Coctier!—My heart—ah! miserable sinner that I am—my heart as Father Francis says, is deceitful and desperately weak. I cannot trust it, cannot trust it."

The King's bed faced a range of windows opening to the west. Above the head a huge canopy projected, the hangings of which had been removed for sake of air; only at the extreme ends were there curtains remaining. These were drawn back as flat to the wall as the heavy silk would pack, but the carved pillars which supported the canopy gave a heavy, cumbersome appearance to the bed. Between these pillars cushions had been piled, raising the King almost to a sitting posture, but with complete and much-needed support.

Never had I seen such an anatomy of a man, and had he not been Louis of Valois I could have wept for pity. His eyes, filmed with grey and colourless from weakness, were sunk deep in a skull to which the skin clung flat, yellow as ancient parchment, and forcing into relief every bony curve and prominence. Naked in throat and chest, the tense sinews played up and down in the lean neck with every articulation, while across the hollow chest the bones showed like white knuckles through the strained skin. His loose sleeves had fallen back beyond the elbow, and the bare arms, stretched downwards on the counterpane, were shrunken to a skeleton. For four days no razor had touched him, and a thin frost lay upon the mouth, framing into relief the cruel straight lines of the sunken lips, through which the gapped and blackened teeth showed at every sneering laugh or outburst of rage. Had he died, and had his father the devil, entering in, raised him to life again, he could not have looked more like a mask of wasted malevolent mortality.

"Coctier!" he went on, slanting his eyes at us without turning his head. "They will kill me, Coctier, if they cross me like this."

From behind the shelter of the twisted pillar of the bedstead a man in a loose suit of grey stuffs leaned over him, putting a cup to his mouth.

"You hear, Monsieur d'Argenton? The responsibility is yours."

"His Majesty sent for—for—this lady," answered Monseigneur doggedly, "and, Sire, truly you mistake. What this—lady fears, is lest your righteous anger should strike more than Monsieur de Helville."

Sucking the liquid from the cup with as much noise and spilling of its contents as if he had been a half-weaned child, the King pointed a shaking finger at me.

"That—that—lady," he said, mocking, "need have no fear. I have Monsieur—how civil you are, d'Argenton, with your Monsieurs and your ladys!—I have the rascal Hellewyl safe, and will hurt neither her nor hers. God forbid!" he went on unctuously, and turning his eyes towards the side of the bed opposite to where Maître Coctier stood. There, a guardian over the soul, as Coctier over the body—and which was the more grievously sick, God knows!—stood a frocked monk, white bearded, white moustached, and rigid as a statue, his hands folded humbly across his breast. "God forbid that I should punish the innocent for the guilty, that would be mortal sin, eh, Father Francis?"

"Then, Sire," cried Monseigneur, "we have your promise?"

"My oath, if you like, man! Why! what a mystery you make about a—a—common——"

"She is Mademoiselle de Narbonne," said Monsieur de Commines, breaking in curtly, as Louis paused to pick his vilest epithet.

Drawing his palms under him at each side, the King pushed himself to such a sitting posture that for very weakness his chin fell forward on his breast.

"Narbonne?" he whispered huskily, his jaw working with sudden excitement. Whether from Coctier's potion or from some stimulant of the devil, fire woke in the dull eyes; and a broad spot of red flushed the skin above the cheek bones. "A Narbonne, you say, d'Argenton—a Narbonne? And yet this rascal Hellewyl——"

"Monsieur de Helville's promised wife, Sire," I cried, crushing back my indignation, and falling on my knees to this loathsome King. "A miserable, broken-hearted woman who pleads for her lover's life. Oh, Sire, Sire! be merciful, be gracious. As God has given you greatness——"

"Bah!" he snarled in a splutter; "be silent, girl!" Then, with a sudden shift to a mocking smoothness, he went on in the same breath: "Oh! we ask your pardon! Give us time to think, Mademoiselle de Narbonne. Narbonne? ho! ho! Narbonne? Narbonne? Come nearer, d'Argenton," and sinking back on his pillows with a moan he beckoned to Monseigneur. "Narbonne? What Narbonne?"

"Cousin twice or thrice removed to Jean de Foix, Sire, and guardian to the young Gaston."

"By God! d'Argenton, we win in the end!" he broke out, shaking his finger at me. "Cousin to Jean de Foix? That girl stands for Navarre, and we'll wring—wring our rights out of her!"

"Oh, Sire!" cried Monseigneur, "your promise, your promise!"

"Your oath!" said a deeper voice, and Francis of Paulo laid his hands fearlessly on the meagre shoulder nearest him. "Dare you forswear yourself—dare you lie in the very ear of God, and the grave open at the bed's edge?"

Round upon him turned Louis, striking upward feebly like an angry cat.

"No oath!" he cried shrilly, his yellow face suffused by excited rage. "I swore no oath, I only said—only said—said——" His voice died away in a quaver as his eyes met those of the white-haired monk set in unshrinking sternness. "I submit, Father, I submit. Heaven is too strong for me, poor weak wretch that I am. But, pray God, heaven is worth a province. It is a long price to pay for a man's soul. But what we must not wring we may win by consent, a consent free from all pressure of compulsion? For that I must—I must think. Mademoiselle de Narbonne, your pleading has moved my pity, as you see, moved it greatly. From my heart I grieve for your sorrow. If—mark, for to-day I say no more than *if*—if Justice allows mercy—it is France who is offended, not I—would you wish to be the one to carry Monsieur de Helville's pardon to Poictiers?"

"If I might, Sire," I answered, my heart beating so fast that I could hardly draw breath.

"And if—not? If France can find no excuse, what then? Would you still wish to say—farewell?"

"Farewell? Not that, not that; give me his life, Sire, give me his life, and in return everything that service, everything that devotion can do——"

"Perhaps," he broke in sharply, "perhaps you can find me excuses for Monsieur de Helville, excuses that will satisfy—France! What will you give—France for his life?"

"Oh, Sire!" I answered, half crying, for it seemed to me he played with my misery, "what can I give France?"

"Navarre!" Leaning his chin on his palm, he bit furiously at his finger-nails. "Navarre! a child for a man. No, no, no, do not answer now, wait till you see Poictiers' market-place clear in your mind as it will be next Sunday at dawn. Wait and think. Go away for to-day, go away. I am tired and must rest, is it not so, Coctier? Only, I would be merciful. Come again to-morrow, and meanwhile, think hard."

"To-morrow, Sire?" I cried, now fully weeping and too confused to grasp the meaning of all he said. "Oh, Sire! there is so little time."

"Tut, tut! no, no, I am not so ill as that; every hour I am stronger, is it not so, Coctier? Take her away, d'Argenton, take her away, there is no more to be said."

"But Monsieur de Helville—Gaspard—oh, Sire, the dawn of Sunday is so near, so very near."

He had fallen back on the cushions, his thin chest heaving as he fought for breath, his eyes closed all but a narrow slit through which the evil beast in him glared at me. As I took a step towards him, wringing my hands, he shook his head, a dry, mocking smile, twitching his lips.

"The greater need to think hard," he whispered. "A child for a man—to-morrow, when I send for you. In any case you shall see your lover, in any case I will send word. Take her away, d'Argenton, lest worse come to her, oath or no oath. A province for a single soul! Ah! Dear Saint Claude! what a price to pay! Take her away, take her away!"

Not roughly, but with a force I could not combat, Monsieur de Commines caught me by the arm, drawing me in the direction of the door, and the last I knew of Louis of Valois was the skeleton head turned towards me on the pillows, the yellow sunken face wrinkled into a malevolent, smirking laugh, and a piping voice that said:

"Are you there, Father Francis? Mother of Mercy! pray for me, for I am very weak."

Not even when we were beyond the door, not till we were midway down the gallery, and so in comparative privacy between two sets of guards, did he loosen his hold. At first I thought he was angry, so urgent was he, so insistent. But no, his eyes were full of pity, and his face, white and strained, was the face of a man in sore trouble rather than wrath.

"You have failed, Mademoiselle," said he, with a kind of fatherly tenderness that sat strangely on one whose hair was still unsilvered. "That was inevitable from the first. But though you have failed, it will be a comfort hereafter that you made the trial."

"But there is still hope, Monseigneur, surely there is still hope?"

"Yes," he assented with a sudden cheerfulness, "of course you are right, and for to-day hope is our best medicine."

"What did the King mean at the last?" I asked as as we walked slowly onward. "He said I was to think hard. But, Monseigneur, I cannot think. My brain is dazed, is in a whirl. He spoke of a man for a child, but my head swims, and I cannot understand."

"Do not try to understand," he answered very gently. I never thought so stern a man had so much of a woman's tenderness in him. "Think only that yea or nay you are to see Monsieur de Helville again. Have you strength for another ride to Poictiers?"

"To Poictiers to see Gaspard? Why, yes, Monseigneur. Poictiers to see Gaspard! That is nothing."

"Then my advice is, rest. Nurse your strength, Mademoiselle; who knows when it may be needed, or for what crisis."

And I did rest, partly because I was worn threadbare, and partly through a draught Coctier gave me. So Friday drifted into the last day of the week end, and on the morrow Gaspard was to die at dawn.

CHAPTER XXXIII
"IT IS THE FINGER OF GOD!"

How the hours of that day passed I cannot tell. They crawled, that was when I sat listening for the footfall of the King's messenger who never came; they flew, that was when I thought of Poictiers' market-place, and what the dawn brought with it. But whether they crept or flew, I was like one groping a way through a maze and forever being turned back.

Twice I tried the stables, but the gear, both bit and saddle, had been hidden away; twice, too, I tried the gates, but was denied passage; none might cross Plessis threshold, even outwards, without the King's permission. Time after time I importuned the guards who kept the outer door of the royal wing—I wept, I pled, I stormed. By turns I was many things, Mademoiselle de Narbonne, Monsieur de Commines' friend and guest, a broken-hearted, despairing woman; but tears, prayers, and threats were alike useless.

So Saturday passed, and the sun went down on the last day of the week.

Through all these desperate hours of failure Blaise and his friend Dâvidd Lesellè went wheresoever I went, and though powerless to help, their dumb sympathy was a comfort. Now, in this growing dusk, they sat with me in silence. I had ceased to weep. To me Gaspard was already dead and I had no more tears. Crouched forward, I watched the western glow fade through amber and palest green to the soft beginnings of the night. Had the sun set in crimson or in cloud, I think I must have shrieked at the omen, so tense and quivering was every nerve. But all was peace, all was calm and tranquillity; and as the purple deepened, deepened, deepened till the stars shone out luminously clear, something of the quiet of nature fell upon my spirit. Then a door clapped noisily, and up the staircase came a rush of feet.

"It is Monseigneur," said Blaise, rousing himself.

On the threshold, Monsieur de Commines stood peering into the darkness of the room. To a sick heart night brings comfort as it brings counsel to doubt, and so the lamps sat unlit in their sources.

"Who is here, and where is Mademoiselle de Narbonne?" he cried.

I, and I, and I, we answered, while I added:

"Oh, Monseigneur, is there hope?"

"God knows!" he said curtly. "Lesellè, dear lad, fetch a light. Mademoiselle, can you ride boy-fashion?"

"Yes, yes; Monsieur de Commines, what has happened?"

"Blaise, you and she are about a size. Fetch her a riding suit, then saddle Bay Zadok and Mesrour; quick, boy, quick!"

"But, Monseigneur——"

"One moment, Mademoiselle, here is Lesellè. Thanks, lad. Listen now. You know the Poictiers road by Sainte Maure and Chatellerault?"

"Yes, Monseigneur."

"Even in the darkness?"

"Yes, Monseigneur."

"I have Sir John's leave to borrow you for to-night. It is a race for life, boy, and there must be no mistakes."

"I understand, Monseigneur. When do we start?"

"In ten minutes: Blaise is saddling the horses. You are to convoy Mademoiselle de Narbonne."

"Mademoiselle de Narbonne? To Poictiers, Monseigneur?"

"Yes, wait in the courtyard till she is ready. Have you supped?"

"No, Monseigneur."

"Then ride hungry, or eat as you go. Off with you now; ten minutes, remember."

But when, catching him by the arm, I would have importuned him, he motioned me to silence.

"One moment, Mademoiselle, one moment," he said testily, and as he spoke Blaise returned, a pile of sober grey stuff on his arm. This Monsieur de Commines snatched from him. "Now the horses, quickly, but with no noise," and at last the door was shut.

"Monseigneur, what does this mean?"

"It means, Mademoiselle, that the King is dead."

"Dead? Louis—the King—dead? That hypocrite, that tyrant—dead? God be thanked for His justice!"

"He was the greatest man in France," answered Monseigneur, with something like a sob in his throat. "He was the greatest King France ever knew. For eleven years he was my master and my friend—and he is dead."

"God be thanked!" I repeated, for my heart was very sore and very hard; how was it possible I could find pity for Louis of Valois? "If he was the greatest man in France, he was also the worst."

"What he was is for God's judgment, Mademoiselle, and it is my belief that Kings do not stand at the same bar as common men."

"But Gaspard? Monsieur de Commines, what of Gaspard?"

A shiver shook him as if he was chilly even in the August heat, but the lines of sorrow softened on his face.

"Take heart, Mademoiselle. Please God, we shall save him yet, or at least you shall."

"I? Oh, Monseigneur! God be thanked! God be thanked! But how? What must I do?"

"The King's death forgives the King's debt, Mademoiselle."

"Ah! Did I not say it was His finger! But who shall tell them in Poictiers, The King is dead?"

"You and Lesellè. Blaise is saddling the horses."

"Eight hours, and thirty leagues to ride?"

"Nearly nine, and not twenty-five, nor is there any spur like love."

"I rode for love's sake two days ago, and it cost me fourteen hours."

"You had but one horse, and lost your way. Young Lesellè knows the road well, and yesterday I ordered relays to be ready at Sainte Maure and Chatellerault."

"Lesellè? Why not Blaise?"

"Lesellè is one of the King's guard, and his uniform carries authority."

"Oh, Monseigneur!" and I caught him by the hand, kissing it, "you think of everything."

"And what thought have you not taken?" he answered. "Now, Mademoiselle, go into that inner room and dress; remember that to-night you ride a race."

Men twit us with the slow niceness with which we women make ourselves dainty to their eyes, and if we failed so to make ourselves dainty they would twit us the more. But that night there was no dallying. I did not wait so long as to untie my points, but slit them open with my girdle dagger, and then thanked God that at Morsigny the daily dressing of little Gaston taught me how to handle boys' clothing. What had taken an hour with a lover's eyes to be met, was undone and done in less time than the saddling of two horses. Tall and slim, my hair coifed out of sight, under the twinkle of the starlight I made as mannish a boy as Blaise himself.

Monseigneur was giving Dâvidd Lesellè his final instructions.

"There is a post to Paris—you can hear their horses stamping now in the west court, and here, in good time, comes Blaise. Join these as if you formed part of the escort. Old Sir John has given orders at the gate, and no questions will be asked. Mount, Mademoiselle, take Mesrour, his motion is the smoother. No, Blaise, no, you must stay with me; God knows what will happen in Plessis to-night, and I may need you for as desperate a crisis as Mademoiselle has to face. Once outside the gate keep behind the troop, and at the river turn south, saying nothing. Is your length of stirrup right, Mademoiselle? Then mount, lad, and I'll talk as we go. Make straight for Sainte Maure; the fords are low, and there is no depth of water to fear. Ride through the village till you see an open door with a light set before it; it burns by order of the King sent yesterday. There horses are ready waiting, mount and ride on. In Chatellerault, at the *Corne d'Abondance* a second relay is waiting, good horses all and do not spare them. Have you strength, Mademoiselle?"

"Please God," I answered.

I saw him nod his head as we rode on in silence, a subdued clatter of life before us.

"At Poictiers," he went on slowly, but though he spoke to Lesellè his eyes were fastened on mine, "I think I would ride straight for the market-place. It was the King's order that—that—all should be as public as possible, and the people warned to attend. Yes, the market-place will be best; waste no time on the citadel, and ride in haste, ride with authority, assume the very powers of the Crown itself, and speak, if needs be, in Charles' name. Remember, that point once reached, delay is life to Monsieur de Helville. Mademoiselle, say what God and your heart bid you. Trust both, and have no fear. And now here are the gates, and there the Paris post is waiting. Lesellè, I think your uncle has held it back for us. He has a kindly heart, and in three hours I have come to know him better than in the last as many years. At times it takes the shock of death to bring men near to one another. Mademoiselle, you are very safe with this lad, young as he is. He is staunch, has a Scot's prudence, a Scot's long head, and a Scot's shrewdness, I can say no more. Lesellè lad, you ride a race for life."

"I understand, Monseigneur."

Few words, three only, and yet they gave me greater comfort than if he had protested devotion for five minutes: the man to have faith in is the man who says little but understands much.

"God bless you, Monseigneur!" I cried, stooping towards him as the gates swung open.

"And keep you, Mademoiselle," he answered, and caught my hand in both his. "From the House of Death to the House of Life; surely it is His mercy and His will, but oh! what a cost to France!"

With that, as the watchman called nine o'clock from the walls, we rode out into the night.

CHAPTER XXXIV
A RACE FOR A LIFE

We rode slowly at first, lagging behind the Paris post, and still slowly when we turned south.

"Not too fast till the horses are warmed to their work," said Leselle, and I, with a fevered, grudging impatience reined Mesrour back to a trot.

But once across the Cher the pace quickened, and on every flat and down every slope, we tore at a gallop. The road was good, smooth, broad and hard, Louis and *corvée* had seen to that. *Pa-lop, pa-lop, pa-lop*! A race for a man's life, said Monseigneur. *Pa-lop, pa-lop, pa-lop*! It was all that, and more than that for me—it was a race for a woman's soul. How could there be a God at all if this monstrous iniquity of Poictiers came to pass? *Pa-lop, pa-lop, pa-lop*! The intermingling beat of our horses' hoofs rang their rhythm in my head; *a race—for the life—of a man; a race—for the life—of a man; a race—for a wom—an's soul*; over and over again, till I almost screamed at the iteration.

A swerve down the hill to the valley of the Indre broke into the beat. With a splash we plunged into the river, and walked our panting beasts up the further slope.

"Do we keep our time, Monsieur Leselle?"

"We more than keep it, Mademoiselle. Accidents apart, there is only one thing to fear."

"What is that?"

"Wolves."

"I am not afraid, Monsieur Leselle."

"I know it, Mademoiselle, nor do I mean fear for ourselves," and with a thrust of the spur we rode on; by reaped cornfields, *a race—for the life—of a man*; through broad pastures, waste lands and commonage, *pa-lop, pa-lop, pa-lop! a race—for a wom—an's soul;* under leafy arches, where the trees, grappling, met overhead and rasped their boughs in a rising wind. What a race it was, and how the blood drummed in the ears, how the courage rose as the night-wind blew cool in the face! *Pa-lop, pa-lop, pa*——Crash! Bay

Zadok was down, and Lesellè lay in the ditch groaning. But before I could jump from the saddle he was on his feet again, stooping over the horse. A minute or two he fumbled at it in the dark, muttering to himself.

"Hurt," he said curtly. "Mesrour must carry double to Sainte Maure. Mademoiselle, shift your foot from the stirrup an instant—yes, I have it now."

In the gloom, I felt rather than saw him grip at Mesrour's gear. With a swing he was up behind me on the croup, but as he steadied himself he moaned.

"Are you also hurt, Monsieur?"

"It is nothing," he answered, grasping my belt, "nothing at all; ride on."

God be thanked, it was not far, and at a trot we entered the straggle of dim grey huts that called itself Sainte Maure. Rounding a curve, a mellow glare flared from a doorstep.

"Monseigneur's posting-house," said Lesellè, and slipped to the ground. "Within there! Horses, horses! In the King's name!"

They were alert and waiting. A head, cowled like a priest's, peered round the jamb.

"Two minutes, Monsieur, two minutes; there is no more than to tighten the girths."

"Better dismount and stretch your legs, Mademoiselle," said Lesellè. "Two minutes means ten."

"Are we on time?"

"Better than that; one third the way, and the hour not much more than gone eleven."

"Bay Zadok?"

"Ah, Mademoiselle! if we could but have put him out of pain!"

"Poor beast! So bad as that? What of your own hurt? Ungrateful that I am, I had forgotten it."

"Nothing, Mademoiselle, nothing at all," and he turned into the shadow of the thatched house, crying out, "Quick with the horses! the King is in haste!"

The King is in haste! A true word. There were two Kings in haste, the King of Life and Love and the King of Sorrows. In my impatience I smote my palms together.

"Will they never bring the horses! Monsieur Lesellè! Monsieur Lesellè— —"

"Here they come, Mademoiselle."

Down a lane between the huts, a lane smelling of unutterable vileness, came the night-capped figure, a bridle on either arm.

"Do you give Monsieur a hand; ride on, I'll follow," said Lesellè, and like a bolt I shot into the dark. This time I could brook no cautious warming into work.

Behind me Lesellè shouted for God's sake to wait; but I only cried back, Follow, follow, follow! and spurred on. It was three leagues before he caught me up, and then only because the Creuse at Port-de-piles stopped me. Six, eight, ten minutes I waited, chafing. But the river was brawling, and I dared not face the water alone. Lesellè's words were a warning. Only wolves or accident can stop us, and I feared the last more than the first.

When at length he came through the gloom he was swaying in his saddle.

"Now I know why you lagged behind!" I cried sharply. "Shame, boy, shame! Monsieur de Commines said I could trust you. Is this a time to drink yourself drunk?"

Steadying himself by an effort he turned to the left, making neither retort nor protest.

"The ford is upstream, Mademoiselle," was all he said.

That he took the rebuke so meekly turned the edge of my anger, righteous though it was, and I followed him without further comment. But as we crossed the stream, I riding on his left, midway my horse stumbled, and I cried out, for the waiting had broken down my self-control. Promptly he dropped the reins from his right hand, catching at my bridle. But reaching across his body he missed it, and I recovered of myself, shaken and out of temper.

"Try your nearer hand next time."

"Yes, Mademoiselle," he answered submissively, and splashing on through the shallow water of the ford led up the road.

But now galloping was no longer possible because of loose stones and greasy ruts. So sure as we pushed on beyond our cautious trot our beasts stumbled, nor did the track improve till we had passed Ingrande. Twice I broke out on Lesellè, once in tears and once lashing him with my tongue as if the fault was his. But he either kept silence and rode on doggedly, or answered, always submissively, that there was no better path, and that the going was faster beyond Chatellerault.

But in Chatellerault there was again a check.

The *Corne d'Abondance* was asleep from garret to cellar, and ten precious minutes were wasted before Lesellé, having beaten the door in vain, at last roused life by flinging a stone through an open window. Then a man leaned out, cursing. But Lesellè cursed him back in two languages, and cried out for the horses that were to be ready in the King's name. But there had either been a blunder or treachery: the horses were ordered for the night following, and again he cursed us for thieves.

"At your peril!" cried Lesellè. "If the King's business miscarries because of you, by God! you'll hang! You know the King's way."

"To-morrow night," answered the fellow, "that was the order, and it is the King's way to be obeyed to the letter."

In the end it was Lesellè's archer's dress that saved us, and thereafter there was no delay. But there had been a desperate waste of time, and as we galloped out of Chatellerault it seemed to me the east was grey.

The road was now a steady rise, with the Clain on our left glimmering in and out of the hosts of trunks that stretched from Mirebeaud to the river's bank. The wind was growing with the dawn, but so buried were we in leafage we scarcely heard the rustle. From the right, not far off, came the short, gasping bark of a fox; that, with the *pa-lop, pa-lop, pa-lop,* of the hoofs on the hard, sound road, was the only life.

So dark was it we dared not touch a bridle, but with a loose rein plied whip and spur in our race for a man's life.

"Are we on time?" I cried to Lesellè, who led the way.

"Please God!" he cried back across his shoulder, and stooping low to avoid the downward thrust of the branches, rode on.

Please God! When a man says, Please God! he doubts. Little by little the strain of the gallop on the rising hill began to tell on the horses, and their speed slackened. The smooth, easy motion shortened to a lumpish gait, and at a very sharp rise they stopped, half stumbling.

"How far to Poictiers?"

"Five leagues, Mademoiselle."

"And the hour?"

All Lesellè's boyish ardour was gone. He rode like an old man, slouching in the saddle, his chin sunk on his breast. At my question I saw him raise his head and look at me, his face white against the overhung blackness of the night.

"Mademoiselle, I have done my best."

"The hour, Monsieur, if you please?"

"Gone four, I think."

"Oh!" and with a savage lash I brought down the whip on my beast's sweating flank. "Dawn in an hour! Lesellè, Lesellè, is there nothing will drive them on?"

"They are only blown, Mademoiselle; give them time."

"Time? Who will give Gaspard de Helville time? God of Love! Is there nothing—nothing to drive them on?"

I have never ceased to count it a miracle, and a proof how, out of evil, the Almighty can bring good. But two things can stop us, Lesellè had said, wolves or accident. Of the two, I feared the last more than the first, and even as I spoke there came the howl of a wolf through the silence, a howl caught up and answered again and again from right and left till the vast wood seemed full of howls. As he heard the baying, the beast under me stopped dead still, his skin creeping with fear till the shudder shook me in the saddle; then with a scream he bolted forward, and on we dashed as if the hounds of hell were loose coursing a soul.

"Lower, stoop lower!" cried Lesellè as the horses swerved, still holding the road. "Keep a drag on the right rein, Mademoiselle!"

Instinctively, but without comprehension, I obeyed, and the rasp of a low-hung bough along my back taught me the lad's wisdom. To the left was the river, and at all hazards we must keep the road. Let such a branch catch me across the breast, and my dawn would break more redly than Gaspard's, and sooner by an hour. Such a thing as that I dreaded, but not the wolves. The wolves? Their howl was salvation, and with my face buried in the drifting mane, I thanked God for the wolves.

Jesu! what a race it was! Men have said, Were you not afraid? But with that wild rush of wind in the face, with the swelled veins throbbing under my cheek, with the sobbing catch in the breath growing hoarser almost every stride, there was no time for conscious fear. If I thought at all, it was that the pace could not last, that Poictiers was far away and the dawn near, that the sob was growing hoarser, hoarser, till the breath in the windpipes roared like the rasping of a file. Then Lesellè shouted, "Halt, halt, halt!" and straining on the bit, I pulled the staggering beast to a stand.

Behind was the howling of the wolves, but down the road ahead came the clatter of hoofs.

"Life or death," said the lad, panting in sympathy with his moaning horse, "but in another furlong or two it would have been— —Halt! halt there! Horses in the King's name; horses for life or death!"

No need now to tell that it was for life. A north bound train from Poictiers saved us; but as we rode on the dawn was grey even in the thick of the wood, and on our left the east flared to a red glare as of the Last Day.

Again it was whip and spur, nor, with no more than a scant league to go, was there need to spare the horses. Spare them? We drove them along at the dagger's point. But the throbbing exultation born of that wild burst had died away, and it was a weary, trembling, white-faced woman who, leading the Scots lad by ten lengths, splashed uuhalting through the Clain and galloped up the hill to the newly opened gate, for the sun was fully risen, and down the valley of the Clain the morning mists were all a-swim with glory.

Before the gate the guard stretched themselves, yawning, and when I would have passed, one caught my bridle. But with a wrench I dragged it from his grasp.

"A pardon!" I cried, my lips dry and cracked, my woman's voice harsh and shrill by turns. "The King is dead! Long live the King! I bear a pardon from King Charles!"

With that they closed in upon me, clamouring, and Lesellè rode up.

"Tell them," I gasped, "tell them as we go, but in God's name, let us ride on. Monsieur de Helville!—a pardon from the King!"

The name pricked them.

"De Helville?" cried one, flinging out a level arm to point ahead. "On—on—to the right—in front of Notre Dame; perhaps there is still time."

Oh! that last dash through the still streets in the cool of the morning! At my right was Lesellè, his face whiter than my own. His left hand was thrust through his belt, the palm flattened outwards. Bay Zadok had broken the arm, and all through the night he had ridden in his pain, making no moan. But I had no thought of pity for him, my thought was all with the packed crowd before us, a crowd that filled the square and overflowed into every avenue of approach, choking them. When Louis said, Do this! it was the people's wisdom to obey; and, even under Louis, a Seigneur was not hung every day of the week!

Dropping the reins, Lesellè drew his sword and pushed on ahead.

"God save King Charles!" he cried, standing in his stirrups and shouting till the cry roared down even the buzzing clamour of the crowd. "God save King Charles! A pardon! A pardon!"

How such a knitted throng could part asunder I do not know; who went down under whose feet in the surge backwards I do not know; but the roar, the thundering gallop, and the naked steel cleft them like a plough cutting a furrow through a sodden field, and we burst into the square unchecked.

In the centre was a hollow kept clear of rabble by treble lines of soldiers, and we, looking above the swaying sea of heads, saw what they guarded—a gibbet, a wheeled platform drawn by oxen, and on the platform three men; they were Gaspard, Father Paulus, and another. A short ladder rose slanting above the wheel.

"God save King Charles!" we cried, "God save King Charles! A pardon! a pardon! The King is dead, is dead; God save the King!"

What a silence fell upon the crowd! what a silence! It was stiller than death itself. Then a roar broke out, drowning our puny outcry.

"Long live King Charles! Long live King Charles!"

But for myself I say this: another King had indeed come to his throne that day; a greater than Louis who was dead, a greater than Charles who had come to his own; a greater than any King who ever reigned in France; for it was the King of Life and Love.

The Lord God be praised for all His faithful mercies!